LAURA LOUP

ISBN-13: 978-1-7332212-2-1

Cover and character design by Laura Loup

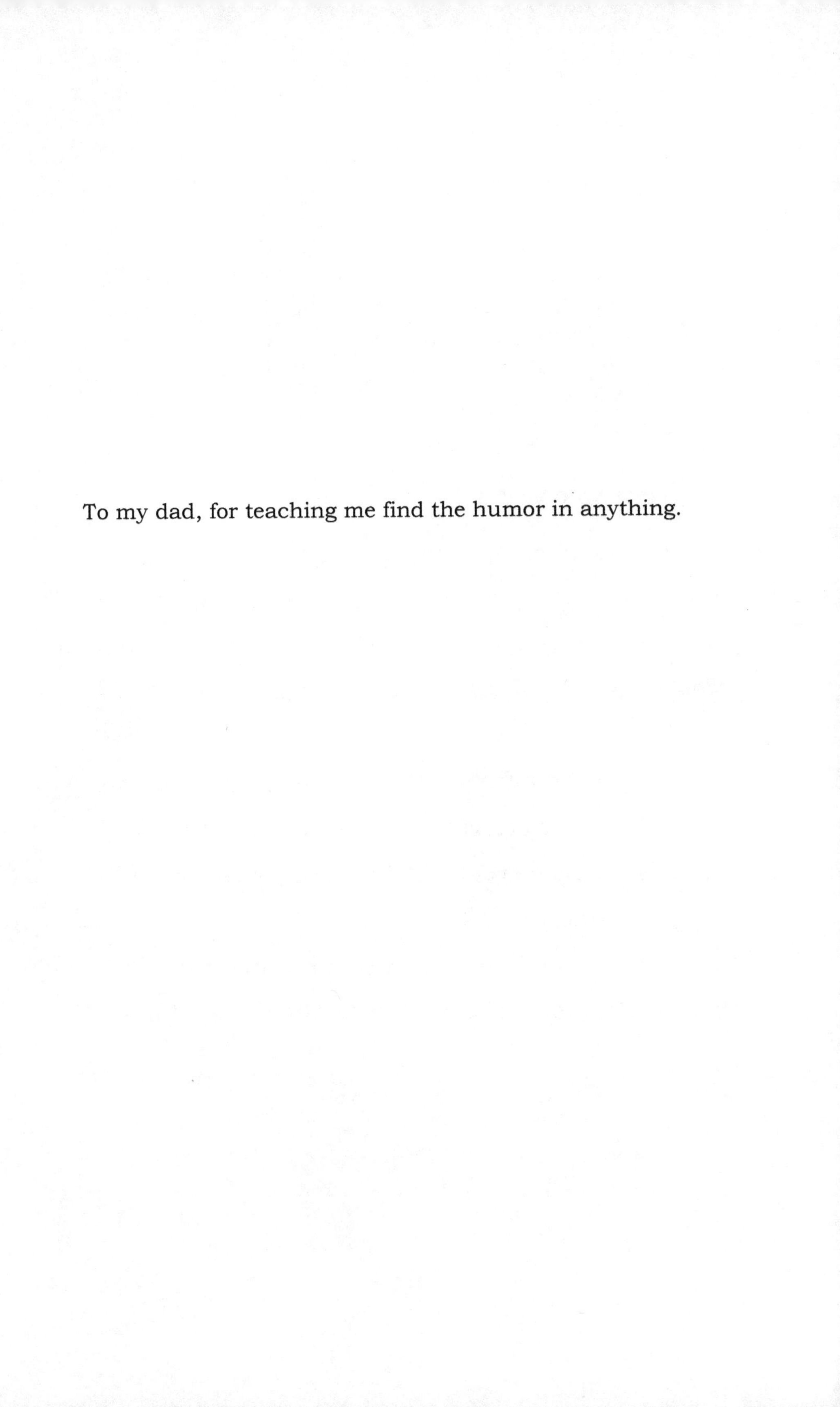

To my dad, for teaching me find the humor in anything.

AUTHOR'S NOTE

If, dear reader, you are just now joining us aboard the Audacity, welcome and best of luck. You'll need your wits about you to keep up, but hey, you're smart, right? You can do it. You can fill in those blanks.

If you're a frequent flyer, I'm sorry. I am so sorry. There are terrible events ahead of us. But there is also ice cream and a happy reunion and limericks and pretzel twists.

As a plastic novelty wall mounted taxidermy bass once sang: "I haven't seen the worst of it yet."

ONE

A SUPERFLUOUS PROLOGUE

There was nothing spookier, thought the lone Tuhntian surveyor, than music playing where music ought not play. In this case, the music was a sorrowful hesteculix piece and the place was on a planetoid which might have been made of dried oatmeal. The music emanated from the abandoned wreck of a warship called the *Innocuous.*

And it was.

Innocuous, that is.

It was one of the ugliest ships the surveyor, who has a name but whose name is untranslatable, had ever seen. It had the uncouth curvature and sickly pallor of a putrefying sunfish, and that's where the pleasantries ended. A host of unbecoming, stick-like limbs sprawled on the dry ground, giving the impression of an arthritic spider.

This planet was *supposed* to be deserted. He had been told that the planet was nothing more than a lump of rock that might, with his help, someday support a thriving ecosystem for a few hundred thousand misplaced Tuhntians.

This was not the first time EnviroDev had been wrong

and it wouldn't be the last.

A wiser Tuhntian might have turned around, reported that the planet was not, in fact, deserted, and moved on. Had EnviroDev been paying him, he would've considered this above his pay grade. Curiosity, however, convinced him to mount the ship's manual entry ladder and climb toward the hatch. His broad shoulders made it through the hatch only after a great deal of twisting and wriggling. At last, he emerged in a hallway which was lit with dim blue light.

The music drifted down the hallway, punctuated by incoherent words.

Spooky, the Tuhntian surveyor affirmed again to himself. Spooky indeed. Harmless, though, probably. And very, very interesting.

He continued down the hallway.

The incoherent words slowly became coherent. It helped that it was the same short phrase repeated on a loop.

Perhaps, he reasoned, the ship was empty after all. Just a recording left running on back-up power.

He reached a set of doors which did not match the sleek gunmetal siding of the rest of the ship. They were intricately carved, half circular behemoths set into the wall. He could see soft yellow light leaking under the doors from whatever was behind them.

"Hello?" the surveyor announced his presence, then leaned into the heavy door.

The tearoom on the other side was brightly lit by an exquisite chandelier and lace curtained faux windows. "Arrest and imprison Xan under Carmnia of Trilly on Tuhnt," said a pink android who sat, her legs delicately crossed, at a doilied tea table resplendent with fine A'Viltrian porcelain and stale tea cakes.

"Ah, poor thing." The surveyor tsked. He pulled a wicker chair up to the table and sat beside her. "May I?" he asked, gesturing to the back of her neck where he knew her reset button was located.

"Arrest and imprison Xan under Carmnia of Trilly on Tuhnt," replied the android.

Taking that as an affirmative, the surveyor reached

around her neck. The android rebooted, blinking lifeless eyes at him in a life-like way.

"Hey there." The surveyor smiled at her. "You were in a feedback loop. How are you feeling?"

"Who are you? Where is Admiral Warders?"

The surveyor sat back in the chair and gave his name which is, as I've mentioned, untranslatable, then said, "I'm surveying this planet for development." He held out his massive, indigo hand to her and she politely shook it.

"Sonan," said the android, then smoothed a napkin over her lap. "Would you like a cup of tea?" She tipped the glimmering A'Viltrian porcelain tea pot over a cup on the table before her. Silence fell between them as the spout hung above the cup, the promise of tea in the air.

The tea did not come. Sonan's face plates crunched inwards slightly with robotic confusion.

"Uh, ma'am, I think you've been stuck in that loop for awhile. Do you know where you are?"

"Yes," she set the pot down again. "Yes, I am in the *Innocuous.* Admiral Warders was just here. He gave me a priority one directive and...Oh my," She paused; her internal clock had updated. "I do suppose that was some time ago now. Did we win?"

"The war?" The surveyor shook his head at her. "No, ma'am, I'm sorry."

"I see. No matter." She set her napkin on the table, pushed herself back in her chair, and looked very much like she was readying herself to stand. She continued to sit.

The surveyor watched her stare at the napkin on the table as she opened and closed digital files in her harddrive. He heard a fan kick on.

"It appears my ambulatory functions have been corrupted," she told him at last. "May I ask a favor of you before you depart?"

The surveyor shrugged. He wasn't in any particular rush to begin scraping up bits of dirt to bring back to EnviroDev. "I'll do my best," he said.

"Lovely. If it's not much trouble, would you please arrest and imprison Xan under Carmnia of Trilly on Tuhnt? It would mean so much to me." Her face plates rearranged into a smile that could have charmed the stripes off a ch'stranda and she patted his arm.

The request, though not surprising, was firmly and undeniably above the surveyor's pay grade. He winced at the android who smiled back. He bit his lip, the smile remained steady. "Ah, ma'am, I'm not really suited to fugitive recovery. Besides, isn't he the fellow who stole the *Audacity*? He's dead. Been dead."

"My criminal database is still functioning and it says otherwise. Please assist me. In the name of justice." Androids were not built with eyelashes, so it was odd that this android had just bat her eyelashes at him.

"You know what? I've got a favor I can call in. Why don't I hire a fugitive recovery agent? Would that help?" The surveyor liked to help.

"Oh yes, that would be delightful! Here is his file." Sonan held out her hand and above her palm floated a criminal record file with the image of a Tuhntian with skin so pale it looked like a blueberry milkshake which had been made with too few blueberries, a long, Carmnian nose, day-glo orange hair which rose into a tentative mullet (a brief but eye-opening hairstyle choice), and a smile that took up half his face.

All Carmnians looked like criminals to the surveyor; most Carmnians *were* criminals. This "Xan" was the first Carmnian the surveyor had ever seen who didn't look capable of committing a crime.

He shook his head, raised his BEAPER, and accepted the file transfer.

TWO

MIND-BOGGLINGLY EXCITING

This deadly ball of laser light was the twenty-second deadly ball of laser light May had dodged in her lifetime. Most of them had been in the past half-year she had spent as a rocket racer; one had been an incident back on Earth involving an electric disco ball with faulty wiring.

"Haven't we run this one before? That deadly ball of laser light looked familiar," May said to her co-pilot.

May was five-foot-six, dark skinned, purple haired, and, for the first time in recent memory, happy with her life.

Her co-pilot, twirling on the hover chair beside her, his gloved hand fishing for crisps in a bag, was Xan who was seven-foot-two, blue skinned, orange haired, and also happy with his life, a feeling which he vaguely remembered experiencing a few thousand orbits back.

"Uhuh, yep. That's why I waved to Selma the Camera Person and said, 'Hey, Selma the Camera Person! Good to see you again.' You were sitting right there. Selma did not wave back. I don't think Selma likes us."

"I can't imagine they do." May could not imagine a camera person liking them because their ship, the *Audacity*, was lacquered in an orange paint so bright it had been known to blow out camera lenses. It had been known to blow out eyes, actually. May and Xan were not popular racers.

They were good.

But they weren't popular.

She twisted the *Audacity* away from the field of deadly laser light and bounced it off the lolling tongue of a particularly sluggish star-whale.

"Crisp?" Xan shook the bag of crisps, which were something like blue-dusted cheese puffs but livelier.

She had learned not to look at alien foods before eating them. Half a year, or seven seasons, as May had sussed out, of culinary experimentation had taught her that Earthlings have the most rugged digestive system in the known galaxy. She plucked out a crisp and bit into it before it had a chance to wriggle much. It wasn't repulsive.

Xan pulled up an inset in the viewscreen that showed the three rockets they were racing against, tiny dots among the stars behind them. He watched the small dots become smaller as they neared the finish planet.

"Blitheon May, we're light-years ahead of them. How do you do it?"

The thrill of touching the ship's fins down on a first place landing pad had dulled to a passing pleasantry, like discovering you still have one pair of clean socks when you thought you were out. It was nice, sure. Mind-bogglingly exciting? Not anymore. Hadn't been for awhile. Still, she parked the ship on Wenshillia Minor and awaited her winnings.

"Beginner's luck?" She took another crisp from him. This one was not only not repulsive, it was also not disgusting.

With the hand that wasn't dusted with blue powder, she tugged on the chain around her neck and retrieved the faintly glowing probability modifier from under her suit. It was quarter-sized, crystalline, and looked like it had been shattered and glued back together several times with wood glue. It hadn't; it just came like that. It was a good luck charm and, as such, couldn't be shattered.

"Or this," May said. "Probably this."

"Right, yeah. It's kind of incredible what that thing can do if you're not using up all the luck on something like ridiculously good TV signal or staying alive without eating for a few hundred orbits."

"You did that?" May licked the salty blue powder from her fingers.

"Me? No." Xan was getting far too comfortable lying to her. "Hey, look! Crystals!" He spun her hover chair around just as a pile of crystals, their winnings, appeared on the teledisc. It would have been an impressive hoard if it hadn't been dwarfed by the crystals buttressing the orange walls of the *Audacity*'s living room.

"Mmmhmm." She knew he was lying. She also knew that no amount of pointing out that he was lying would get him to admit it. She changed the subject. "The next race is in a beoop and I need to check the fin alignment, run a test of the guidance system, tighten the loose bolt in the nose casing-"

"May?"

"Apply for that minority species racing grant, polish the thrusters-"

"May."

"Reply to the fan mail, workshop clever retorts to the hate mail, for which I'll need your help, of course-"

The crumbled bag of crisps wafted toward her face, brushed it, and drifted to her lap.

"May!"

"You threw trash at me," she noted.

"I did." He parked his hands on her shoulders. Now that he had her attention, he wanted to keep it for a few blips. "Why?"

"Why what?"

"Why do you have to do all those things?"

She tossed the crumbled bag into the refuse bin under the control panel. "The...the race is coming up."

"You just won a race. You just won ten races. You haven't stopped."

"I've slept!"

"Right, yes, at the control panel. During a race. You told

me to take over."

"That was wrong of me. We lost that one."

Xan's mouth twisted into a tight line at the corner of his face for a moment before he replied, "You need a break."

"It might be different in Tuhntian but in English 'need' is a strong word. I don't *need* a break." May did, however, need to yawn. She tried not to think about it. Trying not to think about it made the need worse and she attempted to yawn with her mouth closed.

Xan watched the internal battle wage across her face for a moment. Humans, or at least this human, were stubborn things. Tuhntians don't yawn, but Xan had quickly figured out how to trigger one in an Earthling. He stretched dramatically, opening his mouth wide in an impression of a yawn.

"Don't do tha-" The word was cut off with the yawn she couldn't repress. "Okay. A *short* break."

"That's the ticket," said Xan. Earth idioms had been a subject of discussion recently, and he was particularly fond of that one. He reached over her to plug coordinates into the autopilot and pressed the Button Which Typically Made The Ship Go. "You'll love Taeloo XII. The creamiest cream sea I've ever seen. And ice cream. And a beach! How do you feel about sand?"

"I'm fine with it as long as it's not touching me," May replied through another yawn.

"It's...May, it's a beach. I suppose I could carry you around but-"

"I'm kidding! I like beaches, just not sand."

"How complex of you." Xan laughed, leaning back in the hover chair.

"I try to keep life interesting."

THREE
DAVID ATTENBOROUGH

The twin suns of Taeloo XII which warred against one another daily for title of "brightest, most obnoxious thing in the sky" were about to be humiliated.

The *Audacity*, a ship brighter and more obnoxious than any star could ever hope to be, gracefully slid into orbit and sunk its three silvery fins into the pink sand which skirted the Cream Sea.

The Cream Sea, confusingly, is not made of cream and it is not a sea. Rather, it's a spring which produces something like skim milk. Tourists tended to shy away, however, from the "Watery Milk Spring," and thus the misnomer was adopted.

It's not uncommon, especially in older planetary systems, to find naturally occurring dairy springs. What *is* uncommon is to find a dairy spring with bacteria-eating tasseled moyhobbins. The tasseled moyhobbins keep the dairy in the Cream Sea fresh long enough for it to be harvested and processed into ice cream which is then served to the millions of interstellar tourists who frequent the many themed ice cream dispensaries along the beaches of Taeloo XII.

It was here that the *Audacity* landed. It cleared the beach. Disgruntled tourists shielded their eyes, muttering oddly appropriate phrases such as, "The audacity of some people" as they went.

May and Xan teleported down to the beach, and out of habit, they posed rakishly together awaiting photographs, interviews, autograph requests, and tort claims regarding the blinding nature of their ship.

"No one's taking our picture," Xan told May out of the corner of his smile, still holding the dashing pose he had spent a season perfecting.

"Nope. Alright break formation." May confirmed, uncrossing her arms. She wore a sparkly yellow skin-tight swimsuit which appeared to be painted over her curvy body. She and Xan (and now, of course, you) were the only people who knew about it, though, because over it she wore the old "That is, is it not, Yurkunfle" t-shirt which left absolutely everything to the imagination.

Xan also wore something sparkly, yellow, and skin-tight. Just that. And not much of it, either.

"What now?" May asked.

"What do you mean?" Xan dropped to the pink sand, reclined against one of the ship's fins, and began flipping through a battered paperback copy of "The Time Machine" that had, many orbits back, come through the mysterious wormhole in the *Audacity*'s basement. It perplexed him that Earthlings had apparently invented time travel but not space travel.

In the wider galaxy, time travel is thought to be both impossible and a bad idea. There are legends, however. There are sonnets, haikus, even limericks about time travel. Xan had, in his developmental orbits, studied tomes full of time travel related limericks. It's all fiction, naturally. Absolutely ridiculous. It's all complete and utter falsehood.

Sorry, I can't go on like this. The limericks, though Xan did not know this, were not fictitious. The sonnets were. The haikus? Fifty-fifty.

Xan peered up at May, silhouetted against the twin suns which set in defeat. She furrowed her brow at the

Cream Sea.

"I mean," she said, "what are we going to *do*?"

"N...nothing." He set the book down over his thigh.

"Oh." She leaned against one of the fins, then noticed she was next to the service ladder. She began to climb. "I'm going to check the rivets."

"Nuh-uh, nope, I am metaphorically putting my foot down. Wait, hold on." He held his place in the book with his thumb and stood up. "I am literally putting my foot down." He did. "You need a break. Please. Suns-set!" He gesticulated in the direction of the twin orbs which sulked their way toward the skim milk.

"Can't I at least check the rivets first?" She gazed up at the ship, but not for long. When she looked at it, all she saw was one long list of error codes and blinding orange glow.

"She'll still be busted after the suns-set. *Audy*'s always busted. She's an old ship. I promise you'll never run out of things to fix." He dropped back down and patted the sand encouragingly.

May dismounted and sat cross-legged beside him. She tried, she really honestly did, to relax. She watched the white line of waves roll up to pat the sand near her toes, rear back to see if she'd do anything about it, then pat the sand a bit closer to her.

It was maddening.

"Can't do it. Come on, we're going to explore." She stood and vigorously slapped the sand from her thighs.

Xan dog-eared the page he was on (interesting to note: before holobooks became the norm on Tuhnt, books were always dog-eared from the bottom corner, not the top, and a book un-dog-eared was considered a book unloved. There is absolutely nothing wrong with dog-earring books.)

"Why do I have to come?"

"Commentary. Also, what if I think of something clever and no one's there to hear it?" May had gone most of her life without someone to appreciate her clever quips. No longer.

"Wouldn't want to miss that." It was a traditionally

ironic phrase, but he delivered it unironically. He, too, had gone far too long without someone to appreciate his quips. He disappeared from the beach, returning a blip later without the old book but with a sack of crystals.

The offended beach goers had congregated further down, so a long stretch of the beach was empty. To their right, a sheer gray-green cliff face chunked out a piece of the pale sky, and to their left the white sea undulated passively over the riprap.

They set off along the line of riprap, searching the dark crevices for things of interest.

After a while, May noticed that Xan was humming. Something strangely familiar.

"Is that the song Big Mouth Billy Bass sings?" she asked him.

"Whom?"

"The fish. The plastic mounted fish that sings when you press a button. 'Take Me to the River,' I think."

"Right, that's the one." He began singing with the kind of voice that might have made him a superstar in a small town karaoke bar assuming everyone was at least two drinks in.

"How do you know the whole song? I don't even know the whole song and I grew up on Earth."

He shrugged. "I picked it up a lot in orbit. 'I Love Lucy' isn't the only thing floating around out there. It's most of the things, but it's not the only thing."

A great hulking arm of the cliff encroached on the beach ahead, gurgling suspiciously. May approached it with a latent curiosity and watched as a trickle of milky white fed an opaque tide pool which occasionally spluttered.

"What are those?" She pointed to the rocky edge of the tide pool which, as Xan got closer, he realized was alive. Or at least mobile. Whatever it was blended in so well with the rock that the rock itself appeared to undulate.

"That's, uh, tasseled moyhobbin. It's like a kind of fish. Not the singing kind."

"Do David Attenborough," May suggested.

A season or two back, they had discovered a small

asteroid in the vicinity of Betelgeuse which was, inexplicably, lousy with signal from BBC One.

Xan sighed, perched on the edge of the rock overlooking the tide pool, and affected a British accent which was, for someone who wasn't even technically speaking English, not horrible.

"The tasseled moyhobbin is often regarded as a primitive life form, entirely void of sentience. However, the truth, as it so often is, is much more nuanced, much more complex. These amazing creatures exhibit many of the same behaviors found in intelligent life. Ten percent of all known subspecies of moyhobbin, for example, can recognize the difference between 'it's alright' and the more passive aggressive 'it's fine' and behave accordingly."

"Excellent. How much of that is true?" May asked as he jumped from the rock and they began to walk again.

"I'm not a biologist, I wouldn't know! I mean, I knew a biologist and, goddess, she liked to gabber on. Picked up a lot. Dropped most of it. You would have liked her. Or at least, I assume you would've. She was a lot like me and you seem to like me so...just extrapolating there."

"Can I meet her?"

Xan's mouth had been closed. It closed tighter. The words "Recalculating Route" scrolled across his expression.

"Ice cream?" he asked, though it wasn't a question.

They were approaching a boardwalk.

Alien planets, May had found, were often uncannily like Earth. Cultural universals - the desire for shelter, protection, belief in some higher power, for example - are a vital aspect of the humanoid condition. Ice cream is one of these cultural universals. Given time and a means by which to make things cold, every culture will eventually invent something like ice cream.

Every culture which is near a body of water, or in this case, near a body of dairy, will also at some point invent the boardwalk. And boardwalks, by nature, attract tourists. Tourists attract people who like to take advantage of tourists and that, in turn, attracts more tourists and the cycle begins anew.

Which is why this alien boardwalk, on a pinkly sanded and milky-oceaned beach, under two small and competitive suns, thousands of light-years from Earth, hosted several hundred ice cream parlors with garish marquee signs in various stages of deterioration.

Xan pulled on the pink plastic lobster which inexplicably formed the door-handle on a shack called Yusko's Fabulous Forty Flavors, and gestured for May to go in.

"Ladies first," he said, recalling one of the many English idioms May had taught him.

"Ah, but age before beauty," she replied.

"Uh...don't put the cart before the horse?"

May stared at him for a moment, her mouth open in a half-smile as she tried to figure out what exactly that meant in this context. "You don't know what a horse is, do you?"

"Of course I know what a horse is. It's something that should never go after a cart. It's also something that ought not be looked at in the mouth when given as a gift."

"You're a ham," May told him.

"Ah! I am. And pearls before swine so go on."

"That's not what that means," May said, but stepped into the dimly lit ice cream parlor to end the conversation.

While the facade of the ice cream parlor was familiar to May, the interior was more difficult to place. A colorful, banded glacier of ice cream pressed against the far wall, signs denoting flavors rising like survey flags from each band. Around the perimeter, orbs which might've been the offspring of a fungi and a bean bag chair glowed a welcoming orange. In the center of the poorly lit, heavily air conditioned shack, a display of novelty sunglasses, a glass jar, and a bucket of colorful plastic ice cream scoops took up a table. Above the jar, a sign.

The sign had originally read, "Pay what you want" in cheery bubble letters. This had been crossed out by hand and beneath it, in red scrawl, someone had written, "Pay what you can." Below that, in thinner, shakier handwriting, "Please for the love of Paatnu pay something."

The jar contained a few broken shells, a couple half polished rocks, and a smattering of crystals.

"Strange business practice," May said as she read the sign. "Can't imagine it's profitable." She watched Xan empty the sack of crystals into the jar, then, unsure of what to do with the sack, fold it neatly atop the pile.

"Looks like it's working to me! Grab a scoop," he said, picking one for himself along with a pair of sunglasses with pink, star-shaped rims.

"Well, you're one in a million. There's another idiom for you."

"Only a million? At last count there are around thirty-one centillion sentient beings in the known galaxy."

"Fair. You're one in a centillion."

"Huh. Thirty-one exact copies of me out there. I hope they're having a nice day."

May smiled, shook her head, and followed him to the wall of ice cream.

The flavors were a translation chip's nightmare. Tangerine was fine, mixed starches seemed slightly off, but got the point across (the point being that she ought to avoid that one), but things like tittering corcunasnatch and humpterfuge didn't have any English approximate. The chip attempted to shift May's focus toward the flavors it had an explanation for.

She followed a vein of pale blue to a sign which read, "Blueberry."

"Is this actually blueberry? Does it taste like a blueberry?"

"Yes! Well, a Tuhntian blueberry anyway. No idea what an Earth blueberry tastes like. Probably like a Tuhntian blueberry," Xan said in between testing licks of a suspiciously translucent twirl of ice cream.

"You're a Tuhntian blueberry," she said, digging the scoop into the side of the colorful, frozen monolith to extract the blue.

Xan stopped mid lick, retracted his tongue, and inclined his head at her. "I can't tell what that was. Was that an insult?"

May laughed and licked the ice cream which tasted like

it had known a blueberry once and learned a lot about life and love but they eventually drifted apart and hadn't spoken in years.

"It was an observation. This is good," May said, collecting more of it in her scoop.

"Great! So, is a Tuhntian blueberry anything like an Earth blueberry?" He scraped some purple off the wall before flopping into an orange orb which yielded under his weight.

May curled into the orb beside the one he had chosen. "Close enough," she tasted it again to confirm. "Speaking of Tuhnt. What, uh," she tried to sound casual, "what happened there?" About three things May was absolutely positive. First, the planet Tuhnt used to exist. Second, it no longer did. And third, Xan had something to do with that second thing.

Xan made a face like he'd found a toe in his dessert. "Naw, that's not ice cream talk. Ice cream talk is, 'What a beautiful day!' 'It is, isn't it?' 'Do you think it will rain tomorrow?' 'There's a chance of it, yes.' 'What do you suppose the purpose of life is?' 'Oh, nothing much, just tottering about till you're killed or die at an obscene age due to the inability of your body to account for simple yet vital functioning processes.' That's ice cream talk."

The blueberry ice cream had begun to drip steadily down the scoop. May, fearing for her fingers, focused on licking up the melted cream before answering.

"So," she licked, "you won't talk about it during unpleasant times and you won't talk about it during pleasant times."

"That's about right." Xan chomped passive-aggressively on the ice cream, swallowing half of it in one go. "What's it going to take to get you to relax for a blip?"

May didn't think it was possible to angrily eat ice cream until now. "I don't know. Are there any good opium dens out there?"

"Well sure, Truglian X is well known for their opulent opium dens."

"Great. Soft pillows?"

"Naturally."

"Hygienic?"

"The hygienic-est."

"Let's go."

"R...really?" Xan sat up. "I thought you were joking."

She laughed and wriggled deeper into the soft, round orb. "Just trying to see how long you could keep it up."

"Heh, right. There *are* opium dens on Truglian X, though. Not hygienic. Wouldn't recommend it. I used to get sent there all the time via The Agency until I caught a nasty strain of florntulutz. Lasted ninety orbits. Obviously I blacklisted..."

May finished the ice cream and closed her eyes, half-listening as Xan rambled on about his escapades as an interstellar sex worker. Rocket racing was a great deal easier, more profitable and, May was beginning to suspect, safer.

Just as a fine tendril of peace had begun to tickle her psyche, Xan's soliloquy ended mid-sentence with a nervous, "Um."

The tendril of peace curled away like a thread of nylon touched by a flame. She gave a questioning groan, too comfortable to open her eyes.

"The probability modifier isn't glowing anymore," he said.

She looked down at the lump of rock which hung around her neck.

It had been glowing.

It was supposed to glow.

It was not, as Xan had noted, glowing now.

The star-shaped novelty glasses perched on his head fell over his eyes as if to shield her from the intensity of his horrified stare. "May," he said with a nervous warble, "I think our luck has run out."

FOUR

HORRENDOUS REPERCUSSIONS

"It'll be fine," May said as they walked back to the ship. Xan had taken the probability modifier from her and was turning it over in one hand, holding a scoopful of ice cream in the other. "It's not like we'll have *bad* luck now, right? Just the normal-" May stopped talking when the *Audacity* came into view down the beach.

Ice cream is not the only cultural universal. Parking tickets, I'm sorry to say, are also universal.

The *Audacity* had ten now, plus two light pollution citations.

"'Horrendous repercussions,' Yvonne told me." Xan put the modifier around his neck for safekeeping, tore one of the citations off the ship, and skimmed it. "'Horrendous. Repercussions,'" he repeated, removing all the citations and crumpling them in his free hand.

"We might as well pay them. We've got the gem." She held out her hand and he dropped the wad of citations in it.

A frenetic beeping sounded over the beach, heralding a single-wheeled, triangular robot with a red marquee across its chest which scrolled the words "Parking

Violation" as it jetted toward them, bouncing over the dips and hills in the soft pink sand.

"We're leaving!" May shouted at it, then grabbed the BEAPER on Xan's wrist and teleported them back into the ship.

Once inside, she scurried to the control loft and pressed the Button Which Typically Made The Ship Go.

Typically. Not today. Not when they *needed* it to go.

Xan's face appeared beside hers so suddenly it might have made her jump if she hadn't been used to that sort of thing. "Parking brake?" he suggested unhelpfully. May never forgot the parking brake. *He* forgot the parking brake. Not May.

"Maybe the fuse blew. Osy can fix that." She reached into the space under the control panel where Osy liked to lounge, but the small chunk of semi-sentient sponge was not in its usual hiding spot.

"Xan, do you have Osy?"

"No, I never have Osy."

Pulling her bangs back from her face, she rested her forehead in her hand and leaned heavily on the console.

"That was a kid, wasn't it?"

"What? The tiny mustachioed Udonian at the spaceport who asked to borrow Osy then bolted off with it never to be seen again? Yeah, I thought you knew that."

"They had a mustache!" she said.

"Well of course they did, they were Udonian. All Udonians have mustaches. The ones that don't have mustaches shave every other beoop. Never can have a decent conversation with a mustache-free Udonian, they're always skittering off to shave the stubble."

"Damn mustaches," May muttered as she ran the diagnostic program. A horde of error codes marched soldier-like across the viewscreen: Party hatch malfunction, mold in the coolant tank, ice cream in the cruise control—

"Xan!"

"Sorry." He licked the ice cream scoop clean, then tossed it in the refuse shoot.

May returned her attention to the screen, reading aloud

the error messages as if she were reading a criminal's long list of charges. "Temporal paradox in the muffler, stale coffee in the...of course. Rocket ships aren't *supposed* to run on coffee."

"Right, yeah." He sat in the hover chair and spun it. "That was the probability modifier wasn't it?"

"Clearly."

May pressed her forehead into the edge of the console and tried to panic gracefully.

"Okay." She sat up, slapped her hand on her thigh to show she was serious, and began to think out loud, a technique she had picked up from Xan. "What do we have? The nearest station is in orbit, but we can't get there without fuel, and we can't get fuel unless we're there."

Xan nodded encouragingly. He thought maybe she had a plan. It certainly sounded like she had a plan.

"If we could go back in time, we could fuel up before we land, and we wouldn't be stuck here."

Xan leaned in enthralled by the conviction of her problem-solving monologue. And time travel was a plus. He had been wondering about that.

May blinked a few times, her jaw clenching and unclenching in time with her merry-go-round of a thought process.

"So time travel," said May. "You've invented that by now, right?" she asked him.

"Me?" Xan asked.

"In general. Someone's done it?"

"Oh. Sure! Yeah. But only in the one direction. You know: forward. And at a rate of one blip per blip." He bent closer. "I don't see how going forward in time at a rate of one blip per blip is going to help, though. Since we're currently doing that."

"I..." May began, then stopped to think once more. All her thoughts read like mental error messages. "I don't know what to do."

It wasn't that there weren't perfectly valid options. A simple call to the outpost in orbit would've told them that a fuel-run to the planet would only cost a handful of crystals.

It was that she was tired.

She only had so many good decisions in her on any given day, and since her last nap she had completed three races and made exactly 72,903 pretty decent micro-decisions. So, naturally, number 72,904 was a dud.

"Well," Xan huffed, dramatically preparing to stand, "might as well get more ice cream. There are at least thirty-nine flavors left to try. Possibly more. Possibly an infinite number of flavors and flavor combinations! We could kill a lot of time trying them all-OW!" He yanked on the chain that hung around his neck. The probability modifier spun slowly on the chain and gave off a weary glow. "Weird. It must have had a...uh...a circuit thing."

"A short circuit?"

"Yeah." He observed the glowing rock for a moment, as if it might insult him.

May was tempted to observe it too, but stopped herself and pressed the Button Which Typically Made The Ship Go before the charm had a chance to die again.

The Waschu fuel station in the nicer part of Taeloo XII's lower orbit was fancy. Or, at least, someone with a degree in marketing wanted you to think it was fancy. The station itself jutted from the side of an asteroid like a chiseled jaw jutting from a face that knows it's attractive. Its walls were solid sheets of glass which were at once opaque and transparent in a way that made eyes water, whether out of pain or as a reaction to the beauty of it was difficult to pin down.

On the way there, Xan had held the probability modifier in the way one holds a baby bird which has fallen out of a nest, as if its tiny life would escape the second he stopped staring at it.

The reason, May realized as she priced rocket fuel, that they had more crystals than they could reasonably spend in her lifetime was that races generally assume the rockets are running on rocket fuel and set their prizes accordingly. A pot of coffee is so infinitely less expensive than rocket fuel that the cost difference is impossible to write without filling at least three pages of this book with zeros, so I will forgo the specifics.

After paying for the ship's tank to be cleaned of coffee gunk and re-filled with proper fuel, the burden of the crystals was a great deal lighter. Still, without the help of the probability modifier, it was well over weight-recommendations.

"We need a bank account," May suggested, for the thousandth time, to Xan as she sealed the fuel hatch. "We can't keep lugging around crystals."

"Or! Or. And this is a fun idea. We could start a grant. For uh...for humans. Who want to race. A human grant! You know, diversity and whatnot. Buy some poor lost human a racing rocket or two. Charity!"

"Sure, we could buy the five or six humans out here a racing rocket. But what are we going to do with the several million crystals we'd have left after that? We need a bank account."

Xan threaded himself through the lowest vent hole on the *Audacity*'s fin, draping like a flaccid spaghetti through the hole in a spaghetti serving spoon. "We'd have to go somewhere in the Flotluex System to get it," he said, addressing the fin of the ship rather than May.

"So you say."

He made a noise that sounded like a rusty meat grinder working over a steak. "The unrelenting cooking similes are making me hungry. Want to get a snack?"

"I want to get a bank account. And don't mention the narration. It's weird." She gazed around uncomfortably, as if someone was watching her every move and writing it down to later be published.

"Okay, I'll be straight with you." He grunted as he twisted himself around in the hole until he was staring at her upside-down.

"Please don't be," May said, the edge of her mouth tilting up.

"Huh?"

"It's a...a joke. Forget about it," she said.

"I'm not really comfortable going to the Flotluex System

because—oh! Oh I get it. Because in human sexuality 'straight' means...oh, May, that was clever."

"Why," May leaned against the fin and looked down at him, "don't you want to go to the Flotluex System?"

"Remember what happened to Raskov?"

She did, but wished she didn't. Raskov had been incinerated by the police right in front of them and, though a large part of May felt he deserved it, it hadn't been fun to watch.

"You think that'll happen to you? We haven't exactly been laying low."

He shrugged with his eyebrows. "That's a point."

"A good point?"

"It's *a* point. I suppose we better figure out something to do with the crystals before the good luck charm dies again." He let the rock fall from his fist and bounce on its chain. It was glowing, but he could have sworn it flickered. "And as long as this is working, I probably won't be incinerated. It hasn't let me die yet and believe me I've-"

"Don't," May interrupted.

"Right, yeah. Alright!" He pulled himself up and slid out of the fin vent, slinging the probability modifier back around his neck. "Let's be quick about it, at least. And you're getting the account. Last thing I need is a face scan."

"Camera shy?"

"More like incineration shy but sure. Sure. Let's go."

FIVE

A CAREFUL CRASH

The Flotluex star system contains a number of habitable planets, a flock of scenic moons, a baker's dozen of friendly asteroids, two uninhabitable planets which, top astrologers believe, are a touch lonely, and one other uninhabitable planet which, top astrologers believe, rather enjoys its solitude.

Rhea I is among the habitable planets and waffles between begrudging acceptance and a casual dislike of its inhabitants. It is the largest, greenest, and most popular planet in the system and it knows it.

It was here that May and Xan landed. Really, it was more of a careful crash than a landing, and here's why:

The moment the gentle gravitational tug of Rhea I snagged the *Audacity* like an unwitting fish and began to reel her in, Xan made a noise which troubled May and the *Audacity* made a noise which troubled her further.

Both noises were something between a whine and a groan and seemed to describe the sum total of all the dread anyone had ever felt in the Universe up until that point.

"Don't tell me."

"The good luck charm's out again," Xan told her, leaning forward in his hover chair to take a fearful look at the *Audacity*'s read-outs.

"I just told you not to tell me!"

"I thought you were kidding."

"Why?"

"Alright, well, you only mean what you say about half the time and you know, typically—usually when someone doesn't mean what they say, they use some kind of modified intonation but you just put it all out there, flat as a harmonium, dry as smoked zipnite, and I'm left to wonder, 'Was that verbal irony or is she really interested in examining the lifecycle of the common dractifly?' A hint, even just a tiny one, every once in awhile, as to your intention would be appreciated."

By the time Xan stoped talking, the ship was parked, relatively unscathed, in an enormous lot which fringed an enormouser city.

"I'll keep that in mind."

"See! There. Will you really keep it in mind, or was that ironic?"

"It..." May sighed. "It was. I will unironically keep it in mind that you can't always tell the difference. Now let's try to find a bank."

Xan stood, stretching. "Terrific."

"Aha! You do it, too," May said, with a *soupçon* of *schadenfreude.*

"Yeah, well, I suppose it's catching. Ah!" The probability modifier crackled in his hand. "We're in luck again!" He slung an arm around May's shoulders. "You'd think, you really would, that a good luck charm would be lucky enough to never run out of power. Better get down there before it zilches out."

"Shouldn't we change?" May asked, grabbing a bag of crystals.

"No time. What if the charm goes out? Why, do you think this is too modest?" He hopped onto the teledisc and modeled his tiny, shiny golden swimsuit.

"Only by half," she said as they, still in swimwear, fizzled out onto the silvery surface of the planet.

Now I'm not about to pretend that procuring a bank account is the most exciting adventure one could possibly have in the whole of the universe. Not by a light-year.

Being's Choice Interstellar Limited knew this and did what they could as a company to make the process more personal. Which is why when May entered the bank on Rhea I, the tellers appeared to her as fortune machines; rows of animatronic old women in ornate golden boxes with glowing crystal balls, mounds of costume jewelry, and headscarves.

As May approached the nearest box, the form appeared to shift and wiggle like a lenticular printing.

"Eugh," Xan said over her shoulder. "Technology. What do they look like to you?"

"Uh..." She tried to see what they really were, whatever was hiding behind the illusion. "Have you ever seen those fortune teller machines? With the animatronics in them. You press a button and it prints a fortune out. They look like those. What do they look like to you?"

"You know the geodesic domes with the salt and pepper hair that sing the news and lotto numbers?"

"I do not."

"Right, well. That's what they look like. Aren't you going to show it your DNA?"

"That's not something I can really-" The fortune machine/geodesic dome they had been standing in front of extended its coin slot and pecked May's hand. She yelped and jumped away from it, but Xan was crouched behind her, trying to be inconspicuous.

"How can Mama Scarlet direct your destiny?" asked the machine in a thick, crackly voice.

"We, er..." She felt Xan shake his head frantically behind her, his face hidden in her bushy hair. "*I* would like to open an account."

"Mama Scarlet can do this for you. In return, give her six thousand crystal and one business bloop to complete your authorization," said the animatronic.

May dropped the bag full of crystals into a hatch which opened under the machine. Mama Scarlet's wrinkled eyelids fluttered, her plastic eyeballs rolled back, the crystal ball strobed menacingly, a blue light washed over May's face.

"Ah," said Mama Scarlet, settling down again. "Mama Scarlet senses you are a stranger to this land."

"Ha! She called you an alien," Xan whispered in May's ear.

"The spirits from beyond the veil are reaching out to me," said the machine, its bejeweled hand waving about in a stiff circle. "Yes, yes! They bring you a message. The message is this: access to your account may be delayed three to four bloops. Your account location is coming through. Through from the other side!" A card fell into a tray below the fortune teller and May bent to pick it up.

Along with a detailed explanation of horoscopes using an unfamiliar Zodiac, the card was printed with the teledisc coordinates for deposit.

"That's it?" May asked the paper.

"Yup, that's it," Xan replied, lolloping out of the bank, May jogged to keep up. "They used to chip you. Now they sample your DNA and scan your face instead which sounds worse, but the chips would malfunction awfully. They'd overheat all the time and—ugh speaking of..."

He ripped the probability modifier off and let it swing in a wide arc.

The thing radiated heat, flickered miserably, even seemed to shiver with the effort of keeping a novel's worth of bad luck damned up.

And then it exploded.

Billions of shards from the former good luck charm glistened on the sidewalk.

"Well, that's a massive, massive problem isn't it?" Xan said, tossing the smoldering chain aside.

"It's fine," May said, her voice a few octaves higher than was comfortable.

"Hope you're right." Xan went from lolloping to sprinting toward the ship.

Xan was not an accomplished runner. Neither was May. In fact, all other factors being equal, they were perfectly matched runners. All other factors were not equal, however, and Xan soared ahead of May on account of his long legs.

Xan reached the ship's teledisc range long before May did and busied himself nervously surveying the surrounding parking lot like a coked-up meerkat. He wondered briefly if May would consent to leg extensions.

"I'm here, I'm here," she puffed, grabbing the stitch in her side as she caught up with him a few hundred feet away from the ship. Xan tapped his BEAPER and they dissolved into their component atoms to be remerged on the *Audacity*.

They were safe. Finally. Nothing bad could happen to them in the *Audacity*, not in their home. Inside the ship, it was soft and orange and cozy and-

They were not on the *Audacity*.

There is no truly secure way to hurl atoms from one place to another; you're playing atomic roulette, and so it is possible, in the field of molecular travel, to intercept and redirect a signal. If someone were to reach out with, say, a well-angled sheet of aluminum, they could redirect that signal.

May and Xan reformed on a ship that was not soft and orange and cozy but *was* plastered with a few well-angled sheets of aluminum.

SIX
JUNKYARD ALIEN ZOMBIE

Far away in a different planetary system which centered on a yellow sun its constituents creatively referred to as "the Sun," General Listay had the feeling that something was wrong.

Organization was key here, she was sure. The most recent memory she had was of enslaving—no, not enslaving—*helping* Earth. Things were going well. And then things were not. The humans had turned on her. Yvonne, driven mad by Chaos, had turned on her. Then it got a touch fuzzy.

She knew this, though: The entire Universe needed to be thrown out so she could start from scratch.

No.

That wasn't it.

She *knew* that she was trapped underground.

It smelled like fertile soil and the curdling blood of all who had the temerity to oppose her perfect and divine will.

Hold on, not that. Not the blood part.

She was decidedly not alone, either. Thoughts that were not her own kept plunging the whole of space and time into majestic chaos, unmitigated final destruction, the whole of the cosmos cowering before her—*NO*!

Kept interrupting her.

She felt a brief suction, like a vacuum hose to her soul, as the shard of plastic lunch-tray which had skewered her was pulled from her chest, then a static-flooded, anti-color vision of something which had no discernable shape formed in her mind's eye.

That was massively unpleasant, thought the vision of energy and light.

Explain yourself, she thought back, trying to grab at the vision without success. Even if she could have moved her arms, there was nothing physical to grab.

*I am the Mistress of Chaos and I require your body. The plan went astray, so we're on to plan...*The voice paused, whispering letters, then numbers, then common names. *Plan Billy? No, not yet. Plan Mistpillia.*

Which is? thought Listay.

Hard reset.

That sounds awful.

The vision seemed to smile, or vibrate a touch brighter. *Oh it will be ever so! All I need is a body.*

Well, you can't have mine.

That's fine with me. Enjoy being dead.

The corners of Listay's sight grew dark and she felt her consciousness falling deeper into the Earth.

Wait!

Excellent, Chaos thought. *You're me now, and I'm the best thing you could possibly be, so shake off that rigor mortis, and let's have a smile.*

And Listay was gone. Mentally at least.

Chaos wiggled Listay's fingers, bringing life back into the stiffened tendons and muscles and sending a few testing commands to her robotic arm. That arm booted up much faster than Listay's organic matter and it was leagues stronger. She dug a steely hand into the dirt above her and began to pull her new body from its shallow grave.

She rose out of the Earth and shook off a shower of dirt, startling a family of junkyard quails.

Chaos felt herself splitting again. The part of Listay which was still Listay had been busy drawing a white chalk line down the middle of her subconscious; a line which, shockingly, Chaos found she couldn't physically cross. That was clever. Frustratingly so. Listay was not being an accommodating host.

What's your plan? Listay whispered in her own head from her side of her brain as Chaos made her body trudge through the junkyard.

"Go back to sleep," Chaos hummed. She had retained control of Listay's mouth.

I have a right to know what you're doing with me. Yvonne might have gotten away with shushing me but don't underestimate how little respect I have for my own body, thought Listay.

"You used to be wild about me! The word 'love' was thrown around. Whatever happened, mun?" said Chaos with Listay's lips.

You murdered me.

"I brought you back."

Tell me what you're planning, snarled Listay's subconscious insofar as a subconscious could snarl.

"Will you help or hinder me if I tell you?"

That depends on whether or not I agree with you.

"Then no."

Listay huffed, a difficult feat now that she couldn't breathe. She thought for a moment. She couldn't breathe. Was she dead? Was she undead?

"Yes."

Zuut!

"What did you expect, mun? I killed you."

But I'm here, I'm still me. I can't be dead.

"Check the pulse, starlips."

Listay put two fingers to her own ashen purple neck and waited. Nothing.

"Thump-thump," said the Mistress of Chaos mockingly. She laughed with Listay's vocal cords. "See? Dead. So you might as well help me out here."

If I stop fighting you, will you find another body? Listay posed.

"As me as my witness, yes. I can't wait to be out of this filing cabinet you call a brain."

And when you leave will I still be alive?

"I'm not sure what kind of answer you're looking for here."

I want you to let me live, zux it, or I'm killing both of us. Again.

"Mortals are such—oh, alright. If it will get you to shut up, I'll pull some strings and keep your string from getting cut."

Good.

Listay's body relaxed.

So the plan? Listay thought again.

"I'm going to find the Sphere of Time."

That isn't a plan, that's an outcome.

"I didn't draw up a blueprint; I was rather busy trying to animate your hefty mound of flesh."

Listay slapped her own face hard and wrested control of her mouth. "Watch it, goddess, I'm not above hijacking this body back," she said out loud. She felt like a ventriloquist's dummy in her own body.

Settle down, Chaos warned, shoving Listay over to her rightful side and seizing command of her lips again. "You're dead and you'd do well to remember that. I own you and it's by the grace of *me* that I haven't destroyed your puny consciousness yet."

Listay very much doubted that grace had anything to do with it. She ambled around monolithic mounds of garbage, most of it semi recognizable as the siding or signage from her perfect Earth. So the humans had discarded all her hard work the moment she was buried. That was upsetting to know. Not more upsetting than being dead, but almost.

At last, she saw something that made her heart give a single, excited beat. One smug, dark blue AMC Gremlin with a dented red door and silver bald patches where the paint had been half-heartedly sanded a decade before crouched amidst the trash.

And it wasn't just a Levi's Edition 1975 AMC Gremlin. It was a space shuttle. Retrofitted with enough A'Viltrian tech to get a solar system or two away.

As an aside, if you haven't read book one, this may not make sense to you. Frankly, if you have read book one this may not make sense. Best to accept it and move along.

Soon, Listay had the shuttle in working order, the headlights helping her sift through mounds of garbage for assets. So far, a nail file and a working plasma zapper had been recovered. Both would be of use to her.

She continued to dig.

What are you looking for? We have a shuttle, said Chaos who had been snoozing in the back of her parietal lobe.

"A wrench," said Listay, surprised that she had control of her own mouth now. "I need to repair the seat belt before we can go off-world."

Chaos groaned insomuch as a thought entity could do so. *For the last time. YOU. ARE. DEAD. Safety standards can shove it, there's nothing left to save.*

Chaos dragged her body away from the pile of garbage. "Get in the car."

Reluctantly, Listay let Chaos tuck her body into the front seat of the Gremlin.

Where are we going? Listay asked the thread-bare chaos goddess in her head.

"Rhea III."

It doesn't exist. I've been digging for over a beoop now. I'm tired, I need a break, thought Listay.

"Woah there. If you stop, it could take me rotations to get you re-started."

Just a nap, Listay pleaded with the goddess.

"Rheans don't take naps. Wake up." Listay's own fingers snapped in her ear and she blinked her eyes open again. "We're going to Rhea—the original one, Rhea III."

There is no Rhea III, it never existed, Listay thought at her.

"Tell me, how long ago were you hatched?" asked the goddess.

She paused, glancing at her BEAPER. *3,068 orbits, five rotations, twelve beoops, and twenty-eight bloops ago.*

Chaos laughed with Listay's mouth. "Oh you're just a

larvae. We're going to Rhea III. I have it on good authority that therein lies the Sphere of Time. If you're very nice to me, I'll go back in time and undead you. Make it so you weren't killed to begin with. Then, of course, I'll restart the Universe and tweak some things early on. Just a bit. Nothing drastic."

What authority do you have it on? Listay thought.

"Have you studied limericks, Listay? I can see you haven't. Here's one for you. 'An A'Viltrian shaman once said / "You can skip Rhea III 'cause it's dead" / but alas, over there / still remains an affair / Designed to screw with Time's head.' Is that enough proof for you?"

No, Listay began, but Chaos forced her fingers to wrap round the gear shift and launch the Gremlin off the planet. Once the coordinates were set, Chaos relaxed her control of Listay's body just enough to allow her to grab the nail file from the passenger's seat and begin filing down a few season's worth of nail growth.

SEVEN

CREAM OF TARTAR

"Oh, excuse me," said May. "We must've had the wrong coordinates." She addressed the back of whoever sat in the cockpit of the small grey ship she and Xan had *mistakenly* teleported into.

Xan made a nearly imperceptible "erm" and nudged her to look at the read out on his BEAPER. The coordinates were right. She didn't need to look to know that.

"Naw, that was me. I interrupted your signal." The silver-clad pilot twisted languidly around and leaned forward into the light, flashing a gravel-toothed smile from his blue face. The smile morphed into a confused pucker as he surveyed his catch, May in only an over-sized Yurkunfle t-shirt and Xan in his shimmering swimsuit. "What's the bark with the swimsuits, eh?"

"We were at the beach," Xan said, holding back the further, more sarcastic comments which threatened to follow.

"Sorry 'bout that, starlips. Name's Rap," he said to May.

"Get us out of here," she whispered, shaking Xan's arm, not daring to drop eye contact with Rap.

"I'm trying, mun." He was. He had swiped up on the teleport signal several times. Would've done more, but his BEAPER had frozen at attempt number forty-seven.

"Not much use teleporting back to the *Audacity,* is there? Seeing as I'm towing it." One half of Rap's upper lip curled up. It was meant to be a sly grin, but presented as more of a, "take a look at this tooth, do ya' think it looks off?"

Xan tried to back up, but only got as far as shifting his weight backwards when his shoulders hit the wall. "Oh? Oh, well hey, we'll just hitch a lift on some other ship. I never liked that rocket anyway!" This was untrue. Xan liked the rocket very much. "We'll get a new one. It's no trouble at all. Just, uh, let us go and we'll be right out of your hair."

May also tried to back up, and also hit the wall. Even backed against the wall, there wasn't much space between them and Rap. The vessel they were on was terribly intimate. She had the sense that she was in a windowless white van which wasn't too far off; it was windowless, and it was white, and from the outside, the cramped MoonHopper did look a bit like a van if you squinted.

"What's happening?" she asked.

Xan clicked his tongue. "Well, May, we've just been kidnapped," he said matter-of-factly, as if he were telling her the time.

"Not kidnapped," Rap pulled a switch and stood as the ship began to shakily ascend. "Xan of Tuhnt, you're under arrest for treason."

May sat on the cold metal floor and scrubbed her fingers through her hair as if resetting her hairstyle would reset the narrative thus far. It didn't work.

"Treason?" she asked Xan from behind her bush of purple hair.

"Ehuh," he confirmed.

"Treason?" she asked again.

The top half of his face cringed, the bottom half smiled.

"And now you have what, some kind of Boba Fett Space Bounty Hunter after you?" she pressed.

“That’s ‘fugitive recovery agent’ if ya’ don’t mind, starlips,” Rap interjected. “Hands out,” he said to Xan and whipped a pink zip-tie from his coat pocket.

Xan’s cheeks flushed a bright green as Rap zip-tied his wrists, but fortunately for him, it was too dark in the MoonHopper for either Rap or May to see.

“What’s that, a laser zip tie?” May asked, parting her hair from her face and trying to smooth it back.

“N-no,” Rap stuttered. “Is that a real thing?”

May shrugged. “You’d know better than I would, Mr. Fett.”

“Stop with the references unless you want to start paying royalties,” Xan grumbled. He folded onto the floor beside her now, hands pinkly restrained.

“What did you do?” May forced the words between her clenched teeth.

“Ohh, careful now! Admission of guilt!” Rap sung. “Naw, just kiddin’. Everyone knows you’re a guilty zuxing trok-licker.”

Xan closed one eye as he thought, then closed the other as he tried to think of something else, then sighed and opened both eyes. Thinking hadn’t helped.

“What he said. Treason,” Xan said.

“That’s a broad accusation,” May countered.

“Okay, well, imagine you’re baking a cake. Not just any old single layer sort of number, no, this cake is going to change your entire life—it’s a magical cake. So you need to collect the ingredients to put in the cake, right? Some kind of nuts, sugar, um...cream of tartar—”

“Cream of tartar? Where did you learn to cook, the 30s?”

“Forget it.”

“Xan, come on. What happened to the cream of tartar?”

“The cream of tartar didn’t want to die an early death in a pointless war and ran away with the spoon,” Xan said.

“So you evaded a military draft? And that’s considered treason on Tuhnt?”

“No, May, I took the spoon.”

“An important spoon,” Rap piped in.

“Uhuh.”

The MoonHopper fell silent as Rap focused on taking them wherever they were going and Xan chewed passively at the zip tie. May tried not to think about the baking analogy. She failed miserably.

In her mind, clearly Xan (the cream of tartar) had stolen the *Audacity* (the spoon). Clearly. But why? And furthermore how? He could barely fly the thing, much less orchestrate grand theft rocket ship.

Every inch of distance between her and the Earth seemed to telescope out before her, making her dizzy. Aboard the *Audacity*, she felt safe. She felt like she had a home. Now she was trapped in a windowless white van—or rather MoonHopper—with a Tuhntian criminal she thought she knew and a Tuhntian sleaze-ball she wished she didn't.

She felt like the gravity switch in her head had been flipped off and tried to bring herself back by focusing on the things she could see, feel, smell, hear.

She saw an offline teledisc (she was trapped), she felt Xan wiggling beside her (she couldn't trust him), she smelled her own sweat (she hadn't taken a shower in a minute), she heard the ship sputtering and groaning (they were hurtling through space in a tin garbage can.)

Right, that hadn't helped at all. Not a bit. Made it worse, actually.

Xan finally stopped fidgeting and went very, very still. He caught her eye and moved his eyebrows in ambiguous communication.

"What?" she mouthed.

He looked pointedly at her, then at her hands. Unfortunately, the translator chip didn't translate meaningful looks.

Curling his lips in with frustration, he lifted his zip tied wrists, then looked at her hands again. He pointed to her, pointed to Rap's back, and mimed decking him.

Ah, he wanted her to fight back. Because she wasn't zip-tied. She puffed at him, gesturing wildly to Rap's back then shooting finger guns and miming her tragic death.

Xan searched the ceiling as if the rust stains would rearrange into a brilliant escape plan that didn't involve turning May into swiss cheese.

After a moment of thought, he sat up with the beginnings of a smile.

"Hey," Xan called to Rap.

"Huh?" The fugitive recovery agent didn't turn around.

"What about May? Is she arrested too, or is it just me?"

The hamster on the wheel of May's brain started sprinting. What was he doing? Trying to *get* her arrested?

"Just you."

"Then what are you going to do with her? You could send her back to the *Audacity*. Then you don't have to tow the ship with you! Solves two problems."

Rap stood slowly, tapping some keys on the dashboard as he did. "You zoup-nog. Need the rocket, don't I? Don't need her, though, that's true."

Rap yanked her to her feet. Should she punch him? Her brain sent a test command to her arm; her arm politely declined. Nope, not punching him.

"Just dropping her at the nearest space port."

"Wait, no. I don't want to be dropped off," she said.

"You're a waste of fuel, starlips. I'm dropping you." He held her in place and kicked the teledisc until the white rim lights fluttered on.

"No," May was caught in a volleyball net between panic and confusion. "Stop!"

Without Xan's BEAPER, she couldn't get back onto the *Audacity*.

Without the *Audacity,* she couldn't get anywhere.

She glared at Xan's cheerful grin.

Everything went white, then a dingy shade of grey-brown.

Then she was alone. A wooden hand-painted sign tilted on a rusted metal wall high above her. "Welcome to Yenuket Municipal Spaceport."

EIGHT

BIG MOUTH BILLY BASS

Yenuket Municipal Spaceport is, like most spaceports, located on a mega-asteroid orbiting a service planet. It has a force that passes for gravity, a shell that passes for atmosphere, and its denizens have social constructs that pass for a culture.

May had been to a few spaceports and had an idea of what they ought to look like. Glimmering airlocks, rows of businesses and restaurants, crisply uniformed beings zooming around on something like Segways.

This, in her mind, was not a spaceport. Large yellow lights quivered apologetically from the far-away ceiling. It smelled like a swamp (if you have never smelled a swamp before, simply obtain an egg, forget about it for a year, then crack it onto a space heater). It looked like the place the Beverly Hillbillies lived before they lived in Beverly Hills.

And all this was still not as wretched as the sound.

In a blanket of crimson powder which had been steel in a past life, sat a tin can robot plucking away at a twangy, metal instrument. Upon closer inspection, she noticed that the instrument was an integral part of the robot's body.

She waved politely. "Excuse me, would you please tell me where I am?"

"CHHGGGGG-TIK-beep-beep-beep," said the robot.

May almost asked again, feeling that perhaps she was the one being unclear. Instead, she began to walk, looking for something that might point her toward something else that might be of use. She still had the *Audacity*'s anchor button snapped onto the inside of her swimsuit. If she could find a computer, she could track the ship. Then she just needed a StarTaxi or a shuttle to take her to it.

It seemed unlikely there was any sort of Earthling embassy out here, and May distracted herself as she walked by fancying that she could erect the first Earthling embassy in the known Universe. She was wrong, of course. Every Earthling lost in space has had this inkling at some point and thirty percent of those who have had this inkling acted on it. There are eighteen Earthling embassy start-ups peppered throughout the galaxy.

May walked further from the teledisc bay, vacant storefronts withering on either side of her. Something that looked like a mailbox dribbled colorfully from its mail slot. A poster, glued to the side of the dripping mailbox, caught her eye.

In her experience, posters were almost always either pushy, passive aggressive, or decidedly unhelpful.

This poster was, rare treat, all three. "Don't do that," it said under a silhouette of a stick man dancing with what might've been an upright dromedary.

"Noted," May assured it.

She kept walking, her dark flip-flops taking on a bronze tinge from the rust that puffed around her feet like fruit flies around a ripe banana.

A dim light flickered from a window in the distance. The metal sign, corroded and aggressively shedding, read "Bezalbum's Baubles." Perhaps Bezalbum and their baubles would have a word of wisdom to share. Or a map. A map would be better.

She checked behind herself uneasily, so used to having Xan nearby that being on her own left her with the constant dull anxiety that she was forgetting something, then walked into the shop.

The walls were papered with a faded damask, the floor was a dust-filled tight weave carpet. Music, the kind which tries so hard to be inoffensive it can do nothing but offend, wafted from an old radio on the counter, serenading the only other object in the room which was a bronze call bell.

Hesitantly, with the distinct fear that she might upset the balance of the room, May dinged the bell.

The door behind the counter creaked. The creaking metal, the tinny reverberations of the bell, the thudding of May's heart in her ears, and the offensively inoffensive music gave the place an atmosphere of enormous dread, and the door opened slowly, as if it were apologizing about whatever it was admitting into the room.

"Bretsy, if that's you I don't want none of your chocolates so slip-off," said an ancient voice.

May had to look over the counter to see her. A wrinkled lump of a Udonian with a wispy white mustache and wispier white hair piled artlessly atop her skull peeked around the door.

"Good afternoon, um, ma'am," said May. Her strategy for dealing with social interactions was to whip out her Sonic customer service voice. "Do you know where I could find a StarTaxi service?" May sucked her bottom lip under her teeth and chewed gently on it.

The wrinkled creature, who May correctly assumed was Bezalbum, brightened like a fluorescent light kicking on three minutes and forty-nine seconds after you've flipped the switch.

"A tourist! Oh indeed, indeed. You, dear, have come to just the right place. Yes. Follow." She curled a finger to beckoned May into the back room.

Had May not been hopelessly lost anyway, she might've left at that point. But here, at least, was some direction that didn't involve doing, or not doing, something to a dromedary. She rounded the counter and followed the green raisin.

This room was darker than the first, the light having

been soaked up by the tchotchkes and doodads which lined the maze of shelving. The pointedly inoffensive music faded into the background, replaced by a crackling sort of chatter. Faintly, drifting over the dusty shelves like heavy curls of smoke, something fishy.

"Take my money, my cigarettes," sang Big Mouth Billy Bass from somewhere in the back of the dark building.

Bezalbum turned to May, wrapping a leathery green hand around hers.

"Never you mind old Billy. He's been singing that song, I reckon, for two thousand orbits, the poor fool."

"You could take out the batteries."

"Hasn't got any, has he?" Bezalbum laughed.

May shivered though the building was warm and damp.

The fish sang the entire song. It wasn't supposed to do that. It was supposed to sing a few seconds of "Take Me to the River" and then a few seconds of "Don't Worry Be Happy." But it repeated the entirety of "Take Me to the River" over and over. May really would've liked to hear "Don't Worry Be Happy" right now. A haunted Big Mouth Billy Bass forgetting his second number felt like an evil omen of horrible things to come.

Xan would've loved it.

They walked past the singing fish as it flopped on a dusty shelf and May determined that she would bring Xan here so he could appreciate the absurdity of a haunted Big Mouth Billy Bass with her.

"Welcome, dear, to Yenuket Municipal Spaceport, the most remote spaceport recognized by the Universal Review. If you've never been to Yenuket, you're not missing much! Or so say the postcards. You'll want this." Bezalbum plucked something from a shelf and presented it to her. It was a cheaply made folding pocket knife with the words "Zux it, it's Yenuket!" laser etched into the wood siding.

May nodded politely. Bezalbum nudged closer to her, the pocket knife cradled in her open palms.

"Ten crystals!" Bezalbum chirruped.

"I'm sorry?"

“The pocket knife, dear. I can see you want it. You’ve been staring at it for some time now.”

And then May thought of something she hadn’t let herself think about in awhile. Earth. Specifically her mother. Specifically being on Earth and eating lunch out with her mother.

Here’s how it would go:

“Why don’t you just talk to him?”

“Who?”

“What do you mean, who? The cutie in the other booth. You’ve been staring, honey.”

“Have I?”

“Yes!”

“I haven’t, Mom.”

“Sweetie, you’ve got to make the first move sometimes.”

“Uhuh.” May would then pretend to be extremely interested in her french fries or sub sandwich, or whatever she was trying to eat at the time. Her mother would then go on about weddings or grandchildren, depending on her mood.

For a moment she was back on Earth, for a moment she missed it, and then she didn’t. And then she felt guilty about not missing it. And then she wanted a cigarette. And *then* she realized Bezalbum was still staring at her, arms shaking from the effort of holding the pocket knife aloft.

“Oh, no, I just...it was there so I-”

Bezalbum made a loud swallowing noise, her enormous eyes watering.

May rubbed her face. “Alright, I don’t have any crystals on me. Can you take a face scan?” She silently hoped her account hadn’t been opened yet.

A blue flash blinded her, and a directionless voice told her ten crystals had been transferred out of her account. She took the pocket knife and reached through the opening of her t-shirt to tuck it between her boobs. A pocket knife, at least, would likely come in handy later.

“Could you direct me to an information desk? I need to find a StarTaxi.”

“Oh no, dear, no. I don’t sell StarTaxis. Too flashy. I

have got a lovely collection of dolls though. Come along, come to the dolls!" she disappeared around a display of china cups which were chipped so badly their own creators wouldn't recognize them.

May followed her like a cat being dragged on a leash.

One of May's finer points, one of the things she prided herself on, was her respect for the elderly. She had no patience for assholes, drunks, or children, but she had all the time in the universe for the elderly. To a fault, she was now beginning to realize.

Bezalbum led her to a bookshelf which bent under the weight of a mob of baby dolls. *Human* baby dolls. *Parts* of human baby dolls. May took a steadying breath which she immediately regretted. The smell of their musty old clothing and decomposing plastic made her cough.

"They're sweet," she lied, "but I really have to go. My friend's in trouble and I need to find him."

"Oh, dear me," said Bezalbum. "I understand all about the yearnings of the heart! I was quite the romantic myself back in my day-"

"No! No, listen," May said. "He's got my rocket." She squinted, that wasn't quite right. "Well, technically, it's his rocket. I just have to find him. He has, as he would say, 'some 'splainin' to do.'"

"Corral your puntls, missy. You wander into my humble shop, buy a cheap souvenir, and now you're galavanting off. Never visiting. Ain't that how it is with larvae these days. All alike are you." She shook her fuzzy green raisin of a head.

And there was the guilt. "I'm sorry, I'll visit soon, I promise!" she said. "Is there anywhere in this spaceport I can get a StarTaxi?"

Bezalbum nodded and began to walk back to the front of her store.

"Fuff." Bezalbum shuffled back the way they'd come, past the haunted Big Mouth Billy Bass. At the counter, she reached slowly, like a giraffe extending its neck for a high leaf, and turned the radio down.

"That way, take a left at the pile of tabloids, then walk until you see the Moonshine Cafe and take another left.

And if you *do* come back, buy more than a pocket knife next time, alright dear?"

May tried to make it look like she wasn't hurrying as she hurried to the door.

"Thank you. I will come back," she threw over her shoulder. And she would. She had to show Xan the fish.

The tabloids clumped together like a papier-mâché monolith in the distance; what they thought they were doing there in the middle of the road was beyond May. As she approached, she found that the stack was as tall as she was and seemed to have been purposefully constructed. The pyramid marked a change in the lighting situation. The yellow lights on this side of the tabloids were practically blinding compared to their counterparts beyond.

She went anyway.

The Moonshine Cafe's sign flickered to her left. This, she thought, might be the last opportunity she would have to eat for some time. It would be wise to grab a snack. She cupped her hands around her face and pressed them to the window to see what was inside the dark cafe. A wooden bar stretched along one wall and a robot with sorrowful eye-lights and a missing left hand slowly moved a dirty rag back and forth over one spot. It had been rubbing that spot for so long, that the dark varnish had been worn through.

It noticed her and looked up dolefully insomuch as an antique robot with stationary features could look doleful.

She decided that food would definitely be available again in the near future at another location. Without a doubt. She took a left around the building and tried to shake the depressing image.

The road ahead was densely murky and she paused, trying to decide whether to turn back and try the other way or to muscle through.

Her brain glitched back and forth. Forward was hope. Forward was the possibility of a StarTaxi. Forward the air seemed to have turned into undulating cherry Jello. Forward had started moaning. Forward was—okay forward wasn't going to happen. A tendril of cherry Jello struck the back of her throat with a warning blow.

"Wondered how far you'd get," said the sharply toothed mouth of a broken shop window beside her. Oh, she thought, now she was hallucinating. That was nice. At least she would die having fun. She explored the source of the words. Perhaps there would be more words. Words that were actually useful to her.

"Hello?"

"No, Jello," the window said.

"Jello?"

"Yes, or at least that's what I think it is. Don't breathe it in."

"Too late."

The window sounded like it shrugged. "Probably won't kill you."

May peered into the dark window, feeling like the first idiot to get picked off in a horror movie. She swiveled her head around to make sure nothing was sneaking up on her.

"Who are you?"

"Who are you?" parroted back at her.

She began to walk back the way she came. Bezalbum would be getting her second visit.

"Hold on, wait, hold on," the window rushed.

May looked behind her to see something crawling out of the window.

And then May realized she was about to, for the first time in her life, be mugged. And she didn't even have a fist full of keys to fight back with. She did, however, have a useful, if sweaty, pocket knife. She fished it out, clumsily unsheathing the small piece of sharp metal with her fingernail.

"I don't have any money," she warbled at the thing.

"Aw, well. I can make you pay in other ways."

NINE

KRYPTONITE

Xan had seen a TV show about Superman once. He picked up so few Earth broadcasts from his cozy spot in orbit, but he knew about this Superman and the terrible effect of Kryptonite on him. He stared at his wrists now, bound with a thin pink zip tie.

Zip ties were his Kryptonite.

Zip ties were definitely, without a doubt, the only thing that could hold him back. He sighed; if only he had laser vision. Hold on. Had he ever actually tried to shoot lasers from his eyes?

He thought back. Maybe once or twice. He felt that this had come up before. But had he tried hard enough those times? Maybe he just needed to believe in himself more.

He gathered all the laser energy that coursed through him into the space behind his eyes, then closed them. His teeth grit from the effort. He opened his eyes to release the power of a million suns upon the little strip of plastic.

A million suns, it seemed, was no match for a zip tie.

"Oy, what was your name? Zap? Dap?"

"Rap."

"Right, Wrap."

"No, ya zoup-nog. Rap with an 'R.'" Rap had been scraping under his nails with the blunt tip of a knife; hygiene was difficult in a ship without a proper washroom, but he did what he could.

"Uhuh, Rap. So, um, where are we going? I mean, Tuhnt's gone, along with, I assume, the entirety of its legal system."

Rap sat back, tying to look casual, succeeding in looking like he was sitting on a lit grill. "Did ya' honestly think there wouldn't be no consequences?"

Xan thought for a moment, his eyes darting around as he tried to come up with an answer.

"Sorry that was—that was a double negative. Yes, I did not think that there would be no consequences. Is that—did you mean 'did I think there wouldn't be *any* consequences?'"

"Blitheon, you're an obnoxious chunk of trok ain't ya?"

"So I'm told. But zuut, I expected something to happen sooner than this. After the first thousand orbits I suppose I did kinda think everyone had forgotten. I mean, really, how many Tuhntians are still out there? And the Rheans don't care, they wanted Tuhnt gone to begin with."

"Ha! I can't even begin to tell you how wrong you are."

"That sounds like an exaggeration. Go on. Educate me," Xan said in the same flat, uninterested tone May used when she was being ironic.

"The Rheans wanted to colonize Tuhnt, for starters, eh? Not destroy it, ya zoup-nog. Ever wonder why there's a Rhea I, II, and IV? As far as the zuxing Rheans figured, Tuhnt ought to have been Rhea III."

"Well, thanks for the history lesson. Back to the original question, though, if you don't mind. Where are you taking me?"

"To Tuhnt."

Xan winked his annoyance. "You've got a time machine, then. Zuut. I told May those didn't exist. When did that happen?"

"Don't be ridiculous, there ain't no time machines. We're going to New Tuhnt. And I'm telling you now so you ain't surprised: it's a trok-hole."

TEN

NASTY BUSINESS

"Excuse me?" May asked the shadow as it lurched toward her.

"I can make you pay in other ways," they repeated.

"What?" May backed up, shifting her grip on the knife.

"For a ride. You could shampoo the upholstery or something. Or you could change the oil out, I've been meaning to do that. Nasty business changing out the oil on a StarTaxi."

"What?" Fight and flight were so busy duking it out in May's head that she hadn't actually understood what they were saying to her.

The flickering light above them felt that perhaps now was a good time to actually do its job and illuminated the mugger.

A willowy Tuhntian with skin the color of a blueberry milkshake with far too few blueberries in it sauntered toward her. A massive pink braid wrapped around her neck like a scarf, and she wore a sharply studded leather jacket over a white t-shirt with the iconic Earth alien face and the words "I believe" scrawled beneath it. May wondered what exactly the shirt meant in this context but could think of no eloquent way of asking, so she let it be.

"Look mun, I can't take you far, but I'll at least get you to a busier port." She held up a gloved hand. Fingerless gloves. What was the point? May stared at it.

"High five?" the Tuhntian asked.

May gently tapped the hand with her own. "Sure. Who are you?"

"Oy, this again. Alright, I'll go first if it's that important to you. Aimz of Tuhnt. Now you."

"May of Earth," she said. Her full name was May June July but giving a full name out here had only served to perplex people so she stuck with her planet of origin.

"Ohh a Terran, eh?"

"I take offense to that. I think," May countered. Xan had told her it was a slur, the equivalent of calling someone a "dirt person," and May had been called it a few times by some of the nastier racers they'd competed against.

"Ah, hey no offense meant, Earthmun. I think it's cute that you're all the way out here. What are you doing off of Earth, anyway?"

"Racing."

"Racing what? You've got a rocket or something?" Aimz looked around as if an entire rocket ship would peek around the corner like a frightened dog and might come running up to her for pets if she whistled at it. If her tone hadn't been so intensely sincere, May would've thought she was mocking her.

"Sort of." May relaxed just a bit. Aimz was much taller than her, muscled, and decked out in spikes, but something in her enormous, earnest smile made May feel like she could trust her. "I've hit a snag. Will you help me get back to my ship or not?"

Aimz shrugged mightily, pocketing her hands. "I had a pretty full day of acquainting myself with the Jello stuff planned but, zuut, that sounds like an adventure. Now..." She leaned forward until her long nose nearly touched May's. May didn't flinch. She was used to that sort of thing from Xan. "About payment," said Aimz. "I also accept entertainment. Know any good shows from Earth? Maybe an operetta? Jokes will do in a pinch, but you better have a lot of them."

"Oh, uh, I thought you were trying to mug me. I've got money."

Aimz's forehead wrinkled extravagantly. "Are you saying I look like a mugger?"

"You're two heads taller than me and have three inch spikes on your shoulders," May pointed out.

"Ha! Oh these? No, mun, these aren't for you. They're for someone I used to know. He was a leaner. Always hanging on one shoulder or the other, I swear my shoulders are still misaligned because of it. What do you think?" Aimz straightened up, tried to even out her shoulders. "Left one's a touch off isn't it?"

May shook her head, sighed, shrugged. "Yeah maybe a bit."

"Shame. Alright, come on. The taxi's out back. You got an anchor for the ship? Or are we stealing a ship? Be honest, now. If we're stealing a ship I'll have to find my sunglasses." Aimz strode back to the busted window, May had to jog to keep up and briefly wondered if she could get leg extensions.

"I have the anchor, but we'll have to use your BEAPER," May said with a tinge of regret. She could've gotten a BEAPER. Several times she'd thought about how useful it would be to have a BEAPER. Several times she had put it off, thinking one BEAPER between the two of them was plenty. It was not.

"Eh, we'll use the taxi's computer to trace it. My BEAPER's on the outs at the moment." She climbed over a jutting tooth of broken glass and held out her wrist. It sparkled like a Fourth of July novelty firecracker and the holographic display glowed weakly above it, proclaiming that she had a new message.

Aimz squinted at it, brought it closer to her face, then attempted to accept the new message several times before it worked.

"Tell her I'll be back in a bit," said a voice which sounded an awful lot like Xan's.

May paused on the other side of the window, and looked at the BEAPER as if it suddenly turned into a crested gecko and licked its eye at her.

"Who was that from?" she asked.

Aimz gave her BEAPER the same face May had given it.

"Doesn't matter. It's old. Wasn't for you."

It probably wasn't, thought May. The voice recording was scratchy and warped, like it had been put through a blender, but it was uncannily familiar. May had two inklings. One of them was wrong.

She climbed in after Aimz, more carefully. Her shorter legs meant that there wasn't nearly as much clearance between her and the shards of glass.

The inside of the building smelled like old motor oil and stale corn chips, but when Aimz walked in, a host of organic lamps flicked on and revealed a well furnished apartment, if said apartment had been slowly consumed by a discarded craft supply fungus.

"Do you, um, live here?" May asked.

"I'd be an absolute fool if I did, don't you think?" Aimz laughed hoarsely as she tugged on an unyielding metal door toward the back of the room. "Yes. Yes, I do live here."

"It's charming." May had never in her life used the word 'charming'. Not once. This was absolutely and positively the first time it had ever actually come out of her mouth. May would never use the word again.

"Ha! You're a laugh, Earthmun. It's not. Don't worry about it, I'm moving soon. I've never broken lease in my life, but I'm starting to think the landlord's not actually planning to fix that window."

"Oh that? I hardly noticed," May said of the window and Aimz laughed a broad laugh that May swore made the lamps glow brighter.

The door screeched open and revealed a long wooden boardwalk which stretched out from the spaceport like Adam's finger reaching out toward God's. Only God, in this instance, was a ship so small that May would have had no trouble believing Aimz if she said her laugh alone could power it.

A curious thing happened to May, poised on the edge of the rotting wooden planks and surrounded by space. She suddenly had a fear of heights. Someone who'd spent some time in space, who raced a rocket ship for a living, theoretically would have an agreement with heights by now. And she did. But this wasn't just height. It was depth, it was breadth, it was the whole general everything, and it was horrifying. Some invisible atmosphere must extend over the boardwalk, thought May. Some amount of gravity must be present in order for them to walk across it.

Aimz put a hand to her back. "You steady?"

"Huh?"

"You look like a wyrntensil in a maelstrom."

"I'm fine. There's atmosphere and artificial gravity out there right? On the boardwalk?"

"No, see, the idea is that you're supposed to empty your lungs then crawl across the boardwalk before you freeze to death. Of course there's atmosphere and gravity. Go on, just don't look down. Or up. Or to the sides. Or—you know what? Just look at the StarTaxi and you'll be fine."

The hand on May's back started to push her forward and they strolled into nothingness with only a few planks of wood keeping them tethered.

May wondered how far the force field extended. If she jumped, would she be lost to the cosmos forever? What if she fell? Would she re-gravitize to the underside of the boardwalk? Was it even really an underside?

The science of the boardwalk was troubling at best and impossible at worst, so May decided to focus on the StarTaxi as Aimz had suggested.

When they reached the taxi, Aimz pressed the tip of her thumb into a soft button on the side of it, and the door puffed into atoms, allowing them to pass through. Inside, the StarTaxi was dimly lit by a string of blue lights which skirted the ceiling and the soft glow of stars through the digital viewscreen at the front. The taxi rocked as Aimz tucked herself into the pilot's seat, and May crawled into the back. There were four seats, but none of them had accounted for passengers that had legs.

Aimz popped a panel off the dashboard and twisted a pair of worn wires together. With a sizzling zap and a flash of light, the engine began to purr like a geriatric puma.

"Great! There's at least one more trip in this rust sack. Button?" She reached her hand into the back seat, her palm open.

May dropped the pocket knife back into its make-shift pocket, then snapped the button off the strap of her swimsuit and pressed it into Aimz's palm.

"It's a Class 20 Racing Rocket," May said as Aimz popped the button into a slot on the dashboard.

"Really? Don't see many of those anymore. Color?"

"Orange. Really, extremely orange."

Aimz twisted around, scrutinizing her with bubblegum pink irises that appeared to glow in the low light.

"Not Obtrusive Orange, is it?"

May nodded, but slowly, half her brain telling her to run and the other half asking the first half where the hell it thought she ought to run to. "Yes, how did you know?"

Aimz ignored the question.

"And this rocket ship...are you the rightful owner, or did you steal it? Or did you buy it off someone? Who did you buy it from?"

"I'm paying you to take me to it," May said, wishing they had gone through this before she gave away the anchor button. "Not to interview me about it."

"Where is the owner? What happened to him?" Aimz was suddenly nose-to-nose with her in the back seat. It was like being interrogated by a stretched-out, angry pink gummy bear.

"I don't have to tell you anything." May tried to worm her way into the front seat to retrieve the button, but Aimz's fingers were tiny steel girders digging into her shoulders.

"Where is Xan?" Aimz snarled.

"Why do you want to know?"

"Tell me, or you're not getting back to the *Audacity* ever." Aimz released May's shoulders and defiantly crossed her arms to prove that she had no intention of flying the StarTaxi until she knew.

"What do you want from him?" May asked.

"What do *you* want from him?"

"I asked first."

"Ah, but I own the taxi."

"Which I'm paying for."

"I'm bigger than you, you know. Scary mugger-type, remember?"

"But you're bluffing."

"Why, uh—why would you think that?"

"Call it a hunch."

"I..." Aimz straightened her back, "I don't have a hunch. What?"

"I mean I know exactly who you are and why you want to find Xan," May said, feeling smug for the first time in a long time.

Humans, as a species, are terrific at connecting the dots. The concept of constellations doesn't exist, or at least not in the same mythic capacity, anywhere else in the universe. Where one species would see a random peppering of distant stars, humans see an ageless struggle between a hunter, his trusty dog, and a bear. Or a ladle. All humans see patterns, but the creativity of the interpretation of those patterns varies.

May had connected the dots now. The dots were vague, the connections relied on an astonishingly high coincidence factor, but astonishing coincidence was no stranger to May.

"What? You couldn't possibly. Could you? Zuut, you could. Wait. Who do you think I am and why do you think I want to find Xan?"

"You tell me first. I'll tell you if I was right."

"Ahah, that's not how it works, mun."

"If you are who I think you are, you at least want him alive."

"More or less."

"Less?"

"Right, well, he's not winning any awards for favorite brother this orbit, mun, I can tell you that!"

"Ha! I knew it."

"Ah, Blitheon's zuxing trok," Aimz cursed at herself. May smiled.

"So you'll help me find him and not kill him?"

"Oh, I'll help you find him."

"And not kill him?" May clarified.

"Right, yeah, fine. Whatever."

"Promise?"

"I promise not to kill him on purpose."

"Good enough. He's been arrested by a bounty hunter and as far as I know he's wherever the *Audacity* is."

The taxi's computer dinged proudly, spitting the anchor button out of the dashboard like a slice of toast.

"Found him!" Aimz stomped on the taxi's accelerator and made for New Tuhnt.

ELEVEN

TRASHED

Rhea III, as Listay insisted, does not exist. It did, though. Some 32,500 orbits ago it existed, then was abandoned, forgotten, re-discovered, christened Pontoosa: The Wackiest Rock in the Solar System by a band of renegade entrepreneurial Tuhntians, abandoned again, forgotten again, and finally, re-discovered by EnviroDev and claimed as the site of New Tuhnt.

So it was here, to the nearly but not quite deserted New Tuhnt, that Chaos brought Listay to seek out the oft limericked about Sphere of Time.

Listay struggled with the door for a moment, pulling on the inside handle until she heard a crack. Giving up, she unrolled the window and shimmied through it, despite her thickly muscled thighs and persistent rigor mortis.

From a tent in the distance, the Tuhntian surveyor, who has a name but whose name is untranslatable, watched as the Rhean emerged from the window of the AMC Gremlin and trundled into a patch of sprouts he had been tending for the past three rotations.

This was no EnviroDev supply ship. In fact, he had only ever seen a ship that ugly once before, during the war. It was a *Peacemaker* shuttle. A shuttle from the ship that had destroyed Tuhnt. And it was trying to destroy New Tuhnt, now, apparently. One patch of sprouts at a time.

The uniform was that of a Rhean general. Before Listay's body had had a chance to crawl to her shaky knees but after Chaos had begun cursing through her stiff lips, the Tuhntian surveyor offered a hand to help her up.

Chaos tried to wave his hand away, but Listay was less concerned about appearing weak and more concerned about eventually getting off the ground, so she used the surveyor's arm as leverage to stand up.

"Thank you. I'd like to apologize in advance for my behavior, I'm afraid I've been possessed by an ancient Chaos goddess and she's a real—" Listay paused, forgetting for a moment how to work her tongue. The surveyor waited patiently. "—ly magnificent sight to behold," Chaos finished with a smile.

While the surveyor wasn't willing to say that she *was* possessed by an ancient Chaos goddess, he couldn't look into her unmentionably clouded eyes and say she wasn't.

And she was armed. He watched the plasma zapper strapped to her thigh suspiciously, as if it might leap out of its holster.

"What's the zapper for?"

"Nothing so long as you cooperate."

This conversation was quickly morphing from suspicious to vaguely threatening. He needed to confer with someone and the only other someone on the planet was Sonan. "Let's get you inside." He gestured to the wreck of the *Innocuous* behind him. "Sonan will want to meet you."

"No. You will take me to the Sphere of Time immediately." Chaos was accustomed to being obeyed. She was also accustomed to having power over reality. Now, though, she was little more than a persistent intrusive thought trapped in the brain of a zombie. For a being whose *modus operandi* was intimidation, this was not ideal.

The surveyor, at the risk of being uncooperative, had to protest. He protested carefully, though.

"I don't know where or what that is but Sonan might." He gave her an encouraging smile. "So come with me?"

Chaos filled Listay's lungs with dusty air to prepare for an obstinate huff. Instead, she coughed, squashing any possibility of intimidating him.

"I will come with you," she wheezed. "But know it's of my own volition. If I wanted to, I could smite you right now. This place could use the fertilizer. What are you called?"

The surveyor gave his untranslatable name, a no-nonsense, practical Tuhntian family name which Chaos herself had used to refer to a plan four or five plans back.

Why don't you possess him? Listay thought as they followed the mountainous Tuhntian.

"It's almost as if you *want* to be dead again," said Chaos.

"Excuse me?" the surveyor paused.

"Inside joke. Not about you."

If I were to possess him instead, Chaos told Listay with her inside voice, *your body wouldn't survive a blip out here. Is that what you want?*

No, thought Listay as they reached the *Innocuous*'s access hatch. She stared at the ladder leading up to the hatch. Clearly, he was waiting for her to mount it. Clearly, she wasn't going to.

"Do you need help?" he asked quietly, embarrassed.

Chaos shook her head and attached Listay's metal arm to a rung. After a moment of mental prodding, she got her organic arm to follow suit. From there, it was only a matter of time before her left foot found the first rung. And now the right foot...

The surveyor wanted desperately to help her, but he knew that there were some things that had to be done alone, and it seemed like climbing this ladder was one of those things, so he waited until at last she paused, resting her forehead against the side of the hatch, and looked down at him.

"I've only just recently resurrected this body from her grave and I would appreciate some praise at this point," said Chaos.

"Oh, uh, well done. That's...that's very good," said the surveyor, then clapped a few times to show he was sincere.

"Are you patronizing me?"

"Not at all. I would imagine resurrecting from the dead is quite an ordeal," he said.

"Perhaps if you're very lucky, you'll find out one day," she said and opened the hatch, crawling into the dark hallway of the *Innocuous*.

The surveyor followed her inside, sealed the hatch, then led her to the stodgy tearoom door.

"Sonan?" the surveyor asked, rapping timidly on the door. "I've got a visitor for you."

"You may enter!"

The surveyor laughed lightly. "Don't let her intimidate you. She's really very sweet," he told Chaos who was more irritated than intimidated.

They entered the brightly lit and doilied room to find Sonan sitting where she always sat, pouring another cup of tea, and smiling with stiff android lips.

"Welcome to New Tuhnt," said Sonan. "Would you like a cup of tea?"

"I'm looking for the Sphere of Time. Do you know where it is?" Chaos asked, working Listay's features into a scowl.

"No, I can't say I do. Cup of tea?" Sonan poured a second cup now and gently pushed it across the table toward Chaos.

"I don't want your zuxing tea. I know it's here and if you're hiding it from me I will rain my vengeance upon you first!" She flung aside the wicker chair nearest her.

The surveyor, mortified, lunged for Chaos and pinned her arms to her sides.

"Sorry about this, Sonan. Should I put her in the holding cell?"

"Not at all. We will be requiring that cell when Rap returns."

"Respectfully, it's been orbits since we last heard from him."

"We will need that cell," she insisted. "Throw her away."

"What in the-the compactor?"

"Of course."

Chaos tested Listay's upper arm strength against the surveyor's. Had she not been dead for so long, she would've overpowered him easily. Chaos was beginning to regret having murdered her new host body.

"Yes ma'am," said the surveyor to Sonan, then, to Chaos, "I am truly sorry about—"

He stopped. Listay's body had gone limp. He shook her slightly, watching her head loll from one side to the other.

"Sonan? I think she's dead," he said to the android.

From Sonan, nothing. She had shut off.

The Tuhntian surveyor sighed, hefted Listay's body over his shoulder, and brought her to the trash compactor, dropping her corpse, respectfully, into the pit of garbage.

His BEAPER dinged. Sonan had been correct; they would be needing the holding cell.

TWELVE

AIMZ THE CH'STRANDA

The StarTaxi puttered through space with a sound not unlike a Shriner's tiny parade car.

"Where are you?" Aimz's BEAPER was talking again. Talking with, what May now knew, was Xan's voice. "I've been thinking about getting a ch'stranda!" it said.

May hurled herself over the back of the pilot's seat and stared, along with Aimz, at the busted BEAPER.

"I told him he could have one if he could catch one," May said. "Can you let him know we're coming?"

Aimz shook her head. "These messages are a few hundred orbits old. The range on this thing's terrible; they're only now coming through because we're near. Also, if he knows we're coming to get him we lose the surprise."

"Right, so I got a ch'stranda. Named him Aimz. Hope that isn't weird," said the ancient recording of Xan.

Aimz laughed. "It is, you slorpfignut," she said under her breath. The BEAPER sparked and sizzled, its holographic screen zilching out of existence.

"Ouch! Alright." Aimz removed the smoking BEAPER and set it in her lap. On the viewscreen, the spitball which was New Tuhnt was slowly gaining size.

"Go to the *Audacity* first. If you help me deposit some crystals, you can take as many as you can carry."

"Not a bad deal. I can carry a lot. Big hands," Aimz said, proving it to May by flexing her gloveless fingers at her.

"And you're not actually going to try to kill Xan if we find him, are you?" May pressed.

Aimz mulled slightly longer than May would've liked. "No, but I want him to think I'm going to. You in?"

"I mean, he just got arrested. Does he deserve that?" He did.

"Oh yeah. Yes. Yes he deserves that. He told you what he did, right?"

"Via a baking analogy."

THIRTEEN

PERPLEXION

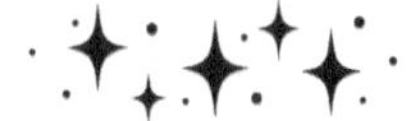

New Tuhnt was a trok-hole. Xan could now confirm it. The planet they had landed on wasn't so much a world as it was a rock. Not even a pretty rock. The land which expanded beyond the MoonHopper's viewscreen looked like dried oatmeal, only somehow less appetizing.

"Okay." Xan paused to tug at the zip tie with his teeth. "Alright, so there's a New Tuhnt. But the question remains," he gnawed. "Why? Because the original Tuhnt wasn't all that great, really. I mean if it's all you know, sure it does the trick. But if I'm being honest this place looks even worse."

"Shut up," Rap said as he checked his landing stats, which were dismal, then shut off the MoonHopper.

Still nibbling on the zip tie, Xan, from the corner of his mouth, said, "Nostalgia, I bet. Isn't it? Everyone missed having somewhere to be which was called 'Tuhnt' and decided to call something else 'Tuhnt' and thought that would make it all right and good but I'll tell you what, once it's gone it's gone. You might as well start with something fresh, eh? Speaking of fresh, does anything even grow here? I mean like fruits and vegetables, not just bacteria."

"Shut up," had become something of a motto for Rap since meeting Xan. He said it again now, urgently.

"Sure...but, really, what's the statute of limitations on something like this? A millenia and a half is a long time."

"There's not really a statute of limitations on genocide, no," Rap said pressing a call button on the MoonHopper's control panel. "We've landed. Want to help me out here? Bringing him to Sonan?"

"Hey Rap, good to see you," the deep voice of the Tuhntian surveyor sizzled through the MoonHopper's communication line. "Been a busy rotation here. Sonan's preoccupied right now. Would you put him in the holding cell?"

"Aye, tell me about it," Rap replied.

"Ha, well, to begin I discovered a strain of bacteria that actually grows here," crackled through the speaker.

"Right get on with the interesting stuff."

"I had to throw someone in the trash compactor today."

"No way. Alright, I'll deal with Xan, then we can catch up."

"I'll be here."

"Shift it." Rap hoisted Xan up to drag him out of the MoonHopper and onto the stinking, oxygen starved land.

"Your standards-" Xan coughed, tasting the odor in the back of his throat. "By Quanzar's Laser-Scythe your standards for New Tuhnt were low," he wheezed. "What is this, a landfill planet? Is this the plan?" He coughed. "Olfactory torture? Really, Rap. And another thing—" He stopped talking.

A gnarly-looking StarTaxi snuggled into the space below the *Audacity*. In tandem, Rap and Xan perplexed at it, then Xan disappeared and Rap perplexed alone.

FOURTEEN

ANAT ATTACK

Two things Xan was not expecting happened in rapid succession. The first, and arguably more pleasant, was that he was back in the *Audacity* and the ship was moving. The second was that something heavy was pinning him to the orange shag carpet.

"Look at you!" said the something.

"Ahh!" said Xan.

"Wow!" said the something.

"Ahh!" Xan reiterated.

"You zuxing tchagg, what have you got to defend yourself? And why are you in a swimsuit?"

"We were at the beach..."

His eyes finally focused on his attacker. A neuron that had slumbered peacefully for a few thousand orbits was suddenly jolted awake, handed a fedora and a briefcase, and told it was late to work.

"Aimz?" For a second, it looked like she wanted to squeeze the life from him with her semi-gloved hands. Then, a ball of wires bounced off her forehead and she sat back just enough that he could shimmy awkwardly away.

"Hey, what?" Aimz shouted at May.

"You looked like you were about to go for the neck." May said, hopping down from the control loft. She dug out the lighter from beneath a pile of magazines under the coffee table, flicked it on, and grabbed Xan's wrists by the pink zip tie, holding the flame under the plastic to melt it through. Only when she smelled the toxic melted plastic fumes did she remember she had a pocket knife.

"May," he whispered, watching Aimz rub her forehead. "Where did you find that?"

"What, your sister?" she whispered back, flinging aside the melted zip tie. "The one you don't have?"

"That's not Aimz. That is most definitely a cruel shape-shifting Anat which is most definitely after my soul. Where's the marsupian wine? Anat's are allergic to culture."

May had no idea where the wine was and was fairly certain they'd had the last of it a while back after a particularly harrowing race win. Still, she knifed her hand into the couch cushions to fish for the bottle.

"Oh, yeah," laughed Aimz. "Did I forget to mention that I was an Anat? Can't wait to dehydrate your souls and tuck them away in my cave of eternal night. Come over it, you know who I am." She winked, situating herself cross-legged on the orange shag.

"Well I know who you *look* like," he growled. "And I've got to say that's outrageously insensitive of you. That's utterly, entirely, and insanely messed up. You know that? That's just-"

"Found it!" May said, uncorking a strangely angled bottle which swirled with a teaspoon of blue liquid.

"Great, melt her!" Xan scrambled onto the couch as if Aimz were a rat that might charge at his feet.

May exchanged a bemused glance with Aimz who tipped her head back, opening her mouth wide to accept the wine which May poured down her throat.

Aimz collapsed not, as Xan had hoped, in an uncivilized puddle, but in a fit of laughter.

"Xan, you slorpfignut, I'm not a zuxing Anat!"

Xan finally got to his knees and moved closer, examining the face that smiled back at him. "Aimz? I swear to Quanzar if you're trying to have one over on me I'll-"

"You'll what? Kill me? Again?"

Xan launched into her and squeezed her so tightly her back made a sound like a snapping glow stick.

"Zuut! Get off me," she whined, but she made no move to push him away.

He released her, rocking back on his heels. "How on Tuhnt did you survive?"

"Well," Aimz got to her feet, straightened her jacket, and flopped onto the couch. "That's the key, isn't it? I wasn't on Tuhnt. I was on an off-world mission interning with BioTech when it happened. We were collecting samples of a new strain of sentient chartreuse cave skrum they'd detected in the area. Mission was canceled. Obviously. Most of my coworkers had enough gem to get themselves to Rhea but not me. Nope. I got stuck in Yenuket with a two thousand orbit contract with Gertrub's StarTaxis. Which I think I'm in breach of, incidentally, seeing as I left the taxi back there." She jammed a thumb at the viewscreen and a spit-ball sized New Tuhnt.

Xan smiled in a way that made it look like someone had cut out a picture of his smile from a magazine and pasted it onto his face. He sat across from her on the coffee table. "And, uh, do you know what happened to Tuhnt?"

May sat on the couch beside Aimz now. She hoped Aimz didn't know because *she* didn't know, not exactly, and it sounded like Xan was about to tell her.

"Hard not to," Aimz said through her teeth.

The cut-out of Xan's smile began to peel away from his face.

"The *Peacemaker* blasted it to bits. And all because someone stole the rocket that was supposed to distract the *Peacemaker* long enough to destroy it."

Another edge of the cut-out drooped.

"All because some orange-haired groutal-lipped coward pilfered the *Audacity* right before it was scheduled to save the planet from imminent destruction."

The cut-out of his smile detached fully and drifted softly, leaf-like to the orange shag below.

"Are you mad at me?" he asked in a voice that was not his.

Aimz very much gave the impression that she was, in fact, mad at him. May understood now why stealing a rocket ship had caused the destruction of Tuhnt, but not why Xan had done it to begin with. She hoped there was a good reason. If Aimz murdered him now, May would never find out, so she casually began to look for other small items she could pelt at Aimz in the event she tackled Xan again.

"Eugh, I don't blame you. You always were the zoup-nog in the family," she sneered. "I just don't know how you got away with it for this long."

"Luck," Xan said, bitter as orange pith.

A flap on Schrodinger's box was open now, and it was ever so tempting to look inside. "About the family," Xan hazarded, careful not to open the box too quickly.

"Zuut," Aimz sat back in the couch and pretended she hadn't heard him. "Yenuket Municipal was a trash compactor compared to this. You've been living nicely, haven't you? An entire couch, lighting, windows...living like a queen."

"Aimz, my quality of life over the past 1,700 orbits isn't important. I mean, the windows are nice and it is delightfully orange in here but that's not the point. The point is-"

"Ah, no don't say it," Aimz covered her face with her hands.

"You're deflecting. What about everyone else? Tell me."

The face May made as she watched Xan accuse Aimz of deflecting encompassed all the frustration of seven seasons of *his* deflecting, tying it up like a package wrapped in awe and just enough bubble wrap to keep her from shouting something at him.

"They're fine."

"Aimz."

"Eugh, alright!" Aimz chewed her lip for a minute, curled her legs underneath her. "I don't know. I haven't seen another Tuhntian since my coworkers scuttled off to Rhea I. Yvonne's alive, at least."

"Yeah, I'm aware," said Xan. And then he said, through Aimz's BEAPER and a few hundred orbits too late, "It's weird, I'm sorry."

Aimz laughed at Xan's confusion. "I'm getting old messages you sent me. You named a ch'stranda after me?"

"Right, Aimz the ch'stranda. Shouldn't have done that; it *was* weird," he said. And then, via Aimz's BEAPER. "Just tell me if you're alive or not, alright? I miss you."

"I missed you, too," Aimz admitted. "After I stopped wanting to kill you."

Xan cringed. "When did you stop? Exactly?"

"I'll let you know."

FIFTEEN
AN EXCELLENT ESCAPE

The *Audacity* hurtled away from New Tuhnt until it suddenly did not. The ship stopped with enough force to fling everything which was not bolted down against the back-lit plastic wall. Nothing, because someone had neglected standard safety practice, was bolted down.

Xan was the first up, rotating his shoulders to make sure they still worked properly.

Aimz came to a cautious sitting position, holding her head to try to keep it in the same dimension as her body.

May slept peacefully, her consciousness having popped out to explore better, less danger-prone brains.

"What in Quanzar's name was that?" Xan asked no one in particular as he tried to leap up to the control loft, only then realizing that it wasn't his shoulders but his hips which had suffered the majority of the blow.

While Tuhntians heal at a rate so much faster than humans that comparing them is mathematically impossible, Tuhntian joints, like all joints in the Universe, are shit.

"Well, we hit something didn't we? Zoup-nog." Aimz rolled herself up and joined Xan at the viewscreen. A bloody gash on her forehead faded away as she rubbed her left elbow which felt every blip of her 3,500 orbits.

May's consciousness was still galavanting about a few light-years away; it was starting to get a taste for freedom.

Xan studied the screen. "Everything's still on. We should be moving according to this thing." He tapped a dial which was quite clearly labeled the speedometer. "But we aren't moving at all according to the other thing." He tapped an inset image in the screen which was also labeled, this time 'Navigation.' "Maybe we're in a pocket dimension! Maybe we're traveling in time instead of space! Eugh, or maybe we're traveling in another, more boring dimension that isn't time. What if we're traveling in scent?"

Aimz summoned a view from the *Audacity*'s back-up camera. "Or we've run out of rope. I'm favoring that one on account of, there's a rope thingy trailing off behind us and we're at the end of it. Also, scent isn't a dimension."

"That you're aware of," he muttered. "Aimz, really, what kind of rope could stop the *Audacity*? You must've hit your head on the wall. Oh! You know what, I think I've read about this somewhere! I bet it's an invisible aether bog. Like, really thick, sticky nothingness. May, settle a wager, what do you think? Rope or space bog? I think space bog."

May didn't answer. Her consciousness was toeing a silvery pond in the seventy-eighth dimension (a dimension which was not exactly scent itself but did have some correlation with scent).

"That's not how dimensions work!" said Aimz to the narration.

The *Audacity* jarred, then began to crawl backward toward New Tuhnt with a sound like a semi-truck squeezing into a storm drain.

"Probably ought to turn off the engine," Aimz said, searching for the off switch.

"Why? We want to go forward. Let's wait it out." Xan sat in the co-pilot's chair, wiggling around until he found a position that didn't hurt. He settled on one leg bent over the arm of the chair, one leg twisted beneath him, and his arms slung over the back. "May?" He wondered why she hadn't joined them yet. The Earthling who had been on the ship for a mere half an orbit knew more about it than he did. It ought to have been embarrassing, but really he was quite proud of her, if not completely dependent on her.

"Alright, blow out your engines, burn through a tank of fuel. I don't care. Not my ship." But her eyes still searched the console. The *Audacity* shuddered pitifully. "I don't think your Earthling made it, by the way."

"What?"

"I think she'd dead," Aimz said, still looking for the off-switch. "Oh! Is this it?" She pressed The Button Which Typically Made The Ship Go (which also typically made it stop) and the storm drain semi-truck sound ceased.

Behind them in the living room, May's wayward consciousness finally felt a twinge of homesickness. It stopped in its lackadaisical journeying and took a good look around. It wandered for a bit in one direction, then back the way it came. After a few false starts, it realized it was lost and began to hyperventilate insomuch as a lungless consciousness could hyperventilate.

Xan approached May slowly; he didn't think she looked dead. He had never actually had the displeasure of seeing anyone dead before, though, so he had nothing to compare it to.

After a contemptuous snort at The Button Which Typically Made The Ship Go But Also Typically Made It Stop, Aimz crouched beside May and lifted her wrist. "See? Limper than last season's Moringarg."

Xan shook his head. "She's fine! She sleeps a lot." He slung her over his shoulder and looked for the couch. It had made a sizable crack in the lighted plastic wall panel. Xan nodded toward it. "Flip the couch over for me?"

"Okay, but how much are you going to pay me?"

The retort Xan wanted to make slipped out as a strangled sigh, and with his free hand, he dug into an impossible pocket in his swimsuit and collected a handful of crystals which he offered to Aimz.

"Blitheon, mun, I was only-" Aimz shut her mouth quickly, choosing instead to pocket the gem before flipping over the couch.

Xan set May down, folding himself over the back of the couch to think.

Xan, as it happens, was not great at thinking quietly.

"Okay, alright, so," he began. "Maybe you were right, Aimz."

"About the Earthling?"

"About the rope!"

"Oh."

"Yeah." He huffed, then returned to watching May. "We can't pull away from the rope, but can we cut it? Untie it? Burn it? Politely ask it to leave?"

"Sure, I'll just crawl onto a fin and climb down, gnaw it off with my teeth, and we'll be on our way." Aimz sat cross legged in front of the couch. "That rope is strong enough to stop a Class 20 Racing Rocket. Not even *my* teeth could hold up to that, and you know what I've bitten through."

"I do." Xan groaned, pressing his face into the couch. If May were awake, she would be trying to think up another plan. Seeing as she wasn't, Xan had to. He was finding it difficult to think about anything more useful than the tiny paper hats people put on roasted turkey legs in Earth media and wondering what, exactly, their purpose was. His mouth, frustrated with his brain for not staying focused, began to think for itself. "It's not so much a rope, is it?" he asked. "More of a cable."

"I suppose." Aimz prodded May's still hand. "Why don't you wake her up?" May's typically warm brown complexion was more of an ashy taupe now. Xan had noticed this but decided instead to contemplate the color taupe and whether or not the color he thought was taupe was the same color May saw when she saw taupe. He wished he could ask her.

With a whine, he tapped her on the shoulder. He knew little of alien biology, but if he were being honest with himself he knew the g-force had knocked her out and he was worried.

"She's a heavy sleeper," Xan said.

Aimz also knew little of alien biology. However, she assumed that a pulse was an important aspect of life the Universe over. She smoothed a lock of pink hair away from her pointed ear and pressed it to May's chest.

"What is it?" Xan asked when Aimz's forehead crumpled.

"Her heart is racing! I'm surprised she hasn't exploded," Aimz said.

"Well at least it's going, right?" Xan laughed nervously. He bent a quizzical ear to her chest. "Ah, no that's normal for her."

May's consciousness was steadily approaching now, having finally asked directions from a passing cloud of kindly steam in the thirty-second dimension.

It began to trickle back to her and settled in with a sigh of relief.

May shot up, her head thunking into Xan's.

"Ouch. Xan, what were you doing on my boobs?" She rubbed her forehead where a bump was forming.

"See! She's fine," Xan said. "May, settle a wager. What's taupe? No! Not that one, sorry. What do you think stopped us: a rope or a space bog?"

Aimz rolled her eyes so hard it made her head lean back on the coffee table behind her. "It's a rope, Xan, you know that," she told the ceiling.

"What's a rope?" May asked.

"Blitheon, May, don't you have ropes on Earth? Like really thick string?" Xan said.

"No, I know what a rope is, I mean...nevermind." She had noticed that the ship was moving but the engines weren't on. "Why don't we pull away? The *Audacity* can break a rope."

"Not this one. Tried that," Xan said.

"Where's it taking us?"

"Back to New Tuhnt. Listen, don't get yourselves taken in by trying to help me. I'll figure something out. Always do," Xan said, trying to put on a brave face but failing.

"Does 'figuring something out' usually involve genocide?" Aimz dug.

After a long, loud silence, Xan said, "Not usually, no."

"It usually involves the probability modifier," May amended. "Which we haven't got."

"Ha! Oh Earthmun, you had a probably modifier? You're massively zuxed. This is going to be more entertainment than I've had in seasons. You know what happens when those things quit on you?"

"Finding out, aren't I?" Xan toppled into the couch beside May and covered his face with his hands.

"The *Audacity* has the Ultra-Ray-Super-Destroyers." May said, squinting into the middle distance. "No one can get on board without an anchor button, so Rap will have to climb up to the hatch to get in. We could, you know..."

"What, disintegrate him?" Xan asked, peeking through his fingers at her.

"I-erm-well-huh," she stammered then bit her lip at him with a cautious shrug. It seemed the most logical plan but she wasn't sure she could disintegrate someone. She would leave the ethics of it up to Xan. She liked to leave him with the ethical quandaries; she was the ideas person.

He started to provide an answer, but was interrupted when the *Audacity*'s fins dug into the oatmealy soil of New Tuhnt. The rocket tipped drunkenly as it tried to settle itself on horridly misaligned fins with nary a stabilizer firing.

May flung herself off the couch and scrambled toward the console to turn on the stabilizers. The rocking of the ship knocked her to the floor, and giving up, she curled her fingers into the shag carpet until the rocket stopped shaking.

At last it stilled, and May finished scrambling to the control loft.

On the planet below, two bipeds were quickly bipedaling toward them.

"I see them!" May aimed the *Audacity*'s Ultra-Ray-Super-Destroyers at the pair who looked, from that distance, like green plastic army men spray-painted silver. Aimz joined her at the console.

"Are you going to shoot them?" Aimz asked, excitement twinged by concern in her voice. She both deeply needed to see them blown to bits and was terrified she'd have to watch. She was a Tuhntian of dualities, and this was something she both loved and hated about herself.

May held a finger to the trigger, as if she were holding down ribbons and waiting for someone else to tie a bow. As they got ever closer, she had to keep re-adjusting the crosshairs.

Was she going to shoot them? Fuck if I know. She chewed thoughtfully on the inside of her lip wondering what sort of person she was if she couldn't disintegrate two strangers to save her best friend, wondering what sort of person she was if she *could*.

Finally, Xan, the one-person ethics committee, joined them. "Alright so, considering the circumstances, my vote probably doesn't mean much, but I do know that blasting someone to bits with six enormous Ultra-Ray-Super-Destroyers is morally repugnant." He scrunched up his face. "By Quanzar I'm going to regret this but..." He moved May's hand from the trigger and disengaged the lasers.

May didn't mind.

Aimz didn't mind much.

"And poof," Aimz said with the help of an explosive hand gesture. "There goes our advantage. Are you enjoying that moral high ground? Nice view up there?" Aimz laughed. "Appreciate it while you can because I don't think one good deed is going to fix the garbage fire that is your busted karma."

A thunk resonated in the ship as their pursuers mounted the ladder.

"Wormhole," May said, hopping down the control loft stairs two at a time.

"Really?" Xan squeaked. "The basement wormhole is unpredictable; we could end up absolutely anywhere as absolutely anything. We could be shredded! We could end up anywhere as shreds!"

The manual access hatch shuttered. The green plastic army men who were silver had reached it. The green plastic army men who were silver were trying to open it.

Aimz accompanied May to the intershoot. "That's a myth," she said. "Most wormholes are harmless. And fun!

Come on, what could you lose?"

Xan groaned, but also tucked himself into the cramped intershoot. "I don't know. A leg. I could lose a leg," he said as they plummeted to the basement.

It was eerily silent, the air stale as if the wormhole had sucked out all the oxygen. The only hints to the wormhole's physical existence were the slight distortion of light that seemingly came from nowhere pulling at its center and a gentle gravitational pull that made it slightly easier to walk toward it than away from it.

"Any idea where it comes out?" Aimz asked, trying to peer through to the other side.

"Not as such," said Xan. "As far as I can tell, this side is stable and the other side moves around occasionally. It's spat out junk from across the universe. We could end up in a different galaxy altogether."

"They won't find us there," May said and, closing her eyes, leaped into the wormhole.

"Zuut, May, wait!" Xan followed her, and Aimz plunged in after him.

The wormhole enveloped them like a blanket made of everything that ever was. All of existence expanded and contracted around them, moving them on to their destination. It was extremely pleasant in an accepting-your-own-death sort of way.

SIXTEEN

IT WAS NOT

May, Xan, and Aimz landed gracefully atop a spray of rusty orange grass. The air was cool, but not cold, and smelled of wet coffee grounds and metal. Disoriented by the journey, May patted around the thick orange grass and tried to figure out why it was so oddly familiar.

No, not grass. Carpet. Shag carpet. May looked up.

The glowing orange walls of the *Audacity*'s living room greeted her. "Whew, thought I'd lost you lot for a minute there," the walls said. "It's sure great to have you back," they said. "By the by, who are these two large Tuhntians who've just broken in? Friends of yours?" they finished.

Two pairs of thick black boots and silver-shod legs stood like prison bars a foot from May's face.

"Zuxing useless wormhole," Xan grumbled to her left. He rolled onto his back and tried to remember a time when he was less pleased to see the *Audacity*'s living room than right now. Never, probably.

"So this is him? Why is he in a swimsuit?" the voice of God, or at least a near neighbor to it, asked.

"They were at the beach, *obviously*. Scrawnier than you imagined, ain't he?" said Rap.

The owner of the first voice was, in fact, the Tuhntian surveyor who has a name but whose name is untranslatable.

"We were at the beach." Xan said absently, weighing whether or not it would be wise to stand up.

"Ha!" Aimz laughed. "This is why probability modifiers were banned. Outrageously bad luck, right? Guessing we're all arrested now." She stood and thrust out her hands, wrists knocking together cheerily, waiting to be bound.

The surveyor's face cracked open with a wide, white smile. "Not yet. You've been invited to tea." It was among the top ten most threatening invitations to tea in the history of the universe.

"What do you mean we've been invited?" Xan said. Everyone else was standing now, so he stood, too.

"To tea," the surveyor repeated. "It was a sort of-"

"What? A catchphrase?" Aimz goaded.

"N-no," said the surveyor. "Look, just come along. Sonan wants to see you. In her tearoom. For tea," he clarified.

"I think I'll pass," said May's mouth before her brain had time to stop it.

"You don't have a choice." Rap pulled a plasma pistol from his belt and aimed it at her. Xan dodged behind Aimz and scooped May behind himself. Aimz glanced over her shoulder at him.

"What?" he whispered up at her from behind her hair. "You like getting shot at, and May's all squish."

"Um," said May.

"Everyone unpin it," said the surveyor. "Especially you, Rap. We've got the ship, they aren't going anywhere. Sorry, about him." The surveyor held out a friendly hand to the conglomerate which was Aimz, Xan, and May, in that order. He introduced himself.

"What was that?" May asked, slipping out from behind Xan.

He said his name again.

"My translation chip must be acting up," she said. "It sounded like you said your name was Precious Butler."

Everything went silent. Even the gentle buzz of electricity coursing through the ship hushed in fear of what might happen next.

The closest English approximate for the surveyor's name was, in fact, Precious Butler. Unfortunately, the words "precious" and "butler" translated back to the surveyor as "Sweet person who performs services" which is a rather nasty thing to call a prostitute in Tuhntian culture.

Precious Butler's reaction was impossible to decipher. Confusion and hurt played tug-of-war with his face and they were fairly well matched.

No one breathed. Except for May, who didn't see why she ought to stop.

At last, Aimz doubled over in a bursting guffaw which Xan tried to ignore but ended up catching like an infectious disease until the two of them were engaged in a chorus of laughter that only grew louder as they became more nervous about what would happen when they stopped.

May and Precious Butler stared at each other, May unable to understand why what she had said was funny, and Precious Butler unable to understand why she had said it.

To keep himself from laughing, Rap shot a blast from his plasma pistol into the ceiling. "Hey!"

The plasma blast zoomed into the wormhole which had inexplicably moved to the ceiling of the *Audacity* and exited the wormhole in the ship's basement where it disintegrated an unopened package of glow sticks.

Interesting, if somewhat unsatisfying, to note: in an alternate reality, May and Xan had found these glow sticks and held a two person rave. This meant that the glow sticks were not there to absorb the blast from the plasma pistol which instead hit a can of hairspray, causing an explosive fire which, when it reached the fuel line in the *Audacity,* obliterated everything within a hundred miles of the ship.

Not in this timeline, though. In this timeline the only casualty was the package of unopened glow sticks, which is still an awful waste, but not a series-ending tragedy.

The blast achieved the intended effect: everyone shut up.

"She's, uh," Xan said on the tails of dying laughter, "she's from Earth. Translation error," he explained to Precious Butler.

"What did I say?" May asked Xan, *sotto vocce.*

"It's a derogatory term for a prostitute."

She scrunched like a raisin. Not only had she insulted their captor, but Xan had been a prostitute when they first met.

Before she could apologize, Precious Butler held up a large, dark hand. "Don't worry about it. I better confiscate that, though." He looked pointedly at Aimz's belt.

"What?"

He sighed, unhooked her belt, and pulled a silver laser gun from a hidden pocket.

"You had that this whole time?" May asked.

Aimz looked equally surprised. "Oh, yeah! Ha, I forgot about that."

"You forgot about a seven inch laser gun attached to your belt?"

"It's a pocket belt. It removes a dimension from anything you put in it, then gives it back when you take it out. There's junk in there I haven't used in orbits. It's really hard to find something if it has no depth. How'd you know about it?"

"Weapons scan. I wouldn't mind, normally, but under these circumstances I feel I ought to." He clipped the laser gun to his own belt and held out his hand. "And your anchors, please." He gave Rap a glance which either said, "I am shaken to my very core that someone who professes to be a professional fugitive recovery agent did not have the presence of mind to confiscate his prisoner's anchor button," or, perhaps more succinctly, "Idiot."

They dropped their anchor buttons in his hand and shuffled onto the teledisc.

On the planet's surface, May tried to take a deep

breath, but the thin air on New Tuhnt made her lungs feel like an aluminum can being crushed in a trash compactor. She squinted away from the blinding light of New Tuhnt's sun which was unimpeded by the feeble atmosphere. A hulking mass of grey blobbed out part of the horizon, giving the impression of a beached whale.

Precious Butler and Rap led them toward it.

May blinked, and the ship had become some kind of wood-wind instrument, shivering like a heat wave.

"Xan?" she puffed, looking around. There were two moving shapes beside her now, one seemed to be a shopping cart filled with bags of oranges and cartons of orange juice. The other was a tall belt, flopping upright on its buckle.

The sky over the horizon burst into a million Skittles which fell like rain and bounced into the red-lipped mouths which now dotted the landscape.

Something picked her up—some sort of dark blue cactus was carrying her now—but she continued to move her legs as if she were walking. She thought she laughed at the cactus. In reality, she coughed amusedly at it.

The cactus brought her to the wood-wind instrument, hefted her up into it, and plunged her into a cold, blue hallway.

She filled her lungs—this time with velvety oxygen. Lights began to dance in front of her, then grow until they touched on images that were beginning to make some semblance of sense.

The cactus reformed into Precious Butler, who was now helping her stand.

"This one's a lightweight. What is she?" said Rap. May heard, instead, "Thith one'th 63%8 a light j2$6. What is $ct7?"

"$ct7'th a human, you thnoffle-eater. $ct7 needth othygen." It sounded vaguely like Xan, to May, but his voice hissed on the 'S's like an old TV.

"Are you ^8%3?"

May shook her head. She could hear a whirring like a tiny fan in her ear.

"Am I what?" she asked.

"Ith it your 87/m\dfjsn(?" He tapped the side of his head to indicate the translation chip.

"&9+9nfj, I'm 83~fh7 ct7 ^hd0-." Precious Butler put a lions-paw of a hand to her back. Whether it was there to keep her from running or to help her stand she wasn't sure.

"^82 your 769$5," Aimz told Xan.

"!@79 it," he hissed at her.

Each word made the thing in her head sizzle and pop like bacon in a frying pan; she wished everyone would shut up.

"(3nd^ can't 9>k0i3??" Xan was starting to panic. Usually, when Xan panicked, May held it together; and when May panicked, Xan held it together. But since he was panicking about her and her inability to understand what anyone was saying, she was beginning to get pulled in by the undertow.

May shook her head again, lifting her shoulders. She had never heard Tuhntian spoken before; it had always been translated through the chip the *Peacemaker*'s doctors had installed in her. It was both fluid and metallic, like a typewriter clacking underwater.

"Can you understand me?" she asked.

"&39n(," said Xan.

"Gestures, Xan!"

"Yes," he said in a strange accent, nodding his head.

Xan was a Tuhntian of few skills. Two, really. One involved glitter, and the other was linguistics. He had an honorary degree in the former and an official degree in the latter but, with the advent of the extremely popular, surprisingly affordable, and nearly infallible A'Viltrian Translation Chip, his degree, which was already practically useless, was now utterly useless.

Languages then, necessarily, had become a hobby. A hobby which he frequently indulged in during his long stay in Earth's orbit. All of the English he knew had been learned by holding a strong magnet to his translation chip and watching "I Love Lucy." Some of the English he knew was, as a result, Spanish.

"Well there's that," May said, then smiled as a thought

occurred to her. “You know English?”

“A little.” He had the pained look of wanting to say something else but not having the words. He always had words. Just not English words. “With Lucy!” he added, satisfied.

“My chip must’ve shorted out. Do you think it’ll turn back on?”

“Yo no se,” he said.

“I...I don’t speak Spanish.” May said, wondering how much of the English he thought he knew was actually not.

“Zuut, &93 Bd%42 &jen(jf @gts$! ^hdf-”

“I don’t speak any Tuhntian!” She winced against the whirring of the chip trying to restart in her head. She tried to stop walking but the hand on her back pressed her forward.

Xan bit his lip and shrugged. “May, (7^g ^hn zxu%.”

SEVENTEEN

HURTFUL BLURTINGS

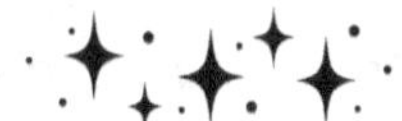

Meant for drunk crew members or the occasional hitchhiker, the holding cell aboard the *Innocuous* wasn't designed with comfort in mind. The ceiling was inconveniently low, as if someone had taken the average height of a Tuhntian and subtracted one inch precisely.

The walls were grey aluminum and molded into a single, mattress-less bed on one side. Everything was grey. It was horrible. That, to Xan, was torture on its own. Grey walls.

The fourth wall of the cell was made of yellow laser light which was easily entered, but deadly to exit.

"Wow, couldn't think up anything more creative than this?" Aimz said, breaking the fourth wall as she strode through it.

"Aimz, we're not under arrest," May said. "We didn't do anything wrong."

Precious Butler smiled apologetically. "You're both accessories now. Please go in?" What he meant to say was, "Go in before I make you go in."

They did.

"Thanks," he said. "Be careful of the laser wall now. If you try to exit from that side, you'll be fizzled."

"Fizzled?" Xan repeated.

"It's worse than it sounds." Rap leaned against the wall, twirling his plasma pistol in one hand. "Job's over then, isn't it? Got what you wanted?"

"Sure. You've officially paid me back for getting you a job with EnviroDev," Precious Butler said as they left together.

May perched on the shelf which thought it was a bed and rammed the heel of her palm against her temple.

"Say something?" she asked Xan who came to sit beside her.

"Can you understand me now?"

She winced as the chip zapped her. Again, she thwacked her temple.

"Okay, say something?" She anchored her gaze to a seam in the floor panels to stop herself from straining her eyeballs by trying to flip them around and look at the chip inside her head.

"Now?" Xan sighed.

She groaned. Obviously not.

"Well," Xan leaned back against the wall, making himself as comfortable as one could possibly be on a shelf, and closed his eyes, "at least we can-"

"Listen," May stopped searching the floor and turned to Xan. "Every time you speak Tuhntian this thing zaps me. Could you please stop talking? I know it's a lot to ask of you," she said with more vitriol than she had intended.

Xan opened an eye at her to see if she was kidding; she wasn't. He gave her an affirmative sort of "hmpf" sound and hoped it hadn't hurt.

Aimz had busied herself with inspecting a corner of the cell, scraping at something on the floor with the edge of a thumbnail sized laserblade she had pulled from her pocket.

If anyone could fix the chip, it was Aimz.

If anyone was least interested in fixing the chip, it was also her.

Xan decided he would *make* her interested. He started to tell May this, but stopped himself. He tried to pat her knee in a comforting way, but stopped himself. Instead, he sighed and joined Aimz in the corner.

"Whatcha doing there?"

"Science," she said, scraping.

"Right, well, uh, speaking of science...have you reset a translation chip before?" He looked back at May to make sure she wasn't trying to listen.

She was doing nothing of the sort. In fact, she had curled into herself, burying her head in her arms and thinking terribly hard about not letting this get to her. The more she thought about not letting it get to her, the more it seemed to get. Fear or anger or exhaustion, or likely a muddy swirl of all three, were eroding the pink beach in her head, and no coastline erosion mitigation plan had been proposed, much less voted on and put into action. The sea turtles would have nowhere to nest this year.

Aimz continued to scrape at something. "Yeah, at BioTech," she said.

"Could you...do it...again now? I'll let you punch me as hard as you want if you fix it." Xan offered, trying desperately to be more interesting than whatever was on the floor.

Aimz stopped scraping and wiped the laserblade on her shorts. "It's in her head!" Xan slapped his hand over her mouth.

"Don't let her hear you!" he whispered. May couldn't hear anything over the sound of the ocean.

Aimz licked his hand, which was to be expected, and he snatched it away. "Besides I don't need you to *let* me punch you. I can just do it." She did, to prove her point, but there was no feeling behind it, and he only swayed sadly backwards.

"Pleeeeeeeeeease?" He drew out the middle of the word, hoping to annoying her into helping.

She clicked her tongue thoughtfully. "It's on her auditory cortex. Not exactly easy access. How am I supposed to get at it? Claw it out with my fingernails? If I had a scalpel, maybe. Or a skewer."

"Right, or a laserblade. Shame we don't have a laserblade, Aimz. Absolutely an absolute and horrible terrible shame we don't have access to a laserblade, don't you think?"

"Oh this?" Aimz held up the laserblade between them. "I've been using this to scrape up skrum samples. I can't cut her head open with it. That's disgusting."

Xan winced with his whole body and leaned against the wall to think. He tried to put together a phrase in English. Something easy like, "Hey, mun, don't worry about it. Aimz is super smart, I have complete and utter confidence in her ability to fix your translation chip if we can locate something extremely sharp and relatively clean that you wouldn't mind having shoved in your head."

Lucy had never had the occasion to say "translation chip" or, as far as Xan could remember, "utter" or "relatively."

He would have to paraphrase, a skill he had never gotten the hang of. Again, he sat on the shelf beside May, tapping her shoulder to let her know he was there and wanted her attention.

May twisted her face off her knees just enough to look at him.

"Any ideas?" her voice was muffled.

"Yes," he said, nodding to emphasize his meaning. "We," he gestured to Aimz and himself. "Have an idea. Need a..." He opened his mouth to say the word he wanted to say but couldn't find it. He looked over at Aimz, but it wasn't there. He searched the feebly glowing forcefield of the cell, but it wasn't there, either. Charades, he decided, were in order.

He chopped one hand into the other and made a sort of slicing motion at May. She squinted.

"Need a...?" she pressed.

Aimz, tired of watching him struggle, crawled over and brandished the laserblade, which Xan pointed to ecstatically.

"A laserblade?" May asked, her voice rising. "You mean to get to the chip?"

Xan bit his lip until it started to bleed. He wanted to pretend he hadn't understood her, but he nodded, then quickly held up two fingers to show her it would just be a bit.

"Can't you use that one?" May asked.

Xan shook his head. "No, we can't, it's dirty," he said in something like a transatlantic accent.

"It's a laser! A laser can't get dirty."

"Is this so?" Xan silently asked Aimz . Aimz pulled him awkwardly down to her level and whispered to him in Tuhntian, "Right, so, technically it's not dirty per say, it's just the principle of the thing. And it's dull. Also I don't want to do it."

"Well I'm not going to do it!"

The chip, in a valiant attempt at translating the whispers, shorted and sent a jolt through May's head that turned everything white.

"Fuck! Please stop talking." May held her head until the blinding white had faded to something of a fuzzy grey. She waited for the grey to clear, but it still floated around the edges of her sight.

"Sorry," Xan said in English and reached out to her. In the absence of words of comfort, he was hoping perhaps a hug would work.

It did not.

"Stop," May pushed him away. "Stop, okay?" She rubbed her eyes hard, the fuzzy grey frame around everything refused to clear. Xan looked enormously hurt and entirely too grey. He never looked grey. Blue, usually. Green okay, sure, he could be slightly green at times, but he was never, ever grey.

May realized that she was in something of a unique position. She could talk to him now and he had to listen. He couldn't deflect. He couldn't start telling her about wonderful unusual things and distract her from her point. So she talked.

"You lied to me, Xan. You said we could visit Tuhnt. You said you didn't have a sister. You said you didn't kill anyone and that's not true, is it?" The ocean of fear, anger, and exhaustion became choppy. The tide was coming in. "And now you've probably killed me, too. How long do you think they'll try to keep you here? A couple hundred orbits? That's fine for you, but I'll be long dead by then. If you'd just told me *why* you were going to get arrested on Rhea, we could've avoided this." May blinked a couple of times; the grey was beginning to recede.

Aimz was delighted.

Xan looked like a salted slug.

"If you'd told me all this earlier, I wouldn't have stayed with you."

Xan didn't know enough English to reply. He didn't know enough Tuhntian to reply and he was brilliant at Tuhntian. He probably could have made a jab at it in the lyrical and poetic ancient A'Viltrian, but she wouldn't understand that either.

It was then that May remembered why she made a point of letting him do most of the talking. She always knew exactly what not to say and, unchecked, she was given to saying it.

She shook her head and sloughed off the rest of the grey that had edged her vision. "Now I'm lying to you," she said with a tiny, testing smile which he did not return. "I wouldn't have left you to fend for yourself out there in the Universe. And if I hadn't insisted we go to Rhea we wouldn't be here."

Xan nodded emphatically, but, wisely perhaps, said nothing.

"I'm so fucking stubborn. How do you stand it?" she asked.

"I love-"

"You better finish that sentence with 'Lucy,'" May interrupted.

Xan brightened. "Lucy. Yes. I love Lucy. She's stubborn, too," he said in English.

The doors swished open and Precious Butler walked in, alone this time. "Sonan's ready for you," he said it in Tuhntian, but May heard it in English.

"Oh!" she said. "Xan, say something!"

"Babalu?"

"In Tuhntian," May corrected.

Xan shrunk, he had forgotten every single Tuhntian word he'd ever known.

"Personal lubricant," Aimz helped.

May understood her but wished she hadn't.

"It's working again! It must have reset itself."

Xan smiled with his mouth closed; it was an odd look on him.

"You can talk again, Xan," May confirmed.

"I…I have nothing to say," he said.

EIGHTEEN

GOLDEN WAVES OF DEADLY GRAIN

Excited to be anywhere that wasn't Yenuket Municipal Spaceport, Aimz was the first through the heavy wooden doors. She felt as if dying in this cozy, brightly lit tearoom would mean she reset back to her hovel on the spaceport. She began picking curiously at a doily before the smallest and sharpest of "ahems" stopped her.

It was the kind of ahem which you couldn't possibly trust. Half way between an, "Excuse me, what the fuck do you think you're doing," and an, "Excuse me, I have something of a cold I'm just now getting over."

The "ahem" belonged to the cleanest piece of machinery Aimz had ever seen. Usually androids, even the precocious ones, had a tell of some kind. A joint that peeked open slightly to reveal a mess of wires or a rusted hinge in the jaw near the ear. The only tell that this android was not an organic being was that she had no life in her eyes. Whatever spark it took to separate a pair of marbles from living eyes just wasn't there.

Xan and May were the last to enter.

Xan had been expecting an enormous courtroom, each of the many chairs occupied by Tuhntian jurors who had argued beforehand about which of them wanted him dead most. He had expected jeering, things thrown at him perhaps, maybe even a vat of acid in which he would be dipped.

He had not expected floral wallpaper and the tinkling of a tiny metal spoon against fancy dishes. He had not expected quite this much pink nor lace curtains, which waved gently in a draft. This was worse, actually. Acid vat he could've handled; the finger sandwiches put him off.

May hadn't expected anything. One hundred percent of her brain power was focused on figuring out precisely how much she had upset Xan, and what, rounded to three decimal places, she could do to fix it.

"Precious Butler, who are these two and why is he in a swimsuit?" Sonan's voice hadn't always sounded like two identical cassettes being played an eighth of a second apart, but she'd grown accustomed to a habitual afternoon tea, and a few thousand orbits of flooding her system with the beverage hadn't been kind to her electric throat.

"Why does no one just assume we were at the beach before this?" Xan asked.

"We found them with him," said Precious Butler.

"You are familiar by now with the full extent of the mission."

"Yeah. 'Arrest and imprison Xan under Carmnia of Trilly on Tuhnt.' But what if they helped?"

"The others are not important."

"What do you mean not important?" Aimz asked, reaching for something on the tiered cake stand.

"You're free to leave. Thank you and have a nice day," said Sonan.

"We are? Terrific! Twa-don!" Aimz yodeled, slipping out the door and onto her next adventure.

Everyone but Sonan watched the door shut behind her, felt the gust of wind it had made when it closed, wondered where exactly she was off to.

"I'll be on the bridge, then. Buzz if you need me," Precious Butler told her and left as well.

Sonan stirred her tea.

"Unknown entity, you may leave," she nodded at May, but May refused.

"I don't have anywhere else to be," she said.

Sonan set down her tea spoon with an emotionless clink.

"Sit, Xan of Tuhnt and unknown entity. Would you like some tea, Xan of Tuhnt and unknown entity?" smiled the android as she tilted the tea pot over two empty cups. She hadn't actually said it, she had smiled it. Her lips hadn't moved.

They sat. They did not take the tea.

"Drink," said Sonan. "It." With a stiff hand, she slid the cups closer to them, then sipped her own tea as a demonstration, her artificial throat sizzling as the liquid went down.

Xan caught May's eye and, as he reached for the cup, held up a finger to her, telling her to wait until he'd tried it first to be sure it was safe. At that, she resolutely snatched her cup and gulped half of the drink down. How dare he try to be chivalrous after what she had said?

Clearly, it had been sitting out for awhile. It was cold and thin and...

"Oh." May looked into the half empty cup now as if the rest of it had suddenly turned into a chipmunk. "It's good," she said, realizing then that she felt a tad dehydrated and finishing off the rest of the cup.

Sonan's smile shrunk slightly. Ever so slightly. Then Xan chugged what was in his own cup, thinking, reasonably, that anything May could drink without dying wouldn't kill him either.

He set the empty cup down with a louder clank than he had intended and gave May a smile to congratulate them both on making it this far.

"Right, that's not bad at all. I thought you were trying to poison us! Silly, really. I mean, what reason would you have to poison May, right? Me, sure, but May's just a..."

"Human," May cut him off. "After all this time still just a human?"

Sonan whirred gently.

"May, I..." He looked for a moment like it physically

pained him to speak.

"Is anything the matter, Xan of Tuhnt?" Sonan said, sipping her tea with a re-invigorated smile and an electric *zzzttt*.

"What?" Xan had the sense that something was decidedly the matter. It wasn't the decor, though that didn't help. It wasn't that May had unloaded all her anxieties and mistrust on him just moments ago, and he hadn't had a chance to process that yet. It was that...He froze.

"Xan, you look awful." May went clammy, wondering if she looked as awful as he did. Had Sonan actually poisoned them? But aside from fear creeping like thorny vines up the trellis of her back, she felt fine.

"May," Xan said from seemingly a long distance away. "You've been really on edge lately. I think you deserve a vacation." He was having trouble holding his head up and felt it best to let it loll against the back of the chair for now. The shadows in the room turned a bright, chalky pink, throwing off his depth perception.

Sonan hummed at May. "What are you, larvling? You're not Panseen, are you? A Panseen would be dead by now."

"Dead?" May jumped out of her chair, toppling it. "Xan, why did she say dead?" She tried to check Xan's vitals, realized she didn't know the first thing about Tuhntian baseline vitals, and settled with tapping his face urgently as he drifted off.

"The tea is made with barley. Admiral Warders and I used to drink it every evening. He had built up a tolerance to the poison. Truly a remarkable Tuhntian. I must say I'm impressed by your fortitude, unknown entity. What is your name?"

"Fuck!" May whispered at Xan who winced in response to what, to him, sounded like a shout.

"Fuck," said Sonan sagely. "And what are you, Fuck? Clearly you're of hardy stock. Have you ever considered breeding?"

"What? No. What did you do to him? Fix him now." She slammed her fist on the table, thinking perhaps she could intimidate the android.

"Ssssss fine, mun, r'lax." He attempted a cool, casual finger gun at her but ended up looking like he was stroking an invisible fish. He stared at his hand for a moment, confused as to why he couldn't make a finger gun, then slumped onto the tea table.

"Hey, hey," May wriggled her arms under his and tried to coax him up. "Shit you're heavy," she said under her breath. "Come on, Blueberry, stop lying to me. You're not fine."

"Yes, Xan, why don't you tell Fuck the truth?"

Xan tried to help May help him get up. Instead, they tumbled in a cacophony of limbs and chair legs to the plush pink carpet. May crouched beside him and prepared to fight Sonan if she tried anything from the back. Sonan was quite happy sitting where she was.

"Want the truth?" said Xan. The cartoonish brightness of his zesty green eyes was dull, like a shut-off neon "open" sign in a closed storefront.

"Preferably."

"Eugh." Xan closed his eyes, but May tapped his face until he opened them in annoyance.

"Hey, look at me."

"Right," Xan sighed and looked at her. He smiled. "I did a really nice thing with your hair. It looks so good, May. Your hair is so nice." He couldn't keep his eyes open anymore.

The anxiety balling up in May's chest escaped as a tea-kettle whistle of a whine now. Sonan tsked. "I thought poisoning would be a more interesting start to a lifetime in prison. Don't you? It isn't much, of course. I don't have the authority to execute him, but this will keep him docile for a few seasons. You, Fuck, are free to come and go as you please."

"See? Not dying. You're free. Android thinks your name's Fuck which's hilarious. You got out your pent up," Xan wriggled his fingers vaguely at May as he tried to recall words, "*stuff* so you feel better. Everythin's grand." He attempted a smile, but hit a dead end at pained grimace and had to turn around.

"It's not grand. I was wrong. I should've trusted you,

and I feel horrible."

"*You* feel horrible?" he huffed, giving up trying to smile.

"Can you forgive me?"

"Right now? I'm kinda indisposed right now."

"HARD SHUTDOWN IMMINENT," Sonan interrupted.

"Hush!" May shot at the android. "Ever?" she asked Xan.

"Wait, that was weird. Wasn't it? What does she mean h-hard shutdown? Did she just-"

"Xan!"

"It can wait. She's off, let's scram." He flung an arm around the leg of the nearest toppled chair and tried to lever himself to standing.

"WELCOME. ENTER USERNAME." Sonan popped up, her nose dripping with tea, her mouth still. "The Ancient and Powerful Goddess of Chaos," said Sonan with unmentionable cadence.

Xan and May both shivered. May out of fear, Xan because the poison had reached his appendix (useless to an Earthling, on the list of top ten vital organs for a Tuhntian).

"ERROR. USERNAME TOO MANY CHARACTERS. ENTER USERNAME."

"Chaos," said the unmentionable voice.

NINETEEN

MEET CHUTE

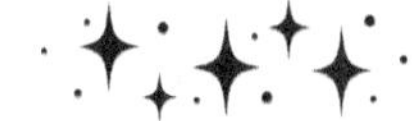

Listay awoke, once again, amongst trash.

What horrible decisions had she made in life to deserve being thrown away twice? Slowly she got to her knees, not wanting to know what slippery thing she braced her hands against. She put a hand to her chest, trailing some sort of slime along with it.

She waited.

She squinted her eyes, focused.

She waited...there! Ha! A single heartbeat like one salvageable line in a phoned-in pop song. Alright, she could work with that.

"Oh, hey, you're alive. Wild," said someone behind her. A pale Tuhntian with ultra-pink hair lounged on a throne of cardboard boxes. "I checked out your vitals a few minutes ago and you were super dead. I hope that doesn't upset you. I'm Aimz."

Listay ran her tongue around her dry mouth. It tasted horrible. "General Listay," she said. "Or just Listay, now. I don't know, does death demote you?"

Aimz shrugged. "I don't see why it should, General. I've been digging around and I found some great stuff in this trok. This funky bit of metal, an unusually long twist tie, and a plasma zapper."

To prove it, she twirled the zapper around her finger.

"Don't-" began Listay.

Zzzaapppp! The zapper interrupted her, creating a molten dent in the thick metal of the trash compactor wall.

"That's mine. I'll take it back now, please," Listay said, holding out her mechanical hand. Aimz tossed it to her and she caught it one-handed with a metallic clink. "Have you found anything that could get us to the hatch?" Listay pointed toward the door she had been tossed through. Earlier, Aimz had jumped through the same door of her own volition just to check out what kind of garbage this ship was packing.

"Would you believe a completely intact, functional metal ladder with those nice rubber grips?" Aimz said.

"No, I wouldn't." The general brushed herself off, pausing to inspect a number of scrapes and bruises on her organic arm and legs. She wasn't healing nearly as fast as she ought to. Death, she supposed, could do that to a person.

"Alright then, not gullible, and you know your own plasma zapper when you see it. No, to answer your question, I haven't found anything. But now that you're alive I think we can reach the hatch. It's not that far. I'll stand on your shoulders then pull you up."

Listay shook her head and laughed darkly. "You'd probably just rip my arm off. I'm not sure what's holding me together, because by all accounts I shouldn't be alive."

"Naw," Aimz squelched happily through the muck toward her new friend. "You look good. Here, let's try a finger. Those are fragile, right? If a finger stays on your arms will be fine." She held out a hand toward Listay.

Too exhausted to rebut, Listay offered her hand. Aimz yanked on Listay's pinky finger with a grin which morphed into a grimace when she felt it pop. "I think I pulled it from the socket, but it's still there."

"Ugh," Listay wiggled her finger painfully. "Yes, it's still there. Alright. We'll need somewhere stable to stand."

Aimz trudged back to her throne. "This is the spot. I'm not sinking in at all here. Come on, I'll let you go up first. Just don't leave me here, okay?"

Listay laughed. "Oh mun, you'd snap if I got on top of you. What do weigh?"

"Eh, about 4,000 crawfish."

It's important to note that Carmnian Tuhntians measure weight based on a species of crawfish-esque bottom feeder which was abundant on Tuhnt. Rheans, however, use metric.

"Right. I'm not getting on top of you." Listay shimmied through the sludge and planted herself beside the cardboard throne.

Aimz put one boot on her shoulder. "You sure you don't want to go first?"

The cry of every tortured voice in hell echoed around them as the trash compactor's ancient gears awoke. Death Herself would pause to look behind her in concern if She were to hear it.

Listay and Aimz reflexively covered their ears, but this wasn't the kind of sound that was heard; it was felt. Mounds of trash clustered around them as the walls moved toward each other like reluctant, hormonal middle schoolers at a mandatory school dance.

"Go!" Listay shouted over the din.

Aimz didn't hear her, but went anyway. She scrambled up Listay, stood on her shoulders, and with a groan that was decidedly "Night of the Living Dead"-esque, Listay hoisted Aimz up to the hatch.

The walls shivered as Aimz stabbed the bit of metal she had found into the crack between the doors and twisted it, wrenching open the hatch enough to slip her fingers through and peel the doors apart. She dragged herself out, rolled onto the cold metal floor of the hallway, nearly took a moment to catch her breath, remembered Listay, and dragged herself back.

Their hands locked, and Listay tried to leverage herself up by scaling the wall, but she could barely bend her knees - not due to rigor mortis, which was clearing up nicely now, but to the compactor's compacting.

"The walls are too close. I can't get any traction!" Listay shouted, the refuse beginning to gnaw at her feet, trying to pull her under.

"I'll pull you up." Aimz quickly realized the sticking point, or rather the slipping point, in this plan as she braced her boots against the opening of the hatch. The general was drenched in chartreuse cave skrum.

Their slick fingers slid wildly as they tried to grip each other. Apart from the growling of the compactor and the pervasive stench of rot (which Listay sincerely hoped was coming primarily from the garbage), it might have been sexy. Giving up, Aimz dove deeper and clutched the sturdy Lay-Flex™ straps on the shoulders of Listay's suit.

"Are you sure you're strong enough for this?" the general called up to her.

"Nope," Aimz said, grunting with effort. It had been a long time since she had last pulled someone from the maw of a trash compactor and that someone had been a good thousand crawfish lighter than this gorgeous hunk of Rhean.

"Don't hurt yourself on my account. I'm already dead."

"Listen, General, I fancy myself something of a biologist, and you most definitely are not dead," she shouted over the cacophony. "Not sure you're alive per-say, but you're not dead, so I'm pulling you out."

And with an obstinate cry, she did. Listay landed heavily atop her, but she didn't mind. Not a bit.

"Well that wasn't nearly as difficult as it could've been, what do you think?" Aimz said centimeters away from Listay's face.

If Listay had any blood to spare, she would have blushed. Instead, she crawled to her knees and peered back into the compactor. The wretched noise had stopped and the compactor began slowly opening back up to allow the far walls to compress.

"Huh," Listay said, watching the walls recede. "We probably could've survived that. As long as we stayed above the trash line."

Aimz crawled beside her and also stared down into the

compactor, absently rubbing away a stitch in her ribs. "Yeah, not a great way to kill someone is it?" She grabbed the piece of metal she had used to open the hatch and stuck it in her belt.

"They thought I was dead already," Listay reminded her.

"Right." In the pale blue light of the hallway, Aimz could actually see Listay. Her mauve face waxy and ashen, her black eyes cloudy, and her thick dreadlocks caked in dirt. She was stunning. Aimz felt she had been staring for an inappropriate amount of time and thought about looking away.

"Why are you staring at me?"

"Oh was I still? Sorry." Aimz continued to stare. "Are you alright? I mean, do you want to talk about it? Death?" Carmnians have a warped sense of manners, but Aimz was really trying this time. There just isn't much precedent for talking to the undead.

"If I think about it too much, Death might realize She made a mistake and come after me." Listay's laugh was dry and shallow, like dirt being flung on a coffin.

"Logical."

"Is it?"

"Eh, maybe. Can I hold your hand?" Aimz asked.

Listay had never met a Carmnian before, and as such, the question threw her off a blip. "Excuse me?"

"Your hand?"

"I suppose."

Aimz snatched her hand, scraping off a glob of the skrum with her finger nail to study it in the light.

"What is that?"

"Skrum," Aimz said. "It's gotten into everything and it breeds like wild. Kinda...zuut what would Xan say?"

"Prolific?" Listay offered.

"That's the one." Aimz licked the skrum from her fingers and bounced up, offering Listay a hand.

"Speaking of, now that I've got backup, want to help me find my zoup-nog brother and break him out of here?"

"Alright. If you help me destroy my ex before she resets the Universe." She took the offered hand and leveraged herself up.

"Easy."
"She's a chaos goddess," Listay clarified.
"Easy and blasphemous, it's a deal."

TWENTY

SMART LUCK

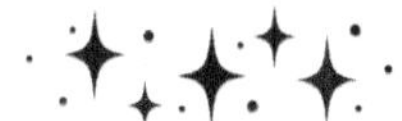

The word "Chaos" brought back unpleasant memories that Xan and May were both fairly certain they had left in the first book. A few seasons of exciting (but not exciting enough to write about) races and epic (but not epic enough to write about) wins had put Chaos firmly out of their minds. Besides, generally speaking, people don't come back from being exploded and sucked into a black hole.

There is no such thing as a coincidence.

It was, however, an astonishingly complex tangle of probability threads that led Chaos back into the lives of May and Xan. So complex that one might be tempted to call it a coincidence just to get out of an hour long lecture on quantum physics and a crash course on modified probability applications.

And so, it was a startling coincidence.

"Hello Tiny Human May, Xan. Fancy meeting you two here. I would call this a startling coincidence but I know better. I know *everything.*" This last part was a lie. Omni-potent, perhaps at her best; omni-present, once she got the hang of it again sure; but omniscient she was not.

Never would be. Never could be. She was right about the coincidence part, though.

Xan wanted to say something, but his tongue felt fuzzy and he was rather preoccupied with that.

"What are you doing here? Why? How?" May ran through the questions which were pertinent to the situation.

"Plan Mistpillia. Do you have the bass yet?"

"I thought you knew everything," May said.

"I do, so I'll know if you're lying."

May sighed, very much doubting it. "I don't have a bass, no."

"Of course you don't. Plan Mistpillia. The idea *was* to reset the Universe with the Sphere of Time, but I've just had a much better idea." Chaos had enlivened Sonan's mechanical eyes, giving her the appearance of a great white shark which had just gained sentience and was thrilled at the idea of its next meal.

A pitiful, miserable glare was Xan's only possible defense at the moment. A better idea for Chaos was almost certainly a worse idea for him.

"I'll go back in time to the moment we first met and do away with you when I ought to have. A touch of revenge never hurt any goddess." This was untrue and proved, once and for all, that she was not and would never be omniscient. Revenge plots account for the spirit-death of nearly twenty immortals every orbit. Incense abuse, in comparison, accounts for an average of thirty-nine spirit-deaths per orbit.

"On the *Peacemaker*?" Xan asked.

"Back in time?" May echoed, wondering if she would have to add lying about time travel to her list of accusations against Xan.

"No, you slorpfignut. The *first* time I met you. Did you not know that was me? Thick. It's been a delight seeing you in this state, but I must be off." She leaned forward slightly, her hands grasping the edge of the table as she prepared to stand.

Nothing happened.

She leaned back.

Again, she leaned forward to stand.

Again, nothing happened. Frustrating.

"Does this zuxing *thing* stand up?"

"Blitheon, I hope not," Xan said under his breath as he also attempted, and failed, to stand. May wasn't even working on standing up; she was working on coming to terms with the incredible coincidence of Chaos's appearance. An impossible task, of course.

"I'll make it," Chaos said via Sonan's mouth, her voice crackling as it pushed through the damaged sound module.

Sonan could, in fact, stand up. It was a function which was built into her. While it was physically possible for Sonan to stand, it had become emotionally impossible.

A good A'Viltrian style android like Sonan has an artificial brain which so perfectly emulates an organic one that it is nearly indistinguishable aside from the blinking lights and well organized mental pathways.

Because of this, androids are not only capable of emotional distress, they are also capable of developing neurosis.

Sonan, after suffering an artificial heartbreak so intense she had no other way to cope, had deleted every line of code related to her ability to stand and was, as a result, completely immobile from the waist down.

Chaos jolted through Sonan's wiry synapses and found the blank spot in her code where her ambulatory functions should have resided. She scribbled something in its place. Something that really ought not have worked. Something so horrifically evil I must omit it for fear of making robotics engineers physical ill.

The android stood. Chaos made her smile, too.

The standing snapped May out of her existential conundrum. It didn't matter that it was impossible, it had happened, and now it was *standing* and about to go muck around in time with the sole aim of ruining their lives. May lunged across the tea table, grabbed the tea pot, and flung its contents at the possessed android. The light brown brew cascaded down her chest plate and dribbled rhythmically to the floor.

"Thank you. I thought she was a touch dusty," said Chaos, tilting the android's head down to watch the tea drip. She regarded May who was still folded over the table and Xan who could do little more than drape over the fallen chair. She shook her head at them. "It really was just dumb luck that kept you alive wasn't it?"

There are a great number of benefits to having an android host body, and one was the standard built-in MilliWave MegaVis scanner which revealed to her a pleasant detail: neither of them had the probability modifier. As such, the probability that the fragile, tiny human and useless zoup-nog Tuhntian could even begin to hope of stopping her from obtaining and using the Sphere of Time was so low, it wasn't statistically significant.

May could think of no clever comeback, but felt she ought to comeback anyway. "It was," she paused to think, "s-smart luck."

Now, May had come to think of herself as the hero in her own story. The protagonist, as it were. Most people see themselves as the protagonist in their lives. However, she was really beginning to wonder what kind of horrible story she was in where the protagonist said things like "smart luck" and stumbled over their words when they said it.

Xan, conversely, hadn't thought of himself as the protagonist in his own story since university. Definitely not a hero. In fact, over the last two thousand orbits or so he had begun to suspect that he was, if not the villain, then some kind of halfwit side character whose only purpose is to create problems for whomever the hero *was*. Being poisoned to death with barley tea sounded like an easy out.

He wanted desperately to poke fun at May for saying "smart luck" instead of something witty and biting.

"Aw, yes, you are smart for a Tiny Human aren't you?" Chaos cooed pejoratively.

"At least I have a body," May said, standing to dust the crushed shortbread off her shirt.

"I can have any body I want." Chaos stepped into the

tearoom's intershoot and disappeared.

May tried again to hoist Xan up; it was like trying to lift a three hundred pound anchor partially lodged in the soft silt at the bottom of an ocean and she eventually gave up in favor of trying to get him back on the same plane of existence.

"Xan, can you hear me?"

"Mpphhffff."

"Listen, I'm sorry about what I said."

"Smart luck?" he wheezed a laugh.

"No! Well yes. That and about leaving you."

"Eh. I'd leave me, too. Given the opportunity."

"Let me apologize, okay? You're my best friend, and I'm sorry."

"Really good best," said Xan, confusingly.

"Uh, yeah..." May agreed. "How do you feel?"

"Ah'm fine," he said. May did not believe him and she had good reason not to. At first he had found it difficult to lie to her, but he had become quite deft at it with practice.

He was lying now.

"I'm going to need you to promise me you'll never lie to me again as long as I live, okay?"

He shot her a bleary, unlit neon sign glare for a second while he gathered the strength to say, "Alright then. I don't want to tell you."

"Don't you trust me?"

"Yeah." He shut his eyes again.

"Why don't you want to tell me?"

"Don't want you to worry."

"Too late for that. *Please* be honest with me. What's going on? Is there anything I can do to help?"

"Yeah, alright," Xan shivered with the effort of looking at her again. "Are you sure you're okay? You drank that stuff, too."

"I'm fine. Barley is pretty common on Earth."

"Zuut, May, you're ridiculous."

"You're the one dying over a cup of tea."

Xan sighed, "I am."

"You are?" May squeaked.

"That remains to be seen, now doesn't it? I mean if the

barley doesn't kill me, Chaos will take care of it."

"Okay, well, that's not going to happen."

"Why, you have a plan?"

"Yes!"

He squinted at her now. "If I'm not allowed to lie, you're not either."

"I'm not lying. My plan is to stop Chaos from finding the Sphere of Time, then to shut off Sonan and untether the *Audacity* so we can get back to work."

Xan chuckled. "Right, okay, yeah. Good plan. Very detailed."

"Fine, it's a goal," May said and tried to get him to stand up again, but he wasn't being any help.

"Eugh, don't drag me along on this one alright mun? You're not the one under arrest here. Just go get the *Audacity* untethered and have fun."

"Absolutely not. I found a haunted Big Mouth Billy Bass on Yenuket Municipal and I have to show it to you," May said and then, through clenched teeth and with difficulty as she tugged on him, "Get up!"

"Ahh stop of the thing don't do."

"What?" May paused, worried her translation chip was busted again.

"It's don't fine worry managed the I did cannot."

"Christ, you're not making sense. Stay here, I'm going to find Aimz."

Xan flopped onto the floor, affecting a masterful interpretation of a washed-up jellyfish. "Aimz, no, wrath. Wrath!" The tea had flooded a rather important corridor of his speech center.

"Wrath?" May sat back on her heels. "She's your sister. She has to help."

His answer was a sigh so heavy and pointed, May swayed back from the force of it.

"I'm going to find Aimz." She patted his cheek fondly. "Hang in there. Take a nap or something."

Xan wasn't used to communicating without words, and he had had to resort to that twice in the past rotation. "Zippy didn't of the chance market," he told her seriously.

Leaving him there felt like the wrong thing to do. But

not doing anything was even worse and if she stayed with him, that's exactly what she would be doing. If you were still trying, thought May, it was impossible to fail. So she tried. She gave Xan one final deeply concerned look, then hefted open the double doors of the tearoom.

TWENTY-ONE
JOGGERS

It is a strange thing, but when two people are looking for each other in an enormous spaceship it actually lessons the chances of them meeting.

This is because it's easier to find someone who has stayed exactly where you left them than it is to find someone who has begun to wander.

May wandered now, because wandering toward help felt more productive than waiting for help to find her, and sometimes the illusion of productivity is all one needs to feel one has the situation under control.

Sometimes.

May did not feel in control of anything right now as the ocean in her head began to swirl into a maelstrom of obsessive thoughts almost too horrible to recount.

As she jogged the dead, twisting, catacomb-like hallways of the *Innocuous*, three thoughts were her running mates:

Firstly, that Xan had a death wish and she was seeking help for someone who didn't *want* to be helped.

Next, that she was stranded on a low oxygen planet with an entity that not only wanted them dead but also wanted the whole of everything crunched up into a tight wad under her heel.

Finally, that she deserved all this because she was too hardheaded to notice when she was actively fucking everything up.

As long as she kept looking for help, the thoughts playing in the back of her mind wouldn't overtake her. Just like a rocket race. She was good at those. She was not, however, good at running.

She focused on drawing a mental map.

A corridor on the left that led to nothing, a corridor on the right that led to nothing, a locked door, two locked doors, she turned down another corridor on the left that led to nothing and also nothing. The next corridor, however, had three locked doors. She turned again.

It was like running through an enormous metal tube sock.

And she was approaching the toe of this sock, a dead end. No more corridors leading to nothing remained. She stopped to recalculate.

Thwack! Something slammed into her from behind. It was "Xan had a death wish." And it had caught up with her, which was unpleasant. She turned around and leaned against the dead end just in time to watch the other two runners slam into her.

"These are things," she said out loud, hoping her wayward brain could hear, "I don't have time to think about right now."

From her brain, a resounding, "Too bad."

Her obsessive thoughts were dusting themselves off from the tumble. Focusing on the image of the map she had drawn in her head, and with a chorus of curses, she launched herself upward again and ran back the way she had come.

Something, presumably an unhelpful and slightly passive aggressive sign, glowed out of the wall ahead of her. If she stopped running, she might not be able to start back up again. This sign, she thought, better be worth the trouble.

And to her surprise, it was. It was a back-lit information

screen which gently illuminated an intershoot. And on the screen, finally, something useful. It was a map which read "Level 2" in blocky, confident letters in the upper left and displayed what looked like a cross-section of a sunfish with rather well-organized innards.

Labeled, even.

And smallish dots. One of which blinked a cheery "You Are Here*" with the asterisk pointing to a note in the lower left which read "Claim made under the assumption you are a not a multidimensional entity." Another dot labeled "Unknown" which blinked, a touch sadly it must be said, in the tearoom.

Clearly, Aimz was not on this level.

She watched the slowly blinking red dot that was definitely Xan. Was it supposed to be red? The "You Are Here*" dot was yellow. What did it mean? It meant, of course, that May was overthinking things. She shook her head to clear the dot discourse and stepped into the intershoot capsule. She would start at the bottom of the ship and work her way up. With a tap to the control panel, the bow intershoot brought her to the lowest level of the *Innocuous*.

Incidentally, the stern intershoot was busy as well.

The stern intershoot was going up and carried two smallish dots (one was blue, the other green, in case you were curious) to Level 2. These dots were Listay and Aimz, respectively.

May darted out of the intershoot pod to check a nearly identical glowing map that read "Level 1." Empty. Absolutely empty. Which was curious for a ship of this size, she thought.

Level 2 was, of course, empty.

Level 3 was empty, as well, but something on this level's map caught her attention.

"Contraband," May whispered to herself. Partially because she liked the sound of the word, partially because she was just so used to hearing Xan gabber constantly that the prolonged silence made her anxious.

"Huh," she mused. Contraband sounded like the perfect place to find a weapon. A weapon sounded like the perfect thing to have as a fragile, fleshy human trying to stop an unspeakable and ancient evil.

Aimz could wait; May was tired of being unarmed. Seasons in space and the deadliest weapon she had had her mitts on had been a spanner. It was time for flashy, sci-fi heroics. At last.

She counted the doors from where she was standing, the fifth door down. Her pick of fantastical alien weaponry was just five doors down. She jogged to the fifth door in a way that honestly wasn't much faster than a speed walk but did look slightly better and slid it open with a tap on its control panel.

A note about starship door security follows: There is none.

The contraband storage facility was a great deal less exciting than May had envisioned. Rows of lockers gaped dustily open, revealing nothing but sticky grime. As it turns out, most contraband aboard a Tuhntian military vessel was food-based and had rotted away long ago. Not a single deadly weapon. However, the fourteenth locker she peered hopefully into gave her something to be hopeful about. Two black anchor buttons with softly glowing green indicator lights rested atop a particularly sticky brown stain which almost seemed to form a smile of recognition beneath them.

"Hello anchor buttons."

TWENTY-TWO

THE LIMERICK

Chaos was an accomplished stormer.

Sonan, however, was not.

Because of this, Chaos in Sonan's robotic body didn't so much storm as she did drizzle haltingly onto the bridge of the *Innocuous*.

Precious Butler sat at the ship's enormous main computer, fiddling with what appeared to the untrained eye to be some sort of pixelated side-scrolling video game but was, in fact, a pixelated side-scrolling planetary environmental development analysis simulation. He dropped a simulated seed in a gridded section of the simulated planet of New Tuhnt. A green sprout popped hopefully up from a beige pixel, then wilted to a simulated 8-bit death knell. Precious Butler sighed deeply, shook his head, and marked off yet another section of his list. The avatar of Precious Butler trudged on through the simulated world, searching for a plot of land he hadn't tested yet.

"You!" crackled Chaos through Sonan's sound module.

Precious Butler, the aforementioned "you," simultaneously jumped, spun his hoverchair, and made a sound he didn't think his enormous vocal cords were capable of making.

"Sonan? What-" He blinked at her as she drizzled toward him, tried to think of a polite way of finishing his sentence, but decided instead to start over. "You're up," is what he chose.

"Yes. I did something unspeakable to this body's perambulatory functions, but I am up. Who are you?"

He gave her a perplexed half-smile. "You must've dropped something out of your memory database when you did that. I could take a look at that for you-"

"That's not necessary. Just tell me who you are in relation to this body."

Precious Butler shrugged. He knew the sooner he gave Sonan what she wanted, the sooner he could get back to work. "Precious Butler. I work for EnviroDev."

"EnviroDev? Interesting. Who are you to me?"

He waggled his head and lifted his broad shoulders. "I, uh, bring you tea, mostly. Dust you sometimes."

"You're not very good at it," Chaos said, brushing off her pink metal shoulders and leaning over the computer console.

Something, thought Precious Butler, was clearly amiss with Sonan. Perhaps one of her sanity relays had hit a snag. Would that have caused the unmentionable glow in her eyes though?

"Done with Xan?" Precious Butler asked, trying to make conversation.

"No. I'm going to locate the Sphere of Time and use it to twist his personal timeline into shlormpaat—" I feel it pertinent to mention here that shlormpaat is an ancient Rhean snack food that is similar to a pretzel in every respect except that it's only ever twisted by the highest and holiest monks belonging to the Monastery of Paatnu the Hungry. "—and then I will shatter every temporal constant in the universe and paste the timeline back together in an order so hideously obscene Time Himself will evanesce, leaving His throne to the unutterable will of She Who Demands The Degradation Of All That Is, Was, And Is To Be. The will of Chaos!"

"Still on the Xan thing, then," said Precious Butler as he returned to scrolling across the simulated landscape of New Tuhnt.

"He's a menace," she said and pushed him aside with surprising strength. She accidentally ended the environmental development program he'd been running for nearly a season. The credits scrolled whitely across a black screen for a moment, then ended with the pixelated logo for the EnviroDev Corp before returning the viewscreen to a dismal display of the oatmealish nothingness surrounding them.

He watched miserably as a season's worth of planetary development research was lost, sighed, and gave Sonan the attention she so clearly wanted.

"And what have you done with Xan and the other one? Don't tell me you just left them in the tearoom unattended."

"I left them in the tearoom unattended," Chaos said, pressing buttons and watching the screen and trying to figure out how the two correlated. "It doesn't matter where Xan is. If I kill him when I should have, he will cease to exist."

"Granted, but shouldn't he be secured in the interim?" He watched her carefully.

Chaos continued to press buttons that did nothing, twisting Sonan's limited facial expressions into something that looked more and more like frustration with every blip.

"I suppose I'll go get them. Again." He stood now, but Chaos seized his shoulder.

"Wait. First you will help me locate the Sphere of Time."

There are certain things that are universal: ice cream, Sunday afternoon listlessness (though the names of the days of the week change, the listlessness remains), and limericks.

Chaos knew every limerick that had ever been written. It was the one exception to her lack of omniscience, and it was inexplicable, even to her, which proved her lack of omniscience. She fiddled with Sonan's sound module and found the setting she was after: a thick brogue.

"There once was a man from Rhea III," she recited. "Who tickled his pickle all dey / When asked where's the sphere?'/ He replied, 'well it's here! / Just west of the Miteran Sea.'"

Precious Butler was used to Sonan saying nonsensical things, but she'd never done it in a brogue before.

"That was lovely," he said, unsure of what she was hoping he would say.

"It was not lovely, it was a clue," Chaos growled. "Where is the Miteran Sea?"

"There aren't any seas here and this isn't Rhea III. There is no Rhea III. I really think I ought to take a look at your head, Sonan."

"This *was* Rhea III. Where *were* the seas?"

Precious Butler sighed. "There's a patch of mineral-rich sediment half a beoop from here by MoonHopper."

"Show me."

He reached for the control panel's primary keyboard, but Chaos stood in his way. "I, uh, need to be right where you are."

"Oh, sorry." She moved, but not much.

"Don't worry about it. I'll just..." He contorted himself around her and fiddled with the buttons until an image of the planet's surface appeared onscreen. In the bottom corner, the *Innocuous* rested like a beached sunfish. "There it is," he said, pointing out what looked like a bruise on the planet's face.

"Take me there. And find me a really big gun."

Precious Butler shook his head. "Sonan, I've got a lot of work to re-do on my EnviroDev report before I head back to Rhea I, and you just left fugitives to wander the ship. I really ought to-"

She fixed him with an unmentionable glare.

"Fine, I'll get you a gun and the keys to the MoonHopper but that's it. You can take yourself to the time thing."

Chaos was used to having lungs with which to huff at people when they didn't do as she asked. She was used to having powers which allowed her to turn people into sentient floral fainting couches. She was used to being able to step into different dimensions and out of them at will. Now, she struggled to get this body to produce a simulated groan.

"That will do," said Chaos.

TWENTY-THREE

SCHRODINGER'S ZOMBIE

Listay and Aimz approached the tearoom slowly, Listay's plasma zapper drawn, Aimz wielding her twisted metal bit. They paused at the door.

"Alright, General. Are you ready?" Aimz whispered.

Listay stood on the other side of the door. "I'll go first," she said.

"Why? I've got a weapon."

"This is my job. You're a biologist," Listay explained in a whisper.

"I'm an adventure biologist."

Listay laughed quietly at her. "I've got a gun; I win."

"Alright, alright, go on."

Listay burst through the double doors, Aimz close at her back. They were met by nothing. Almost nothing.

"Ah, Blitheon's stars what happened to you, mun?" Aimz knelt at Xan's head. He winked up at her, the neon of his eyes flickering and buzzing.

"Oh. Soo," he managed with a vague smile, thinking that he'd very clearly said "Oh. It's you." He was getting the hang of talking again. "Harris day?" he said as a means of asking where May was.

Listay sniffed the half-empty cup of cold tea. "Barley tea," she told Aimz. "Is this your brother? Looks like he just came from the beach."

"Preciminsice!" he confirmed.

"Yeah, that's Xan. What's left of him, at least. That's a shame, isn't it? Just reunited and you get killed on me. Don't mind if I donate your body to science do you?" She pulled out the tiny laserblade and tried to decide if it was sharp enough for an impromptu autopsy.

"Sames op-ed," he slurred, telling Aimz to stop it. He swatted at her swimmingly. "Not homming do suck-sing eye. Unfortunabalmont." Which meant that he was not going to zuxing die, unfortunately.

"Whatever you say, mun."

"What did he say?" Listay asked, joining them on the dense floral carpet.

"Not a clue," Aimz shrugged. "Alright, Listy-"

"Listay," she corrected.

Aimz's cheeks flushed greenly. "I know I just thought it was cute."

Listay's eyebrows scrunched together, then unscrunched slowly, one at a time. "I suppose it is."

Aimz smiled at Listay until Xan decided he'd had enough of the heady silence and broke it with a pitiful moan.

"I think I was going to ask if you had a plan or a girlfriend or something," said Aimz.

"Neither, sorry."

"Don't be sorry."

Listay blinked meaningfully at Aimz. "Your brother has just been poisoned by an android possessed by the Goddess of Chaos who is now loose on the planet looking for the Sphere of Time which she intends to use to end the Universe as we know it. Let's take care of that, then we can flirt."

"We could do both!" Aimz said, hooking one arm under Xan's as Listay got his other arm.

"Mun, half a rotation ago I was dead. I'm not sure I'm ready for that level of multitasking just yet."

Aimz grunted as they hefted him into the chair.

"Xan," said Xan to Listay as she released him. "Of-Tuhnt," he slurred, offering his hand to her in greeting. "Or used t' be of Tuhnt. Not now. Nice meeting of. When is May?"

His hand was still held aloft, so Listay cordially shook it, then gently pushed it down to his lap. "Pleasure meeting you, as well. I wish it were under better circumstances."

"Ah, a circus stance," Xan nodded sagely. "May is and?"

"May? I thought she'd be with you. Did you lose her?" Aimz asked.

The light had flickered back on in Xan's eyes now, but he looked mortified. "Zuut, did I?"

"May is a human he's been taking care of," Aimz told Listay. This made Xan laugh and the laughter seemed to shake out more of his lexicon.

"Other way around. She left to do the, uh, the eyes searching thing."

"Looking?"

"Right. Went to do the looking searching find to found would have found did find was going to have found—"

"Get to the end of it," Aimz snapped.

Xan winced as his synapses dried out. "May went looking for you. Aimz, you, not uh...you, you." He looked pointedly to Listay who didn't catch the hint that he'd missed her name. He sighed. "Xan," he said with a smile, holding out his hand to her.

"We did this already," Listay noted.

He nodded. "Yeah but the one of who you are didn't be forthcoming."

"This is Listay, and I met her first, so don't try to seduce her."

"Really, Aimz, in the state of which I am now I don't have the lexical capacity to do seducorcery."

The double doors slammed open and Listay raised her zapper, lamenting the five milliblip lag she seemed to be experiencing between her brain and her slowly re-knitting nervous system. Even half-dead, her reflexes were better than either of the Tuhntian's.

May rushed in, yelped her surprise at the zapper pointed at her face, shut the doors behind her, and pressed up against them.

"Shinestar!" Xan said. "Right, Listay. Not to shoot her. Important."

"I know you," Listay said to May as she lowered the zapper. "You were kitchen staff on the *Peacemaker*, right?"

May nodded but did not recognize the Rhean who walked stiffly toward her. She'd been so gobsmacked by the abduction that introductions from that day hadn't stuck much.

"Sorry, you are?"

"This is Listay. She's a bit dead, but I think she's getting better," Aimz said before Listay could get a sound out.

"Hello," she said, since the introduction part had been taken care of, and held out her dirt-encrusted robotic hand. May shook it, tentatively. "I gave you a llerke, remember?"

"Oh, yes," May said. Her abduction had been a very stressful day half a year ago and the details had gone fuzzy but she did remember someone giving her a llerke.

"So, you're dead?" May asked

Listay shook her head noncommittally. "It's unclear. I am simultaneously dead and not dead."

May nodded. "Same."

"Same?"

"Well...no. Sorry, I wasn't sure how to reply to that. How's Xan?"

Xan flailed limply at her.

"I found Aimz! You declared that it was you who were going find Aimz but ultimately it was I who did the finding of." She peered around Listay to see Aimz plucking things from the tiered tea tray, licking them, then putting them back exactly where they had been.

"Right, good work, Watson." May patted his head and he pulled her into a hug that made it clear he had forgotten she used her lungs to breathe.

"Can you help him?" May wheezed over the top of his head.

"Eh, he's fine," Aimz continued to lick items from the table as if she were spitefully claiming the entire spread for herself. "Need to find something alkaline to-aha!" she said as she licked something which resembled a peppermint that had been crushed with a mallet and reconstituted. She popped it into Xan's mouth and held his jaw shut. "Swallow, don't chew," she told him. With a scrunched look of annoyance, he obeyed, the sharply pointed thing fighting its way down his throat.

"Eugh, that was horrible." He growled, then, excitedly, "Horrible! My words are working again! Wait. I think. May, ask me to explain something humans don't know about."

"Okay. Why is it that you and Aimz are the only two aliens I've ever seen with back-lit eyes? As David Attenborough."

He threw his head back and laughed. "Alright, okay, wait..." He cleared his throat and put on a serious face and British accent. "The Carmnians of the species have a curious genetic mutation. Tiny fibers in the vitreous gel of Carmnian eyes are coated in thousands of light-producing cells called photophores. This mutation is thought to be the result of Carmnia's diet of a bioluminescent genus of ophiocordyceps fungi and the souls of those who cross her-"

Aimz smacked his arm with the back of her hand. "You know Carmnia doesn't eat souls. She *curates* them." She laughed, which inspired Xan to laugh. May and Listay did not, however. Neither of them knew who Carmnia was, much less why it was funny that she curated souls but didn't eat them. They shared a shrug of solidarity.

Then, above the din of the laughter, the clank of fast-approaching footsteps echoed down the hall.

"Anchor buttons," May informed everyone, opening her fist to reveal the two black disks she had rescued from contraband. The footsteps stopped. The doors creaked. May grabbed Xan's wrist, pulled him onto the teledisc, and told his BEAPER that she would very much like to be back aboard the *Audacity*.

Like a chain of plastic monkeys, May grabbed Xan, Xan grabbed Aimz, and Aimz grabbed Listay, and the teledisc whipped all four of them into a cloud of easily transportable atoms.

TWENTY-FOUR

AN INDETERMINATE NUMBER OF PORCELAIN CLOWN FIGURINES

Sorting atoms is tough. Sorting atoms without knowing how many beings you're trying to sort them into is tougher, even for a sophisticated military grade teledisc.

Imagine you have a box full of an indeterminate number of porcelain clown figurines. Some hooligan drops your box from a fifty story building and the figurines shatter into millions of pieces. Not knowing how many clown figurines you're meant to be gluing back together makes the process all the more difficult, and you're likely to buy new clown figurines rather than go to the trouble of reconstructing them.

The *Audacity*'s teledisc was about ready to buy new figurines.

Fortunately, May arrived intact and one hundred percent her. Xan, however, did not. The teledisc could suss Earthling DNA from Rhean and Rhean DNA from Tuhntian, but the two Tuhntians had proved difficult..

Xan stumbled off the teledisc, clutching imaginary pearls around his neck. Something was very wrong.

Aimz, too, had noticed it and shuddered with revulsion.

Xan was the first to get himself under control enough to speak. "You took my tongue!" he accused Aimz who had and was currently wringing his tongue through her teeth.

"Not intenthonally," she said with some difficulty, going cross eyed as she tried to see it. "You took ny tongue ptierthing."

Xan explored clicking his new tongue. Something metallic clanged against his teeth. He certainly had taken her tongue piercing.

May had the sense that they were forgetting something. "Turn off the teledisc!"

She tripped over herself getting to the teledisc plug which Xan was standing right in front of it, preoccupied with his new tongue.

"You know, actually, I think I like it!" He flicked the metal bar against his teeth, enjoying the thwicking sound. "Whatcha think, May?" He brandished his new tongue at her.

May's cheek twitched. "I think we better stop Chaos." She tossed aside the plug with more force than was strictly necessary.

"Ah, she can't do any harm. Time travel hasn't been invented yet. She's chasing after an old Tuhntian legend, and I say we leave her to it. There's got to be a way to get this tether off *Audy.*" Xan flopped over the back of the couch, his spine cracking in a way that had either made it feel better or worse (it was worse, but he wouldn't know this until he tried to use it again.)

"May's right," Listay said, stepping down from the teledisc. "Chaos is an ancient being; if she believes the Sphere of Time exists, it likely does. She's older than the legend, so she'd know. If she finds it, she could reset the entire universe with her at the center. Any semblance of reason in the universe, any illusion of order and soundness, would cease to exist." This disturbed Listay on a personal level, and she paused for a moment, considering all the ramifications of such a thing. This new universe wouldn't have spreadsheets. Listay shuddered.

There are as many ways to react to stressful news as

there are people to hear stressful news.

Xan was trying out a coping mechanism which relied on him pretending to be a wet blanket. Aimz preferred to sling a few insults at a problem. Listay had been dying lately when things got too stressful. May's cheek had adopted a persistent twitch. She slapped a hand over half her face to still it. "That sounds bad," she said. It was.

"And does she know where this zuxing time ball is, or is this all hypothetical crosh-wopple?" Aimz asked. She leaned heavily on absolutely nothing. It was disconcerting —like there was an invisible counter behind her. "I mean, zuut, I wouldn't mind getting my hands on something like that. I can think of one or two things I'd like to change about the past." She shot a hurtful look at Xan who pretended to pretend to look very hurt.

"Wait, wait," Xan said, swapping the wet blanket impression for one more akin to a bag of concrete which has been rained on and solidified. "If you go messing around with the past, won't it change the present?"

"Obviously," said Aimz. "That's the point. I mean," she barked a laugh, "I can imagine a million different better futures than this one. All involve you not destroying Tuhnt."

"I didn't destroy Tuhnt, Aimz!" He stood up now, eschewing all comparison to inanimate objects.

"Oh right mun, of course you didn't. You just doomed it. Just took off with the one piece of kit that could've saved Tuhnt. Why though? Was it the orange? Because if you stole the *Audacity* because she was pretty, I swear on O'Zeno, I'm going to go at it with a can of blood-green paint and draw ovipositors all over the hull."

"I didn't have much-" he began, then paused, staring over her shoulder and into the past. "That was you! By Blitheon, you painted those ovipositors on Chrismillion's Minicraft." His face flipped far too quickly from anger to amusement.

Aimz choked back a chuckle. "I thought you knew it was me."

"You are Carmnia's larvae," Xan laughed.

"You're one to talk; you destroyed the planet! Classic

Carmnian move."

Xan sat heavily on the couch again. "Yeah." He sighed.

"All we've got to do, I figure," Aimz crashed into the couch beside him, "is find the Sphere of Time and keep you from stealing the *Audacity* in the past. Easy?"

"We need to do it before Chaos does," May interjected, keeping a mental list of all the new questions she had for Xan which would have to wait.

Xan laughed, "Right, yeah, her idea was just to kill me before I could screw anything up. Elegant, really." His demeanor shifted into a shade May hadn't seen before. She didn't care for it. "Why do we have to stop her?"

May looked to Aimz, thinking perhaps some sibling bond would give Aimz the right words to say. She squared her spiked shoulders, regarded Xan thoughtfully, took a preparatory breath, and didn't say anything.

"We're stopping Chaos either way," May said, finally. "Preferably before she offs Xan," she told Aimz who didn't seem to mind.

"Good, then we're agreed." Listay said. "The Gremlin might still run if we're lucky."

May cringed loudly at the mention of luck.

"And if we aren't lucky?" May asked. "What's our back up plan?"

Aimz jumped up. "StarTaxi!" she said, as if it were obvious.

"You parked it beneath the *Audacity*," May reminded her.

Aimz blinked, smiled, then finally had the decency to look confused.

"You parked it under a rocket ship, and then we took off. It's been incinerated."

"Oh, for Blitheon's sake. That was a zuxing rental," she said, more to herself, slapping her own thigh as punishment, then, to the room, "Well, we've got to find the Sphere of Time now. I can't afford to replace that thing."

Listay stared at Aimz for what she knew (for she had counted) was the ninth time since they had met with perplexed wonderment. She blinked it away and carefully took the stairs to the control loft panel. The rigor mortis was beginning to calm down and her heart was up to a solid twenty beats per beoop which, by her definition, was alive but wildly inappropriate.

She flicked on the viewscreen and spun the camera angle until she could see the enormous white hull of the *Innocuous* and the single MoonHopper still parked beside it. Assumedly, Chaos had either started toward the Sphere of Time on foot, or she hadn't figured out where it was yet.

Both of her assumptions were incorrect. Chaos was currently inside the MoonHopper, cursing in a dead language at the MoonHopper's console for not being user friendly. The dead language didn't have a concept of user friendly-ness and, as such, she jumped from language to language like a mosquito sucking indiscriminately from whatever was handy. It was a shame Xan couldn't hear it, because he would have appreciated her lexical dexterity. It was a shame Aimz couldn't hear it, because she would have appreciated the creative use of swears.

"You have weapons on board, right?" Listay asked over her shoulder. "I would suggest you go get them. We need to be ready to move out as soon as Chaos does."

Aimz pulled the twisted bit of metal from her infinite belt, a brightly colored candy wrapper impaled on one end. "I've got this!"

"I have a novelty pocket knife," May said. "But we have a utility room. We could chuck power tools at her."

She pulled back the orange wall to reveal the utility room, which might more accurately be called a utility closet, lined with tools May only knew from the ship's manual. She slipped inside. None of the tools were particularly heavy, a credit to Tuhntian technology but a hindrance to her plan.

Xan scrunched into the closet to look with her as she dismounted a handheld device with an obsolete grey screen.

"What's that?"

"It's a diagnostic thingy. I've never had to use it though; the viewscreen has a digital version."

"Try it out! Diagnose me." He thrust his arms out to the

sides, as far as the space would allow, and looked forward seriously.

The part of May's brain which frantically tapped its watch at her shut off for a blip. She switched the diagnostic thingy on and scanned him with the green light which emanated from it.

"Huh, says here you've got a clothing malfunction. You need a transplant." She nodded gravely to his shiny yellow swimsuit.

"I do! Great opportunity to make a new suit. I'm officially a criminal on the run now, so it's got to be something edgy. I'm thinking shoulder extenders, all black, tasteful ruffles."

"Nothing too tasteful." She handed him the diagnostic device. "That's the heaviest thing in here. How's your aim?"

"It could be better."

"Could it be worse?"

"It could be better," he repeated.

"I see. Just talk her to death, okay?" May said, picking up a fishbowl helmet and strapping the attached oxygen pack to her back. The remaining tools were a thin metal handle with a stubby green light at its end which would do about as much damage as a lit cigarette, an extremely unsafe safety pin, and a jar of something which wibbled. A green light flashed in her peripheral vision, distracting her from her fruitless search.

Xan tapped the diagnostic screen. "Says here that you're still mad at me." He looked up at her wincingly.

"You stole the *Audacity*. We've been racing in a stolen ship. How can you live with that?" she asked, considering a stained pin cushion for a moment before pitching it to the floor. The pin cushion hadn't deserved that.

It was a good question. A question Xan had been playing like a favorite cassette tape in the dusty old walkman of his mind since before walkmans were invented.

"I don't know. I thought I was getting better at it." He ground his teeth and made a face like he was trying really hard to stuff a pair of pants into an over-full luggage case, then at last zipped it up and sat on it to be sure it would stay closed. “Alright.” He went to the coffee maker just outside the utility room and began shoveling grounds into the filter with a ferocity that suggested that he was imagining burying himself beneath the course grounds. “Let’s go confront an ancient Chaos goddess who wants me dead. Again. Instead of just letting her get it over and done with. Endangering everyone else on my account. Because it wasn’t nearly as harrowing as it could’ve been the first time, and I don’t already feel terrible enough about myself,” he said, modifying his intonation so that May would know that it *had* been harrowing the first time, and he *did* already feel terrible enough about himself.

May leaned on the counter, the fishbowl under her arm, watching as he filled the filter one aggressive scoop at a time, then continuing to pile grounds on until they began to tumble onto the orange laminate. She thought it best not to stop him.

“Hey, I know this sucks,” she offered.

“Sucks?” he repeated, still shoveling coffee.

“It’s...” May needed to use older Earth sayings around him. She tried to think of something Lucy might have said. “It’s a bummer.”

“Oh, right. Yeah.”

“It’s the right thing to do, though.”

Xan finally realized the filter was nicely full and plopped it into the coffee maker, using his finger to dust off the extra grounds around the rim. “Yep.” He flicked it on.

“I’ll miss you,” May said.

“Right. Now I’m not going to claim I know anything about time travel, because it doesn’t exist, but if it *does* exist and we *do* go back to make it so that I didn’t steal the *Audacity*, you won’t have met me, so you won’t miss me or the *Audacity* and that’s okay. It really is.” The coffee splattered into the carafe between them, and he stared at the brown stream, willing it to hurry up.

May stared at it, too. She’d be back working at Sonic. Maybe this time she wouldn’t get abducted, maybe she would. There were a million other eventualities to account for. If she got abducted, there would be no *Audacity* to pull her out of open space. If she got abducted, she was dead.

"But I'll miss you, too," Xan said as the coffee stream sputtered to a stop. He drained half the carafe, not bothering to pour it into a mug. "It's a mighty good thing that we probably won't remember how terrible this feels, right?" He laughed and handed her the carafe which she took and drank from with the reverence of a sacred ritual. "Time travel, if it in fact exists, certainly thought of everything."

"Good thing," May said hoarsely, having burned her throat with the scalding coffee. She let her eyes rest on the orange shag carpet, stewing in the silence until it was broken by an obnoxious clicking noise.

"Xan," she said, too melancholy to summon enough energy to tear her eyes away from the carpet, "are you playing with the tongue ring?"

"Uhuh." The clicking stopped.

The living room was densely quiet now, Listay keeping watch on the MoonHopper, Aimz testing the integrity of the sharp bit of metal by carving her name into the coffee table, and Xan and May partaking in a final carafe of coffee together, sadly enjoying each other's company.

Listay wrenched away the comfortable silence. "She's gone, let's move!"

May jumped, startled to find that she was not, in fact, swimming in a warm pool of orange carpet. At some point, she and Xan had started leaning more on each other than the counter. They had forgotten to change.

"Ready?" she asked him, fitting the fishbowl over her head with a thloop, pushing her hair up into it, and sealing the opening around her neck.

"Not in the slightest. You?" He finished the coffee and placed it neatly back on the hot plate.

Aimz leapt from the couch and grabbed their hands, bouncing on her heels as if they were about to take her to a candy store.

"I'm ready. We're going to find a time ball!" She literally dragged Xan and May to the teledisc, but not figuratively. Figuratively, they were still floating in a melancholic orange pool.

TWENTY-FIVE

EARTHQUAKE

The surface of the planet welcomed May, Aimz, Listay, and Xan with a grossly tepid wind. It was neither hot nor cold, just slightly too warm for comfort, like someone had peed in the public pool that was the atmosphere.

All that remained of the MoonHopper were two toasty scorch marks in the dirt and a cloud of residual affront from the ancient curse words.

The Gremlin was exactly where Listay had left it, and as they approached, the tortured machine no longer gave off an air of smugness, no longer wished to be useful in any way whatsoever. It pinged desperately as its engine cooled. "No," it said, "let me die, I beg of you."

Listay did not speak AMC Gremlin and, as such, hadn't understood its plea. She flew to the pilot's door, grabbed the handle, and pulled. The door handle snapped off in her hand. Chucking it aside, she flew to the passenger's door, grabbed the handle, and pulled. That handle also snapped off. Chucking it aside, she flew to the hatchback and pried it open, crawling into the front seat. May squeezed into the passengers side, leaving Xan and Aimz to stuff into the rear and shut the hatchback behind them.

"Right, General, after that MoonHopper! This is fun," Aimz said to Xan, the seat squeaking as she fidgeted. The noise Xan made in response was so unsure, so noncommittal, that it is impossible to duplicate it here phonetically. But I will try.

"Mmmnnnnhhungggmmph," said Xan.

In the front of the car, Listay flicked a switch which was meant to reignite the burnt out pilot light.

On and off, on and off.

Bupkis.

"Parking brake?" Xan said, his face appearing suddenly over May's left shoulder.

"It's only ever the parking brake when you're driving." May pushed his face back, like a dog she was directing away from a plate of food. "Let me try, switch with me." They shimmied into each other's seats, May contorting herself around Listay, thwacking her knee on the shifter, and gaining her tenth bruise thus far. There would be more.

The dashboard was a field of stripped wires, twisted together by hand, and laid out in shockingly neat lines, as if someone had scared them into tidiness. The wires didn't matter, though. The pilot light didn't matter, either.

At its core, the AMC Gremlin was still just that: an AMC Gremlin. And May, with this in mind, turned the key which had been left in the ignition and twisted it to life. Hands grasped her shoulders and she jumped.

"And the human saves the mission. Tint me surprised," Aimz said behind her.

Equal parts flattered and annoyed, May rolled her shoulders to dislodge Aimz's hands and shifted the car into drive, something she hadn't done in years. It was like riding a bike, or, more accurately, like driving a car. Once you've done it, you don't forget.

The Gremlin's belts squealed a litany of complaints regarding their age, the dry air on New Tuhnt, and the fine dusting of sand which coated every surface, interior and exterior, of the car. May was an unsympathetic ear and forced the Gremlin to lurch forward out of the divot it had made in the sand and chase after Chaos.

She convinced the car to reach a speed it had never in its life attained on land: ninety-eight miles per hour. It hated that, vibrating painfully until she brought it down to ninety, which it would tolerate but only just.

Sandy, dry air streamed in from the open window and May was grateful for the fishbowl because the three highly evolved, millenia-old humanoid aliens with her couldn't keep their eyes open without having them sandblasted.

"Do you-pfft," Aimz spat a mouthful of sand, "see anything?"

"Nothing," May said, and then was immediately proven wrong as something appeared over the dusty horizon. It wasn't a MoonHopper, though. It was a billboard with one metal leg crunched beneath it, tilting like a flamingo with vertigo.

"Water Where There Ought Not Be, the Logic-Defying Amusement Pool," May read as they barreled past it. There were more. Hundreds of billboards, some face-down in the dirt, partially buried, others leaning exhaustedly back, their sun faded advertisements impossible to read. Occasionally, May caught one which was legible.

"Visit the Pontoosa Adventure Hole," she read as she drove past another sign, this one with a large green arrow hooking around its rectangular frame.

"There's no zuxing way. Pontoosa Adventure Hole?" Xan shielded his eyes and tried to see what was zooming past them. "All those ancient limericks we studied in literary history of the universe were supposed to be myths! Aimz, you remember them?"

"Must've had that class with Yve, because I remember nothing. What kind of zoup-nog memorizes limericks when someone like her is in the seat over?"

"I see it," May said, interrupting some important reminiscing and pointing to a massive billboard in the distance.

Listay leaned forward and squinted at it. "Don't Miss The Sphere of Time," she read from the enormous billboard they were approaching, May slowed the Gremlin to let her finish. “Ancient Rhean Wonder Lost to the Ages Until Now. Right ahead.”

May attempted to step on it. Attempted to coax the Gremlin to its theoretical top speed of ninety-eight miles per hour. It rattled with the ferocity of an earthquake motion simulator. She slowed down, but the rattle got worse. She braked. A sign which said something about a Hooflatoo Bone Sculpture Museum crumbled in front of them and flopped on the dusty ground like a waterless fish.

The car, May realized, had not been rattling like it was in an earthquake motion simulator. It had been rattling like it was in an earthquake.

Suggestions chorused around her. Listay tried to convince her to drive, Xan mentioned something about seeking shelter, Aimz wanted to get out and explore the shivering landscape.

“Everyone shut up!” she shouted at last, choosing to drive carefully around the fallen billboard and get up to speed again, despite the shaking. If the Gremlin shook apart, it shook apart.

It did not shake apart, but the ground did, swallowing the Gremlin whole.

The AMC Gremlin, at last, had come to the end of its journey. It smoked gently, badly crushed, tires splayed out beneath it like the legs of a newborn giraffe. It had brought them to an underground cavern, surprisingly cold and damp and smelling of wood rot and rust. Clusters of dimly glowing fungus illuminated the cavern, glistening on the shattered windows.

To her delight, Listay was still conscious. To her dismay, the Gremlin was not and would never be again. “Is everyone alive?” She rammed her shoulder against the door until it popped open so she could survey the area.

Aimz peered out at the cavern with bated interest. Not bated for long, though, as she crawled over the front seats and used Listay as leverage to extract herself from the car. “That was zuxing terrific,” Aimz said without a hint of irony.

"Yep, zuxing terrific," Xan agreed with a great deal of irony. "May?"

"Terrific," she said with an inflection which could have gone either way. She shook a shower of glass from her hair. The fishbowl had shattered and, though the adrenaline helped dull the pain, she felt blood dripping down her face.

The door refused to open, so May dragged herself from the broken window of the car, landing on a creaking wooden boardwalk. The dark wood panels had splintered in some places under the Gremlin, so May, not keen on finding out what exactly was under the boardwalk, scrambled off it and onto the softly luminescent blue concrete.

The alcove they had landed in stretched impressively out in every direction and was clearly meant to aid the shuffling of hundreds of people from one place to another. From the roof of the cave hung a marquee sign, supported by two massive cables, reflective sequins glimmering with points of light which told them they were in a place called Ponstoosa.

May removed what was left of her helmet and Xan undertook the arduous task of combing glass shards from her thick hair. Oxygen, she assumed, was precious, so she held her breath and waited for the hallucinations to set in.

"Hey, you know you can breathe, right?" he asked.

She raised her eyebrows.

She did not know that.

"Yeah! Tons of oxygen down here. Almost too much. There are highly suspicious levels of oxygen in this pit." He tapped his BEAPER as if the readings would change.

"Cavern," corrected Aimz from the other side of the Gremlin, snapping samples of the glowing fungi off the boardwalk and pocketing them.

"Same thing."

"Nope."

Xan shrugged; May breathed.

"Huh," said Listay. "Chaos was right. This planet used

to be Rhea III." Her voice echoed in the suspiciously oxygen-rich air.

"What makes you think that?" May tried not to look like she was limping as she walked toward Aimz and Listay who had gathered in the middle of the cavern around a fixture that had at one time been a fountain. With an almost imperceptible whine, Xan wrapped an arm around her, trying not to look like he was helping her walk.

"The historical marker on this fountain says the Pontoosa Adventure Hole was built over the ruins of ancient Rhea III where they discovered the legendary Sphere of Time," said Listay.

Beyond the fountain, May could just make out a large, marbled facade with golden friezes carved along the top. A beam of light shone through the crack in the surface and highlighted a phrase carved into the entablature of the underground building.

"'The Arch of Time, Through Which Lies the Museum of Time, The Gift Shop of Time, the Experience of Time, and Therein The Mysterious and Powerful Sphere of Time,'" May read out loud.

The ground shifted.

"Aftershock," Listay explained. She was wrong. "Let's continue on foot."

Before they had a chance to agree, the concrete exploded into the suspiciously oxygen-rich air.

TWENTY-SIX

THE WYRNTENSIL

The wyrntensil is a heretofore assumed mythical creature with five hundred tiny legs peeking out from a tube-like body, five hundred blind eyes lining its ridged back, five hundred sharp teeth at one end of the tube, and one merciless heart smack in the center.

Little is known of the wyrntensil, because most people who are unlucky enough to meet one end up finding out just how sharp all five hundred of its teeth are.

"Run!" shouted Listay. She didn't have to.

She unclipped her plasma zapper and sunk a few shots into the beast's maw to distract it before bolting after Aimz down the corridor which read "In Memoriam of The Small One".

May and Xan clambered into the trunk of the Gremlin. May, because she knew she couldn't outrun the thing. Xan, because his first reaction was usually to do whatever May did.

Reaching down her t-shirt, she fished the sweaty pocket knife from between her breasts and flicked it open. Tried to flick it open, at least. In the end, she pried the blade from its wonky plastic casing with her teeth.

"That thing ate plasma! I doubt a pocket knife will have much effect," Xan whispered, as if the creature might overhear. It did not have five hundred ears. Didn't have any, actually.

"It has to come in handy eventually," she said, testing the point with her finger. There was no point. The pocket knife had no point at all.

"Does it?"

"I would think."

I will remind you at this time that the pocket knife had no point and May was, in fact, wrong.

The creature gave a record-scratch shriek and slithered around the car, occasionally rolling onto its side, as its eyes were all inconveniently located on its back.

"You've got a plan, right?" Xan asked, scooching closer.

May did not have a plan, but she was decent at thinking on her toes, and as she collected a list of their current assets, something was beginning to come to her.

"Check the glove box for jumper cables. I'm going to try to get the engine on," May said, scrambling into the front seat.

"Check the what for whom?"

"Never mind. *You* try to get the engine on, and *I'll* check the glove box for jumper cables. Got it?"

"Got it." Xan twisted the key in the ignition. No sound could be heard but the squelching of the wyrntensil circling its prey, looking for an opportunity to strike. He continued twisting anyway.

May pulled a length of red and black cables from the glove box and held them out triumphantly. "Not working?"

"I think this was its last life."

"It's fine. Harvey Foster once started a bonfire with his car battery when we were on a camping trip and he didn't have the car actually on at the time, so I think I can make it work."

"Harvey Foster?" Xan asked with a smile, forgetting the key. "Who's Harvey Foster?" It was rare that May talked about life on Earth. And for good reason, too. There wasn't much about Earth she wanted to remember, but

Xan tried to encourage it.

"No one," she said, checking the cables to be sure they were intact.

The wyrntensil was becoming restless. It smacked the car, flinging it onto its side.

"Right. You're getting out of this one for now because we're in mortal danger," said Xan, "but I've got to know who Harvey Foster was!"

"Okay, I'll tell you later. Can you pop the hood?" May said, climbing up toward the passenger door which was now the ceiling. "I'm going to hook these up to the battery."

"Then what?" he said, searching for the hood release.

May ripped into the denim seat covering and extracted a chunk of stiff yellow foam which, she hoped, was highly flammable. "Fire bomb?"

"You think that'll work?" Xan asked, finding the lever under the steering wheel and pulling on it several times before he heard the satisfying click of the hood unlocking.

"Not at all, no."

"But it would be cool," he said.

"Exactly." May handed Xan the pocket knife (which she had not used to open the seat covering, because the stitching was already so weak) and pulled herself out of the car window. "Cover me?"

"Uh," Xan stared at the tiny pocket knife. "Uhhhh!" He had no choice now; he followed her out of the window and held the knife in front of him as he straddled the car door. The wyrntensil wrapped massively around them, an impenetrable wall of thick grey hide that seemed to have no beginning and no end. Which was fortunate because if Xan had seen the beginning bit of the wyrntensil, he would not have faced it with nothing but a pocket knife protecting him.

May propped open what was left of the crushed hood and clamped the cables to the battery terminals, then held the foam between the rusty jaws of the black cable and touched it with the red one, eliciting a frail spark.

The foam did not catch.

The wyrntensil noticed.

It rolled onto its side to get a sense of where May was, then slung the heavy tube of its body around as May frantically rubbed the clamps together. The foam, it seemed, was not as flammable as she had hoped.

"It's coming over," Xan said, watching the creature slither closer to May.

"I've almost got it," she said, though the spark was getting smaller and she was decidedly getting farther away from having it.

The knife would by no means pierce the wyrntensil's flesh, but perhaps, thought Xan, it could distract the creature. He chucked the pocket knife right at one of its five hundred beady eyes. It hit just below the eye, bounced off, and clattered pointlessly to the ground. The wyrntensil continued its threatening slither unperturbed, then began to lift up the front of its body, rearing back to add some drama to the kill.

"Back in the Gremlin!" Xan shouted.

"Throw the diagnostic thingy at it!" May redoubled her efforts, but the cables weren't even sparking now.

"Can't."

"Why not?"

"Lost it."

"Ugh." At last, May dropped the foam and climbed back into the car via the upturned passenger window. The wyrntensil wailed and flung its face against the car. There was a tooth. One of five hundred. The beast roared through the windshield, effluvium from its foul ancient breath stinging May's eyes as she tried to stuff herself under the dashboard.

"Plan two?" Xan asked from the backseat as the Gremlin rocked.

"Wait for it to lose interest." The car rolled again, now onto its roof.

And then it stopped.

"Think it lost interest already?" Xan whispered.

May shook her head. If it had lost interest, it would be slithering away, not blocking the cavern's light with its massive body.

Blips passed. Silence. Stillness.

Maybe, May thought, it had died suddenly. She began to pose this theory, "Do you think-" Tentacles burst through the Gremlin's windows and felt around the inside of the cabin until they wrapped wetly around May and Xan, then retracted, curling back out from whence they came.

May had experienced a lot of terrible things in her life, but being covered in an inch thick layer of worm saliva took the metaphorical cake.

Xan was more used to this sort of thing and only sighed his disappointment.

"What?!" May whispered, squeegeeing the mucus from her face.

"Tend-blugh," Xan paused to spit a mouthful of the stuff. "Tenderizer," he said. "Alright, okay. So, as far as I figure, there's a slim chance I'm making it off this planet alive no matter what happens, so I'll tell you what I'm going to do." He peered out of the window to see what the wyrntensil was up to, decided he'd rather not know, and turned to May again. "I'm going to run, lead it away from you, and then you can look for Aimz and Listay and stop Chaos from, I don't know, eating the universe."

"Can you outrun it?"

He laughed, thinking she was making a joke.

"Then don't try. We'll think of some-" If she was able to finish her sentence, Xan didn't hear it above the racket of the car being pummeled from above. May clambered into the backseat, which was slightly less squished than the front on account of the hatchback.

The boardwalk creaked under the strain, the planks bending and splintering until at last the Gremlin broke through to an underground tunnel where the purple luminance couldn't reach.

Oh how curious, thought the wyrntensil as it came down hard on nothingness. *Not a moment ago I could have sworn I was coaxing two delicious vermin from their hidey-hole.* And then, figuring it was losing its edge in old age, the embarrassed creature slithered back to its nest.

Beneath the boardwalk, squished between metal and

denim, May experimentally wriggled her toes. Those worked. The fingers, too. The plume of ancient allergens around the car hadn't settled yet, and when she opened her mouth to call out to Xan, she got a throat-full of junk that wanted nothing more than to incubate into space flu. She coughed, dislodging most, but not all of the germs.

"Xan?"

"Yeah?"

"Good." She squirmed out of the Gremlin's back window and into the thick darkness of the lower tunnels. She itched. Everything itched. Or was it burning?

Xan joined her, sloughing off globs of wyrntensil saliva. "Eugh, we need a shower."

"First we need to find Aimz and Listay."

"I mean we *really* need a shower." He touched the sleeve of her t-shirt and the entire garment came unstitched and fell as rags at her feet. "That's going to happen to our skin if we don't."

"Fair point. It's humid down here; there must be water somewhere. There's a flashlight in the glove box. If we're lucky."

"We're not," Xan interjected.

"Okay but if we are, it might still work." She dug through the splintered wood around the the car carefully, though a few splinters didn't matter much now that her hands were full of glass shards, and found the flashlight.

She pressed the soft button at the base and, to her delight, it flickered on. Xan's face lit up literally and metaphorically.

"Alright! We've got light; now we can watch our skin melt off!"

"That should be entertaining," May said as they set off down the dark tunnel in search of water. "Mine will probably go first, so don't freak out on me."

"At least you have a shirt on."

May swung the flashlight around the corridor. Pipes which were bolted to the rough concrete walls were conveniently stenciled. "Gift Shop," read one. "Storage," read another. "Croosflarten," read a third.

"We'll go to the gift shop," she said. "Maybe we can find

something to towel off with."

"Right, let's hurry, I don't have much clothing left to lose," Xan said, picking at his disintegrating yellow swimsuit.

TWENTY-SEVEN

RETAIL THERAPY

The gift shop, like all gift shops, was replete with logoed goods, still lovingly arranged, as if one renegade restocker, after whatever cataclysm had led to the place's abandonment, had returned to straighten a pile of shirts or refill the keychain bin one last time.

Unlike all gift shops, however, this shop's ceiling was a net of tightly woven threads, cocoon-like in their organic precision, clinging to the ceiling and bathing the place in a bright glow which was not unlike fluorescent lighting. It even occasionally flickered, though whatever lay behind the cocoon shell was completely still.

It was eerie, and Xan said so.

"This is eerie," he said, peering in from the utility door. "I'm getting a strong 'we shouldn't be here' vibe off this place. What say you?"

May pushed her head under his arm to look through the cracked door.

"Cobwebs," she said, and forced the rusty door open enough that she could slip in.

"Those aren't-"

"Cobwebs," she insisted. She knew they weren't. She

also knew that her swimsuit straps were disintegrating and wouldn't hold up much longer. Sneakily, she crossed her arms over her chest to keep everything in place.

"Oh, right, yeah, silly of me to think otherwise." When Xan followed her in, the friction tore apart his swimsuit and he snatched the nearest novelty item he saw: a triangular flag on a stick which proclaimed "I had fun in the Adventure Hole!" He covered up with it.

"Take what you want, I-" May had turned around. The absurdity of the flag made her laugh and when she went to cover her mouth, her straps snapped and she quickly doubled over to keep herself decent. She laughed harder. "Right, I'll close my eyes, you find us towels."

"Already done."

He tossed a towel at her which draped over her head, and she used it to rub the wyrntensil spit from her skin, beads of dead skin sloughing off with it.

Wyrntensil saliva would someday in the far future be harvested and developed into a multimillion crystal industry on account of its natural exfoliants. May did not appreciate the silky smoothness nearly as much as future generations of wealthy socialites would.

"Are you decent?" she asked Xan once she had toweled off.

"Well, yeah, I guess. Could be better. But I'd like to think I'm a decent person, sure," he said, scooping on the nearest garish t-shirt and novelty shorts he could find.

"Are your clothes on, I mean."

"People usually say I'm decent when my clothes are off," he said with a chuckle. "But yeah. Yes. Your eyes are now safe from the intricacies of my strange alien anatomy."

As she began the search for clothing which would fit her, a challenge when average height for a Tuhntian was around eight feet and May barely made five-and-a-half, she got the sense that something was wrong. Not the mysterious ceiling cocoon, she was accustomed to that now. Not the shockingly pristine state of the clothing she found either; alien fabrics were wonderfully dexterous. It was Xan.

"You don't look like yourself," she noted.

"Eh, I don't feel like myself. Good match I guess," he said, folding the sticky towel and setting it neatly atop the pile, since, of course, he hadn't paid for it.

The gift store was hung wall to wall with gaudy outfits and he had somehow chosen the cheapest, most unflattering items available. This, above any passingly suicidal remark he had made, worried May.

"Blueberry," she said, grabbing the smallest suit she could find off the rack for herself, "you're not going to die. And even if you were, you should at least go out looking like yourself. You'll feel better."

"I will?"

"Superficially, at least." She snuck behind an extremely tall mannequin and slipped into the fresh suit. When she emerged, she found Xan lumped on one of the display tables, like a half-melted mannequin. It was almost unseemly how unkempt he looked. His usually perfect pompadour had fallen into his face, and she had never seen him wear a t-shirt that wasn't knotted up to reveal his midriff. It felt like a bad omen. She had to fix it.

She yanked the outfit off the mannequin she had hidden behind and brought it to him. "You'd look good in this," she offered.

"You're really bothered, aren't you?" he asked.

"I don't want you giving up, and this looks like giving up."

His response started as a sigh, made a hard left turn into a groan, meandered into a whine, made a u-turn as a sharp intake of breath, and hit a dead end with an anticlimactic, "Okay."

He took the outfit and slipped behind the nude mannequin to spare May the show.

"Ah, zuut, May you know me too well. I look fantastic in this."

She turned around to see him fixing his hair in a shiny bit of chrome siding on the wall. "Feel better?"

"Marginally so." His shoulders drooped. "I don't have any crystals on me. Do you?"

"No, why?"

"Uh, we've got to pay for this stuff. We can't just take

it,"

May shook her head, but smiled. "I don't think anyone will mind."

"I mind! That's stealing."

"You stole the *Audacity.*" May noted - a touch accusingly, thought Xan.

A high-pitched whistle, like a boiling kettle, drifted from the be-weaved ceiling and the luminescent creatures cocooned therein began to stir.

"Let's go?" Xan suggested, watching the ceiling like it might eat him as he picked up the flashlight.

"Let's go."

TWENTY-EIGHT

IN THE UTILITY CORRIDOR

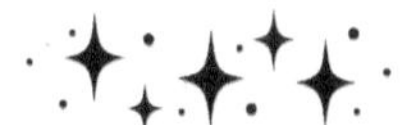

They shut the gift shop door and bolted it closed. An urgent tapping followed on the other side of the door, but they were too busy legging it down the corridor to care, the light from the flashlight in Xan's hand bouncing along the walls.

"Xan, do..." May paused to breathe. "Do you think I could get-" She breathed again.

"Leg extensions," they said in tandem, Xan slowing to let her catch up.

He patted her back. "Yeah, sure thing, mun."

None of the pipes had been stenciled with anything along the lines of "You're going the right way," and so they guessed. Heading first toward the "Incredible Glasses of Milk Museum" and then toward the "Water Where There Ought Not Be Utility Access" before they slowed.

"Water Where There Ought Not Be," May said with a smile. "Sounds like my apartment."

Xan laughed at that because he knew he should. "Speaking of your personal history, who's Harvey?"

"Harvey Foster? Just a guy I knew in high school."

"And you two were..."

"Friends. Until he wanted more. Then we were ex-friends."

"You're not the romantic type, are you, starshine?"

"I was busy," May said.

Xan considered this for a moment. Never in his life had he been so busy that he couldn't start a romantic entanglement. In fact, romantic entanglements were typically what he was busy with.

"It's alright, you know, if romance isn't your thing. I mean, I'm not sure how it's done on Earth—everyone on 'I Love Lucy' had at least one spouse—but on Tuhnt, it's okay to not want any."

"Good to know."

"So you, uh...don't want that, right? With anyone? Ever?"

"Nope," May said. "I told you something, now you tell me something. Why did you steal the *Audacity*?"

"I-I didn't—I mean..." He stopped. "I guess I did," he said, as if someone had just irrefutably proved to him that he was his own great-grand-father. "Zuut, I stole the zuxing *Audacity*."

"Yes, I know. Why?"

He dropped the flashlight and it rolled slowly along the uneven concrete, illuminating nothing but dust as it winked in and out. In and out. In and out.

"Blueberry?" May asked, trying to put out a hand to find him in the darkness. He was not where he ought to have been. May shuffled, arms outstretched, but ended up kicking him while he was down.

He was too busy panicking to notice she had kicked him, to notice he had dropped the flashlight, even to notice that he was no longer standing but lying flat on the dusty, damp ground.

There was a voice in the back of his head. It wasn't his...or it was but it was wrong. It sounded like it had been run through an old radio, the bass turned up, and fitted with an evil rasp he didn't think he was physically capable of.

It had been there for a long, long time, and he had always been able to shush it with a stern inward glance and a bit of humor, but it was like chucking handfuls of sand into a pit dug with a track-hoe.

May was saying something to him now, but her words weren't nearly as loud as his head voice, and they came through as a low rumble, like a distant motorway.

The worst part was that the voice in his head wasn't angry when it told him he was better off dead. It wasn't sad, either; it didn't lament what it was making him think. It was confidant, serious, and strict, but somehow kind.

"You've done enough damage in this lifetime. You failed miserably, but it's okay. Just die now before you ruin anything else," said the voice in an even roll, accompanied by an all-consuming yearning to obey.

Now, usually, Xan had a pretty good handle on this voice. Throw some coffee at it, say something self-deprecating, watch "I Love Lucy" with the volume up so loud it made his translation chip cut in and out. But now, there was no coffee, there was no "I Love Lucy," and he was using his lungs to breathe, so he didn't think he could talk. He would try, though.

The part of him that was still him gave it a go, offering up a few possible jokes he could spew. Something about overstaying his welcome? No. A hearty jab at his awful luck? Not that. He didn't care enough to keep trying. He knew his fingers were shaking, so he shoved them into his hair and held on at the roots to keep them still. Maybe, he thought vaguely, if he pulled out his hair, the voice in his head would go along with it.

"Xan!" May's shout finally reached wherever he had gone.

"Uh?" he managed between breaths.

"What the hell happened?" May got to the ground and found two points of dull green phosphorescence so she knew what part to talk at.

"Remember when you asked me if I was depressed?" he said, grateful she couldn't see him in the darkness.

"You said it didn't translate."

"Yeah, well, you probably won't be surprised to know I lied."

"I'm not."

"Blitheon, May, why'd you come looking for me? And why didn't Sonan just kill me? And why can't we just go back to the Gremlin and wait for Chaos to kill me? I don't honestly care. I just want it to be over."

"Hey," she said. The tunnel seemed to get a few degrees colder. She chose to think that some kind of ancient air conditioning system had finally kicked on. "I came looking for you because I wanted to."

"Because I have the *Audacity*?" he asked, turning the AC up just a touch.

"N-not just that." It would be a lie for her to say she hadn't been interested in getting the ship back. It was her livelihood and her home, after all.

"May, I stole it." Talking was helping, even if he didn't like what he was saying. As long as something was being said, he didn't have to think.

"I am aware of this. I know you, though. You must've had a good reason."

He shook his head. "Not good. If Chaos goes back and kills me before I steal the *Audacity*, Tuhnt will be safe, and you'll be safe, and everyone can get back to doing whatever it is happy, planet-having people like to do."

"Stop it. I don't want you to die."

"It's healthy to disagree on things sometimes."

"We need to agree on this. It's important. You're important."

"What, to you or cosmically?"

May gave him a helpless "Nngph" before she answered. "Fuck, Xan I can't speak for the cosmos. You're important to *me* and I'm a selfish, stubborn asshole and I want you around."

Xan chuckled. "You are not."

"Want to test that? Tell me why you stole the *Audacity*. I need to know," she said, trying to keep her voice even.

"Fine, alright. But," there was a hint of a smile in his voice again, "only if I get to tell you in the form of a dramatic flashback scene."

"Ideally you would."

TWENTY-NINE

INSERT FLASHBACK SOUND EFFECT

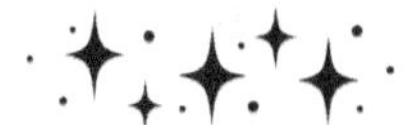

"Right, so this happened during final age of the War of Reversed Polarity, in the darkest booth in the farthest corner of the seediest sub-bar in the city of Trilly on the continent of Further Masedon on the planet of Tuhnt in the system of Flotluex, and I had just received a message on my BEAPER.

"'Mandatory Draft in Effect,' it read.

"My first instinct was to dunk the BEAPER in my Electro-Blitz and fry the circuits, but that, obviously, wouldn't get me anything but a busted BEAPER.

"Brooding, at that point, was my only recourse. I knew it wouldn't make a difference, but I wanted to look absolutely as put-out as possible. The Universe would know, I thought. But it didn't. Turns out the Universe is nearsighted! Someone else noticed, though.

"'You look absolutely put-out,' said the someone.

"I agreed before looking up. Likely, I should've looked up first, because when I did I realized this person was military and I was about to be officially zuxed. Or zuxed by an official. Ha! Because I was having sex for gem back then, and I thought maybe he was about to proposition me. That was a joke. And I'm getting a 'wrap it up' glare from the actual narrator so let's move it all along.

"He introduced himself as Admiral Ranken Warders, told me he had an offer for me and asked if I wanted to hear it.

"I didn't want to hear it, so I asked him if I had a choice.

"Then he said, in a gruff old man voice," and here, Xan attempted to affect a gruff old man voice. He didn't pull it off well. "'Well of course you do, my lav. But something tells me you won't say no.' Then he winked, and that's what really got me thinking I was about to be propositioned.

"I leaned across the table and gave him a kind of sexy scowl I'd been working on. Don't ask me to do it, by the way, it was not sexy. Dropped that one a few hundred orbits back.

"I asked him how much. No less than a thousand crystals a night, I thought, but I quickly talked myself down to five-hundred. Two-fifty, maybe, but absolutely no kissing in that case. I was always underselling myself back then."

"Still do," May interrupted.

He huffed humorlessly at her. "The Admiral said he had it on 'good authority' (whatever that means) that Operation *Audacity* had an eighty-nine percent chance of backfiring horribly and destroying Tuhnt.

"That, obviously, concerned me a bit. And clearly the proposition had taken something of a u-bend. That is, unless he was about to tell me the only way to save the planet was to take my pants off. I know that *sounds* unrealistic, but it has happened. More than once, too.

"Then he produced an anchor button from the inside of his coat pocket and handed it to me, like I was supposed to do something about it.

"He told me the *Audacity* was a diversion ship, meant to distract the *Peacemaker* from their heavy hitter, the *Innocuous*. Without the *Audacity*, they couldn't end the war, but at least Tuhnt wouldn't get zuxing smithereened.

"I still wasn't too clear on what he was getting at, and I was out of Electro-Blitz so I had nothing to distract me.

You ever ask someone for clarification and then they act like you've just told them you've never heard of the sun before? Because this guy had some kind of attitude.

"And then, he told me this: 'I want you to steal the *Audacity*. Can you fly a rocket?'

"And I could! Kind of. Tolerably, anyway. Bearably, I could. I told him that, staring at the anchor button in his hand. He'd been holding it out too long; I had to take it. It was becoming uncomfortable.

"Again, I had to clarify. You really can't over-communicate, you know."

"Is that a jab at me?" asked May.

"No," he laughed quietly in the dark tunnel. "It's a jab at myself. Anyway! I asked again, 'You want me to steal a military vessel to save the planet from imminent destruction?'

"I mean, he was an Admiral! I would zuxing wager he could have done it himself if he really wanted too. Probably some sort of political trok.

"Apparently, questioning an Admiral is considered 'gross insubordination' but you live, you learn, you get arrested for destroying a planet, right?

"So, I was absolutely green with embarrassment. I told him to ask someone else, as if he had asked me for a spare zipzam.

"He was massively plivered, but then he went extraordinarily calm which was a great deal scarier. I know this must sound zoup-nogged, but I swear on Blitheon he spoke without actually moving his mouth when he told me it had to be me. He told me 'she' wouldn't let me die.

"Still no hint as to who 'she' was. That was odd, really. An odd thing to say..."

Xan paused for exactly too long, re-wondering about what the Admiral had said. May nudged him.

"Right. I didn't have time to ponder that back then because the Admiral flicked his photon gun in a way that suggested that if I didn't stand up, too, I would find out exactly what setting the gun was on. He told me to take the offer.

"And I... I guess I did."

"You guess... you did?" May repeated.

"Yeah. He shoved me in his MegaCruiser, we were in the thick of a sub-blizzard and I was wearing a mauve faux bufatalo coat. It wasn't important, I just always liked saying the words 'mauve faux bufatalo coat' with my mouth. Mauve faux bufatalo co-"

"Go on," May prompted.

"Right. He brought me to the *Audacity's* rocket silo which wasn't lit from the inside because it didn't need to be. The ship was so bright, it sucked up any light it could find and multiplied it faster than breeding zipnites. Would you believe the *Audacity* is actually faded now? From star exposure. Yeah, she used to be the brightest thing in the sky. I mean, she still is, but she used to be more so.

"She was so gorgeous, I couldn't stop staring. It turned out to be an issue. Do you know, every time I close my eyes I see the after image of a cyan rocket ship? Photic Retinopathy, it's called. Fun fact. About my eyes. You're getting a lot of eye facts lately."

"That probably should've gone away by now," May said.

"Probably. Hasn't. Eh, that's the way the chip crunches.

"Anyway. He forced me, at gun-point, to teleport into the glorious orange tube.

"I had only ever flown a StarTaxi and, for a sense of scale, the living room alone can dock seven StarTaxis comfortably. The console was covered in buttons and switches and levers and things I didn't even have a name for. I hoped most of those switches had to do with mood lighting."

"A good sixth of them do," May said.

"I don't know how I did it, but I got the ship on and pressed the Button Which Typically Makes the Ship Go," he said.

"Without opening the silo roof?" May asked.

"Eh-huh... that was a *sound* I can tell you that. I guess I expected the admiral to open the silo. Not sure why. He hadn't given me any indication that he was particularly helpful, had he?

"I do remember forgetting to turn on the viewscreen, though. For the first few blips I was flying blind. Should've kept it off, too. When I turned it on all I saw was the tops of clouds and several military grade missiles headed towards me and you know what? Seeing the clouds from the wrong side honestly bothered me more than the missiles. Isn't that crosh-wopple? The things you focus on when you're stressed. Speaking of...I can't quite recall what happened to that mauve faux buffalo coat. Must've been traumatic, loosing it. I loved that coat."

"There were missiles?" May prompted, trying to keep him on track.

"Right! Yes. The missiles. I set a flight path! And that flight path was so horrifically fool-hardy that it circled back around into being fool-proof! The missiles couldn't figure it out. Neither could I, honestly. Then, and you'd be proud of me for this, I took stock of my assets. That's a very you thing to do, but I did it, and it worked!

"The StarTaxis I knew how to pilot barely had a drive, but this thing had a *hyper*drive.

"Now, I'd like to think I would've been able to figure it out faster if I hadn't been flung to the other side of the ship and into the artificial gravity lever! Hurt like a splice in the duct, pardon my Rhean.

"It's odd that the ship has an accessible artificial gravity lever, right? I can't imagine why anyone would want to turn that off. Alright, perhaps I can. I can imagine a couple of reasons someone would want that off, but certainly not military related reasons."

"Sex reasons?" May asked.

"Sex reasons. Yes. But you've got to agree it's odd to have such a feature on a ship whose express purpose was to zoom about and blow things up for the government.

"I had nearly got my hand back around the lever when the ship jerked again, punting me face-first into the viewscreen."

May hissed through her teeth, the viewscreen got exceedingly hot. "Did it burn you?"

"You know, it did? But once the dead skin peeled off my face was ultra soft. Actually, I did it again once on purpose before an important client. Not the pleasantest facial, but zux if it doesn't work!"

"I'll take your word for it."

"Probably best. How're your palms, by the way? Still hurt?"

May shrugged, though he couldn't see it. "Mostly back to normal. I'm fine. Finished out your story."

"Well, the flight path was nearing its end. Soon I'd be on a straight course again, and it would be like shooting a dractifly in a radiator.

"I found the hyperdrive, managed, after a great deal of fumbling and some curses I think I forced myself to forget because they're so foul. Then I broke the color barrier for the first time and was well off the mark of those missiles.

"After I got the artificial gravity back on, I realized just how far away from Flotluex I was. How far away from Kalumbits and Aimz and Zilla and Yvonne...and I couldn't go back, was the thing. I didn't know if I'd be executed or what, but I knew I couldn't go back.

"Eventually I tried to delete the draft alert from my BEAPER and noticed a new message from Aimz which read, 'Kalumbits-"

Xan's voice glitched like a scratched record player, but May's translation chip was working just fine.

"What did it say?" May asked, leaning in.

"Kalumbits was our favorite aunt. The message said, 'Kalumbits wants to know when you'll be home.' I sent her an audio blip. Told Aimz to tell her I'd be back soon."

"And that was when?"

"A millennium and a half ago."

THIRTY
THE MANUAL

The floor of the utility corridor was cold, damp, and bulged in exactly all the wrong places. Regardless, May was now lying on it next to Xan, both staring at the black ceiling which occasionally dripped. She figured if he was enduring a crude kind of water torture, she ought to as well.

"So-" *drip* "an admiral forced you-" *drip* "to steal the *Audacity*?"

"Eh, wouldn't say forced." *Drip*. "Not entirely."

"He had a gun."

"Alright, yeah, but I wanted it, too. I didn't exactly-" *drip* "resist. I didn't actually do anything to stop him."

"You also didn't want to be shot." May sat up now, tired of being dripped upon.

"Well-" *drip* "you can be my lawyer. The point is, what I did got Tuhnt destroyed and whatever Sonan or Chaos wants to do with me, they're right. I mean, Chaos resetting the Universe sounds a touch extreme, so I suppose we should try to do something about that, but even if I get out of that, I'm staying here." He rolled up, patting around the ground until he found the flashlight, and flicked it on again.

"That's not fair."

"It's entirely fair. It's just about the definition of fair."

"But I don't want you to," May said, choking on the "to" like it was a stale saltine. She needed a glass of water. "And this is another thing we cannot agree to disagree about."

Rather than reply, he sighed.

"You need a hug?" she asked.

He nodded.

She wrapped her arms around him and focused on transmitting some semblance of a zest for life to him. He hugged her back in a way that let her know it might have been working.

"How did you find out about Tuhnt?" May asked.

"What?"

"How did you find out that Tuhnt was destroyed?" she repeated.

"I was on a job and the guy told me before we started. You'd think that'd be a mood murderer, but he gave me a huge tip and a great review. You know, now that I'm thinking about it was probably a pity thing." Xan had one dusty chuckle left over from earlier that he whipped out now. "Definitely a pity thing. Not that I'm not good at what I do...er, did. I'm just not an extra hundred crystals worth of good. And I definitely wasn't on that one. Nice of him, I guess."

"Do you miss it?"

"What, being a sex worker? Eh, I'm getting too old for it."

"No, Tuhnt."

"Do you miss Earth?"

"Earth's not gone," said May defensively. She felt defensive because she did not miss Earth, but she didn't think that was the right answer. "It's weird. I don't want to go back to Earth and find out that everyone I knew is dead. If I don't know for sure, then they're fine."

"Eloquent."

"Was it?" she asked.

"Not really."

"It's like Schrödinger's cat," she tried. "You just keep putting off looking in the box."

"It's...yeah. Exactly."

"You don't have to pretend you know what that means."

"Thanks."

"Good thing we worked all this out before making it so that it never happened, right?"

"Oh, definitely."

In other branches of the Pontoosa Adventure Hole, Aimz and Listay fought a swarm of tiny, sentient flying arrows. Chaos neared the resting place of the Sphere of Time. The wyrntensil skulked the tunnels hungrily.

In other branches of the Pontoosa Adventure Hole, Time passed normally at a rate of one blip per blip. But in utility corridor 4B, Time crept carefully past so as to not disturb Xan and May. Time kicked a rock, stubbled and, embarrassed, began moving along at a normal pace again.

"Shit, we've got to find Chaos," May said.

Then standing, dusting off the detritus of their conversation, they started again down the corridor in an urgently contemplative silence.

Near silence. As close to silence as they ever typically got. Xan hummed, "Take Me To the River" and May quietly mumbled the name of every location stenciled on the pipes which ran along the corridor.

Xan stopped humming. "Did you say something about a haunted Big Mouth Billy Bass or did I dream that? I feel like that was a thing that came up."

"Yeah, I found a haunted Big Mouth Billy Bass on Yenuket Municipal," May said. "I want to show it to you, so you're not allowed the die."

"Right. Well, can't fault your reasoning. A haunted singing fish is a pretty tempting offer. I suppose, for the fish, I'll try to not."

"That's the spirit," she said, then stopped. "Here it is."

And there it was.

A door, that is.

A door which read "Sphere of Time Maintenance Access".

"Blitheon's stars, here it is," Xan echoed.

All was dark until May found the light panel on the wall. Amber lights slowly glowed on above them to reveal a cavern filled with plastic boxes full of hardware, old laser tools, and discarded motors which crouched toad-like in the dark corners.

On a work desk, under a layer of sandy dust, or perhaps it was dusty sand, sat something book shaped. May investigated; something book shaped was likely to be an asset. Particularly if it was, in fact, a book.

With her sleeve, she wiped off the cover and smiled.

"Manual!" She held it out to show Xan, pointing to it earnestly.

"Is that," he eyed the yellowed tome suspiciously, "going to help? In any way?"

"It can't hurt. And it's pretty heavy; I could throw it at her."

"I'm not sure androids are susceptible to paper cuts."

May flipped the stiff pages of the index. They weren't made of tree pulp, of that she was certain. What they were made of is a touch horrific but extremely durable.

Her finger flew down the page, then, finding her mark, she flipped to page 395. "Operating the Sphere" titled the page. "Do Not Operate The Sphere" subtitled it in Danger Diophalothene (which, to May's eyes, was a reddish magenta). An illustrated sphere took up the rest of the page with explanatory labels, each asterisked with the warning that never under any circumstances should the sphere ever be used.

The sphere itself looked like a sound board from 1960s that had been melted over an upturned ceramic bowl in an oven.

"What's it say?" Xan asked, fiddling with doodads on the table.

"Some of the words are," May cringed as the translation chip guttered in her head, "unreadable. I don't think this is meant to be gazpacho."

Xan peeked over her shoulder. "It's a recipe, actually. Yeah. That's zipnite gazpacho."

"Really? Why would there be a-"

"Aha! I did it. May June July, you've just been bested at your own style of humor: dry sarcasm. I can now die at peace."

"Not until you see Big Mouth Billy Bass," May reminded him.

"Ah, right, yeah. Singing fish promise."

"Exactly. What does it actually say?"

Xan set down the flashlight and leaned over the book, bobbing his head up and down like a bird until the words were in focus.

"Oof, this is some old Tuhntian. This was back when the word "glosternaoffle" was the plural of "gloasternaof" and they didn't have a concept of specified nebulous pronouns."

"Which is?"

"You know, like 'she, he, or they' instead of 'she, he, or they'?"

"Oh. Right, yes. That."

He gave her a curious glance. "English doesn't have specified nebulous pronouns, does it?"

"Nope, still no clue what you mean."

"Don't worry about it. The tip of the bit is, this writing is old. Long dead when translation chips were made which *means*," he said, genuine excitement in his voice, "I can translate it!"

"You?"

"Yes! I'm a linguist! Well, I was a linguist. Well, that's not completely honest. I was studying to be a linguist before translation chips were invented which sort of put a bit of a squash on that particular career option."

"Great! So what does it say?"

He looked at the page again. "Something about an aria being mortally unsung. That...that sentence doesn't quite work. Wait." Then he was silent until he said, "Oh it's a metaphor. Right. Basically, using the Sphere of Time might tear the universe apart and it should never ever under any circumstances be taunted."

"Taunted?"

He looked again. "No, sorry. Turned on. Never be turned on. The sphere is for display only, apparently. Might not even work."

Then, faintly, they heard something which they could not understand but deeply offended their sensibilities anyway.

"What was that? And why did it feel so dirty?" May asked.

"Well, you know how you can say something in any language and know it's a curse word just by how it was said?"

"Right, like spanner."

"Yeah, like spanner. I think someone just cursed in a dead language somewhere above us. Those ancient curse words were foul. Zuxing foul."

"That's got to be Chaos," May said, looking around as if a staircase would appear now that she'd figured it out. There was no staircase, but the ground did slope up slightly leading out of the cavern. That was something.

So they took the manual and walked, purposefully, like retirees speed walking in the wee hours of the morning through an indoor mall. The corridor twisted around, looping back on itself and wavering off to one side, then switching decidedly to the other.

Whether from the effort of climbing slowly uphill, or from thinning oxygen, May was short of breath.

"We must be reaching the surface," May said, hesitant to continue forward. She leaned against the corridor wall and focused on not blacking out.

"What makes you think?" Xan asked, oxygen not being relatively high on his list of necessary conditions for survival.

"Just a," she took as deep a breath as she possibly could, "hunch." She pointed to the staircase in front of them which was labeled "Surface Entrance to the Sphere of Time."

Xan tried to grab her arm and convince her to run in the other direction, but she refused.

"Gotta get Chaos," she wheezed, "and the sphere." Then looked very seriously at the ground. "Chaos and the Sphere would be an awesome," she paused to breathe at him for a moment, "band name. Xan we should start a band. I can play..." She winked dizzily, "I can be band manager. You and the fish sing. First, though-"

A gleeful, robotic cackle could be heard from the other side of the door. Something was clearly going well for Chaos which meant something was going poorly for them.

"Get Chaos!"

He just stared at her, frozen in place.

"Well?" May said, gesturing to the door.

"Oh me?" He slapped a hand over his heart dramatically. "You meant I should get her? Sorry, I thought you wanted me to not die. Should've been clear about that. Alrighty, no problem. I'll just saunter on in and ask an ageless goddess of Chaos to hand over the Sphere of Time and we'll be off her mark. You think of somewhere you'd like to get a bit to eat while I'm out-"

"Stop!" May whispered harshly once she'd recouped enough breath to waste some. "If you don't, I will. I'm not letting her unravel," she took a painfully deep breath, "the reality fabric."

"Why not? That would be more exciting than going back to life on Tuhnt." He leaned against the stone wall beside May. "Without the *Audacity,* I will not have been there to rescue you from the *Peacemaker* and you will have died a horrible death in the vacuum of space."

"You don't know that," May said. "I might not will have been or would be or...anyway, I might not have been abducted."

Contemplating his own death was one thing. Actively running toward Death shouting, "Hey! Hey, Miss! Did you drop this? It's my immortal soul. Figured it was important," was quite another.

Xan made a noise of roiling dread in response and squeezed what little air May had left from her lungs. "Go back to the Gremlin and think of somewhere you'd like to get a bit to eat. I'll be right back. Probably." He looked at the door like it had insulted his favorite aunt, who he then remembered was dead, and looked at the door even harder. "Hopefully," he amended.

"Hey! I trust you," May said.

And that was the exact moment he decided he wanted nothing more than to be trustworthy, that it was vitally important that May continue having a reason to trust him. He swallowed, gently patted her head, and jumped up the staircase, flinging himself into whatever horrors were beyond.

It was eerily silent in the corridor without him. May expected to hear some sort of stand-off, some quipping, even. The air seemed to become thinner and colder; May shivered. The tug of fresh and suspiciously ample oxygen in the corridor behind her was strong. Xan said he would take care of it. May shook her head, it wasn't that she didn't trust him. It was just so quiet on the other side of the door.

May collected a lungful of air and began to climb.

THIRTY-ONE

A JUMP TO THE LEFT

Xan plunged into light.

This was not the right place, thought Xan. This was likely not even the right planet and, he had a suspicion, this was not, in fact, the right dimension.

Xan had left an ancient utility corridor under the deserted planet of New Tuhnt and arrived in what might easily be confused for a spaceport terminal apart from the eerie green light the entire setting seemed to be made of. The lighting was anxiously bright. The walls were distressingly bare. The seats were made of a molded plastic which appeared to be purposefully ergonomical but was in actuality just wrong enough to not be comfortable for any known species equipped with the ability to sit.

The setting had so thrown off his resolve that for a moment he couldn't remember what he was looking for and why he was looking for it. Then, at last, something jogged his memory.

An orb glowed greenly on the reception desk by the chairs, projecting with an easeful waft the setting which he found himself in.

Right, thought Xan, he was here for a reason and that reason was to find Chaos and nicely ask her to please stop trying to kill him. That was the entire plan. It was a plan, he assumed, which would only make him die faster. But at least he could then say that he had tried.

Chaos was not in the terminal. Or, if she was, she was hiding, which seemed a touch silly. He stalked carefully forward just in case.

The terminal gate was open, and as he approached it, he saw a familiar scene on the other side: the *Audacity*'s original rocket silo complete with an un-dented version of the *Audacity* and, now that he was closer, he could see the admiral's MegaCruiser as well. He was staring into his past.

Everything was as he remembered it, expect for the presence of Chaos.

She stood statue-still, a nasty looking anti-matter cannon poised on her shoulder like a lion perched on the wing of an ibis. I could go into more detail about the make and model of the anti-matter cannon, but it doesn't matter.

Beyond her stood Xan's past self, awestruck by the magnificent ship that towered over them as he stepped from the Admiral's MegaCruiser. Fear gripped him like a giant, clawed hand made of ice cream. He looked curiously into his own eyes.

The anti-matter cannon clicked, made a sinister charging noise, then made an even more sinister discharging noise.

A spectral figure passed through him.

"Watch where you're goi-oh," said Death, looking at him as if She had seen a ghost. "This is unusual." She looked at the soon-to-be pile of ash which was a younger Xan and then at the older version she had just walked through. She shrugged. "Not my problem," she said and floated off to make it his problem instead.

Before he could see what Death was about to do to him, Xan bolted back into the relative comfort of the spaceport and ran to the sphere.

It was completely digital, but the effect of the faux cut-out face was so great that he nearly jammed his finger straight through the tempered glass as he pressed the large, red-rimmed metal button he assumed would make it stop.

The gate closed.

Perhaps, he thought, the past hadn't saved yet.

Perhaps he would be okay.

May burst into the spaceport terminal and was pleased to find that she could breathe again in the atmosphere the sphere generated.

"Xan? What happened?" May asked.

"Nothing important. Hey, unrelated, do you know how to work this?" He tapped the top of the sphere and the simulated spaceport lost its greenish glow, gradating into fuchsia.

She slung the manual onto the desk but didn't need to open it; she had memorized the faux analogue face of the sphere.

"This is the date." She tapped an analogue counter. "And this is for the location coordinates." She tapped another counter. "And you use the dials and levers to set it."

"Fantastic." He frantically tapped the sphere, twisting touch-screen dials, pressing fake buttons, whispering details to himself, trying to remember where exactly he had been the night the admiral propositioned him.

"Where's Chaos?"

"In the past, I think." He looked something up on his BEAPER and set the coordinates.

"What happened?" she asked again.

Xan shook his head. "I don't think I'm going to make it to Big Mouth Billy Bass, but I've got an idea." The gate opened and May jumped back, expecting Chaos to leap from the portal and insult them. Instead, a gust of icy air filled the spaceport. The gate had opened on the snow-laden door to a seedy sub-bar in the city of Trilly on the planet of Tuhnt.

"Alright, get ready," said Xan, his hands on May's shoulders. "We're about to meet an older model of myself and he's not...well I guess I'm not...no. I was not exactly always this put together."

"This is put together?"

"Comparatively so. What I mean is—oh it doesn't matter. I could disappear at any moment if time works the way it ought to, so in case I do, I was in this pub when the admiral propositioned me and you've got to tell me to not take the *Audacity. Capisci*?"

"Still one question," May said.

"Anything."

"When did you learn Italian?"

From Xan, a confused head-tilt.

"Don't worry about it, let's go," May said and they walked together into the gate. They did not, however, walk together out of it.

Xan vanished as quickly as a candy bowl set out on Halloween with a note which reads, "only take one."

"Xan!" she called into the blizzard. He was gone. The moment he left the spaceport, he had disappeared. She popped her head back through the portal. The spaceport was empty and quiet except for the sound of electricity buzzing through the sphere.

Around the portal, the world was dark, cold, and smelled of rust and alcohol. She could hear something behind the pub door; whether it was an angry din or a jaunty chorus, she couldn't tell.

She paused for a moment, her hand poised on the door handle.

If she was about to successfully convince him not to steal the *Audacity*, she wouldn't be here now, which meant that she couldn't convince him not to...she shivered. It was too cold out here to think properly. She entered the pub and was surprised to see that nothing in the pub was terribly surprising.

Sloppily dressed Tuhntians drank and shouted around something akin to billiard tables, well-dressed Tuhntians whiffled their evenings away at a bar tended by a scantily dressed Tuhntian. To her right, a flash of orange could be seen over a row of booths.

"Xan! Listen, this is very important," May slid into the booth across from him and now saw precisely why Xan had tried to warn her about his past iteration.

Instead of his perfect pompadour, something she could only compare to a party in the front, party in the back, rave along the sides mullet.

Instead of a LayFlex™ body suit and shiny gloves, he wore a coat which looked like a skinned muppet and an old t-shirt which was, to his credit, tied up into a crop top.

Instead of greeting her like a dog which had been waiting by the door for her to come home, he glared at his wrist.

"Woah," he said when, at last, he looked up at his unannounced tablemate. "You're short," he said. "What planet are you from, tiny stranger?" Xan asked, his eyebrows pulled together.

"Listen. Don't steal a rocket ship tonight. In case," she paused realizing how strange that must sound, "you were," her head wobbled noncommittally, "considering it."

Puzzlement, then confusion, then concern traipsed across his face.

"You're alright, mun? Can I, um...can I get you a drink or perhaps a psychologist?"

She shook her head, though a psychologist might actually have been nice right then. Her eyes were beginning to sting.

The Xan who was not her Xan patted the top of her head with fingerless gloves (every culture has a fingerless gloves phase and Trilly on Tuhnt was in the thick of it at the time.)

"Ey, mun, it's alright," he said soothingly. "I won't go anywhere, okay? I'm not going to steal a rocket, and you don't have to be sad. I'll beap my aunt; she can help you. Probably." His smile twisted uncertainly.

May declined with a hurried shake of her head. She had to get back to see if it worked.

She wasn't sure exactly how she would know if it worked, but she couldn't find out if she stayed here.

Though this Xan didn't know her, she couldn't help but slide to the other side of the table and give him a goodbye hug.

"Remember," she put a finger on the tip of his long nose, "do not do the thing you're about to do." She ran back through the bar, back into the portal, and closed it.

Once again in the spaceport lobby, she sat in one of the fuchsia chairs. The chair wasn't real, but the discomfort was.

It felt like she was back on Earth, waiting for her boarding pass to be called. She held her head in her hands and tried to calm down. She wasn't waiting for a plane, she was waiting for reality to rearrange itself around her.

Reality didn't bother.

Perhaps just outside the fuchsia tinted bubble of the spaceport lay Earth; perhaps she was safe while she was in there.

Aimz and Listay surged into the scene, plasma zapper and sharp bit of metal at the ready.

"Time ball!" Aimz leapt over the chairs and tapped the sphere, swapping the fuchsia glow for blue. "We found it first. Oh, you wouldn't believe the adventure we had. Absolutely massive cave in, three different kinds of flesh-eating parasite, a sentient box chased us, there was a waterfall and oh! An entire wing of this place is a shrine dedicated to someone named Daniel Devito. Never heard of him. Sounds like an unmitigated delight, though. Anyway, here now, and it's a good rotation to save Tuhnt." Aimz said, hefting May up by the arm. "Did you lose Xan?" Aimz asked.

May nodded.

"Well, let's light this lav up and see about getting him to not commit 'accidental' planetcide." Aimz looked curiously at the sphere. "Wait, did you use it already? Without me?" Her smile faded slowly as she went to inspect it.

This, at last, convinced May to speak. "Chaos killed past Xan, then I tried to convince a further past him not to steal the *Audacity,* and now..." She stopped before her voice could rise another decibel and brought it back to a gentle simmer. "I don't know why nothing has changed."

Listay had wandered off to explore the spaceport with

her plasma zapper, only returning when she was confident they were alone.

Sitting cross-legged on the desk beside the sphere, Aimz pondered.

"Well," she said, her zeal squashed. "If anything changed, we'd remember it right? I mean the new things. We'd remember things happening differently."

"Not necessarily." Listay leaned on the desk and studied the orb. "There are several theories of time travel which state that your memories can't be re-written if you're at the center of the change."

"That would be this," Aimz gestured around herself, "spaceport thing. We weren't in it when they fiddled with time. We should remember something different."

"Perhaps it takes a few bloops to go into effect."

"Or nothing changed," May suggested. "But if that's the case, where's Chaos? Where's Xan?"

Aimz propped her head up with her fingers and thought. "Right, staring at the sphere isn't going to tell us. Let's go back in time and suss it out! Any idea when and where Xan stole the ship?"

"Maybe," May said and flipped open the manual.

The sphere hummed peacefully beside her, unaware of how much it had ruined her day. There was something like a browser history in the sphere, and May's translation chip was able to suss out just enough of the garbled ancient Tuhntian to locate the switch that controlled it.

"I think this is it," she said. "I'm going to go back a few blips and shift it to the left so it doesn't overlap the original portal."

"Good work, mun! Clever Earthling, aren't you?" May tilted her head at Aimz, offering her a chance to rethink her sentence. "Sorry, right, yeah. Intelligent species, I mean." Aimz winked at her and twirled the sharp bit of metal around her finger.

"Into the past!" she said and pressed the red-rimmed digital button. The gate opened again, this time on an orangly lit rocket silo. A military MegaCruiser skidded to a halt.

THIRTY-TWO

OFF-ROADING

The two strangers Xan had met that night differed in almost every meaningful way. Height, of course. Facial hair was another big one. Intent was, undoubtedly, the most prevalent.

The first stranger had told him *not* to steal a rocket ship whereas the second had told him in no uncertain terms that he most definitely should.

Different, too, was their style of persuasion. The first hadn't held a photon gun to him. The threat of having your molecules rearranged into something a great deal less tidy was enough to convince Xan to get in the MegaCruiser which Admiral Ranken Warders was now setting down in the rocket silo.

He twisted around to fix Xan with the photon gun's one-eyed glare and held up the anchor button which Xan had refused to take.

"Get in that ship and take it off-planet, or you will die before anyone else."

While he had promised the first stranger that he wouldn't steal a rocket ship tonight, and he hated to break a promise, he also hated to die, so he took the button and exited the cruiser.

When he did, he saw something beyond the impingingly orange hull of the *Audacity* which he did not expect.

A bluish portal thwapped open and through it came May (whom he recognized as the first stranger), Listay (a third stranger), and, lastly, Aimz (a non-stranger, though she was strange). Admiral Ranken skirted around the cruiser and tried to decide if his gun should be aimed at one of the three interlopers, or at Xan, or perhaps at himself, seeing as there was clearly something wrong with him. He opened his mouth and gurgled his confusion.

"Aimz! O'Zeno's thumbs, why are you here?" Xan's voice echoed around the claustrophobic silo, circling back to him.

She cupped her hands around her mouth. "Trying to stop you!"

"Can you stop *him*?" Xan jabbed a thumb in Ranken's direction.

Ranken hiccuped angrily.

"Who's he?" Aimz shouted back, but before Xan could explain that he really didn't honestly know, another portal opened, this one green tinged, and admitted a pink android with an anti-matter cannon slotted into her shoulder.

The anti-matter cannon was aimed quite purposefully at Xan.

There is a Rhean phrase which goes "like a laser fight in a rocket silo" and means a situation is dangerous, confusing, and completely out of anyone's control. This is because if you fire a laser in a rocket silo, the laser will ping off the curved walls in deadly game of billiards until it fizzles out.

And so, literally and figuratively, when Listay, Ranken, and Chaos discharged their weapons, it was like a laser fight in a rocket silo.

Xan leapt behind the cruiser. The cruiser disintegrated.

Laser beams bounced colorfully overhead, pinging off this, ricocheting off that, and incinerating with gay abandon.

There was only one decent hiding place left: the ship.

Xan caught sight of Aimz charging the admiral with a weaponized sharp bit of metal and trundled into her, flicking the teleport signal on his BEAPER as he did so. Aimz began to throw him off with a punch, was interrupted by being rent atom from atom, then finished punching him once they were both remerged on the ship.

He fell back onto soft orange shag, rubbing his chin. "Zuut, I was trying to help."

"No, *I* was trying to help! Put me back." She tried to reverse the teledisc with her busted BEAPER, which sizzled instead.

Already at the control panel of the ship, Xan tried to work out which was the launch button.

"Wait." She tripped over the rim of carpet around the teledisc, falling into a gangly sort of desperate run. "Mun, I'm a future Aimz, if you take me with you in the past it'll-"

He had found the button. The ship ripped through the roof of the silo like an impromptu can opener.

Aimz tossed herself across the control panel as the ship sped off into the atmosphere. "Zuxing Blitheon's nipples you slorpfignutting prog of a jexafeeb," she informed him.

He looked at her like she had gone off her rocket. "You've just insulted your own queen, you realize that?"

The missiles started before she could tell him that she did, in fact, realize that, and she would gladly insult Carmnia for creating something as dim-witted as Xan. The blast of a nearby missile hurled them to the carpet.

Aimz struggled to pull herself into the pilot's chair and stared wide-eyed at all the buttons. "Well zuut. Do you know how to program a flight path? Because I don't." Then, after a thoughtful pause, "Oh, of course you do. You did all this alone before."

"What?" Xan braced himself between the two seats and groaned at the complexity of the console. "I've no idea. Just start pressing buttons!" he said, having at it.

Aimz felt it better she not interrupt. Somehow, in the past, Xan had accidentally evaded these missiles. Best not to mess with history any more than necessary. Then again, if she was here now, was she always going to have been here?

"Ah, hold on." Aimz squeezed her temples as if it would help her think. "Were you alone when you did this?"

"What in Quanzar's name are you talking about?"

"I suppose you wouldn't know, would you?" Aimz chewed her lip, unsure of which theory of time travel they were meant to be operating under, then eventually decided inaction was better than wrong action and tucked her hands beneath her.

The rocket began to swivel, twist, and turn in a completely unpredictable mess of a flight path.

"Aimz," he shouted over the din of missiles firing just outside the hull, "what were you doing there?"

"I came from the future to save Tuhnt, but you weren't supposed to take me in the *Audacity*. I mean...I'm fairly certain you weren't. I suppose you must have been meant to since I'm here." She shook her head. "How did you survive this?"

"I survive this, do I? That's encouraging."

"Yeah, but don't count your larvae. I'm starting to think the past future is uncertain. You've still got to do whatever you were going to do!"

"Oh, right. This class of rocket has got to have a hyperdrive, doesn't it? Do you...." he paused entreatingly, "do you know where it might be?"

"You're the one who is going to have done it!" She quieted for a moment, mumbling the sentence again under her breath in a few different inflections, trying to figure out if what she had said was at all grammatically correct given the situation.

He stared blankly at the console. "That? Maybe?" He started to reach for a lever that looked particularly interesting when a sudden shift flung him from the swivel chair and into the opposite wall.

Aimz held tightly onto her chair, curling her legs up under it to hold herself there as she felt gravity take an unscheduled sabbatical.

"Aimz," she scolded herself, "no more talking, no more trying to change things. Just let him do whatever he did last time, exactly as he did it and everything will be fine.

Promise? Promise."

"Uh, can I get some help? Aimz?" Xan spun wildly, his fingers just grazing the lever. "Aimz!"

"I can't! If I change the course of this event, you might not survive and, further more, I might not survive, and if I don't survive, I'll be dead, and that sounds extremely unpleasant, so please just ignore me all together!"

The rocket shifted, and Xan smashed into the viewscreen. "Oof!" he said. Then, "That's scourge speech, mun. If we survive this, I'm taking you to Kalumbits."

Aimz nodded; perhaps that was for the best. "Sure but for now, hush up and focus." She went back to trying to make herself as small and unhelpful as possible as Xan crawled beneath the console. He fiddled with a few pedals, then flashed her the reassuring grin of a madman as he switched on the hyperdrive.

There's no known verb which can describe how incredibly fast hyperdrive is. It far outpaces zooming, leaves bolting in the dust, even the classic verb rocketing can't come close to describing just how fast hyperdrive is. And so, they hyperdrove away from Tuhnt.

Xan checked the viewscreen. "Ha!" He disengaged hyperdrive. "That's how you fly a racing rocket," he said as he propelled himself over to the gravity switch, turned it back on with some difficulty, and sauntered to Aimz. "I'd wager you didn't know I could do that."

"I think I did. I mean, I was supposed to know that, but I'm not sure that I did anymore. Now I do, of course."

"Woah, hey, it's alright. I didn't know I could either." Xan crouched beside her and took her cheeks in his hands, checking the pink glow of her eyes to be sure the ophiocordyceps fungi hadn't spread. It hadn't, so that was good. Still, he couldn't help but say, "There's something very wrong with you Aimz. You aren't scourged. Are you on a zipzam popper? Nothing you've said has made a dractifly's toe of sense."

She shook her head. "I know, I'm sorry. You might understand later. Hopefully..." She peered into the middle distance. "Hopefully I will, too. I feel like I've forgotten something important about the future. Or the past. About something that happened in a time that I'm not really sure existed. Aside, have you got any zipzam? That might actually help."

Xan shook his head and sat back in the pilot's chair, kicking his feet casually onto the console.

"Well, we're light-years away from Tuhnt now. I'm not sure I can take you back, either. Maybe we could find someplace nice in another star system? Someplace with decent mental healthcare?"

"No, I need to get back to my own time. Or maybe I could just go back to Yenuket Municipal and live with my past self until I catch up? Wait! What if *you* brought me to Yenuket Municipal in the first place instead? Would that work? Could I just circle around like that? Would I be circling forever? Oh goddess, I should've paid more attention in our time travel theory lectures."

"Mun, I'm genuinely worried about you. Why were you in the silo? Who were the other people you were fighting with? And what makes you think you have to be anywhere?" Xan leaned over and tried to program a flight path that didn't involve getting tossed like a salad.

Aimz puffed a sigh at him. "I think I've been misplaced in time and I need to get back to where this all started: Yenuket Municipal Spaceport. I've got to be there or, well, just thinking about what might happen if I'm not really makes my head spin."

Xan begrudgingly searched for Yenuket Municipal Spaceport on the ship's computer and found its coordinates. "Alright, I'll drop you off there." He looked at her pleadingly. "But maybe we can just stop off somewhere fun, first? I swear I'll take you there afterwards."

She shrugged. "I guess there's no rush," she said.

Xan flashed her an unabashedly bright smile. He might not be able to return to Tuhnt, but at least he had his favorite sister with him. "Where to?"

Aimz promptly disappeared.

THIRTY-THREE

MAY IS MISSING

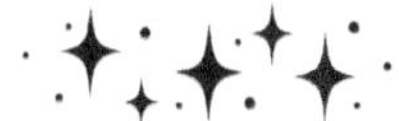

Aimz appeared in the blue-tinged spaceport with the feeling that she had never left. She had a very clear memory of an event that didn't happen which was unendingly unsettling. Thinking, perhaps, that her braid was too tight, she undid it and scrubbed her fingers through her hair. The memory persisted.

"Aimz!" Xan materialized and lifted her into a tight hug. "What happened?" He set her down. "In the past, I mean. Is it different now? Because if it is, I'm missing some massively important chunks of memory, and I'd love you to help me locate them."

"I'm in the same StarTaxi; no idea what happened. I've got a headache about it, though. Aside, do you have any zipzam poppers?"

"When have I ever?"

"Never mind. Look, do you remember taking me with you when you stole the *Audacity*?"

Xan squinted up, then moved his head in a way that wasn't quite yes, wasn't quite no, and was only vaguely approaching maybe. "All I remember is trying to stop myself from stealing the *Audacity* with May. Now I'm here.

I think I'm missing a fairly sizable bit of time, though. It's as if I blacked out for a blip there."

"Blacked out?" Aimz asked. That didn't happen to Tuhntians.

"It's something May does when she's especially stressed. Point is: where's May?"

"In there." Aimz pointed to the gate. "Last I knew."

They peered into the scene beyond the portal. Laser light ricocheted and debris rained from the ceiling of the silo like sharp metal dandruff. And through it all, Listay barrelled toward them.

Listay jumped back into the spaceport terminal through the portal, laden with her plasma zapper, Chaos's anti-matter cannon, and a photon gun and BEAPER which had heretofore belonged to one Admiral Ranken Warders. She tapped the button on the sphere with her elbow, closing the portal behind her. As the portal closed, the sphere faded back into fuchsia.

"Where—sorry," Xan caught himself. "Rude of me. Welcome back, Listay. Where is May?"

She held a finger up at him and leaned on the desk, breathing faster than she had in days. At least, she thought, if she felt short of breath, it meant she needed it to survive.

She unhooked the photon gun from her belt and handed it to Xan in lieu of an answer. The BEAPER and plasma zapper she held out to Aimz.

"So," she breathed, "don't worry, but," she breathed again, "we have to go back further."

"Why? What happened?" Aimz asked, pocketing the new BEAPER in favor of her old one and twirling the plasma zapper in her hand to get a feel for it. It was no metal shard.

"Well," Listay snapped at Xan, "when you decided it'd be a good idea to teleport Aimz onto the *Audacity*, Chaos got May."

"I didn't—"

"You did. Just now, in there." She gestured to the empty wall where the gate had been.

"Yeah, and I was there!" Aimz said. "I mean, I think it

was me. Am I the same me? I remember that but I also don't think it actually happened. How is that possible?"

"I think the timeline has righted itself somehow. But now May is dead in your past which means she can't be here in her present."

Xan made a sound like a moribund squeaky toy; he would've dropped the photon gun had his finger not been hooked dangerously around the trigger. "May is...?"

"And Tuhnt? It's still gone, isn't it?" Aimz interrupted. No wisp of a timeline in her head had it right. Whether Xan stole the *Audacity* or not, Tuhnt was gone.

"My May?" said Xan.

"What about Tuhnt?" said Aimz.

"*My* May?!" said Xan.

"Hush!" said Listay, and she was the one with the anti-matter cannon, so they did. "I disintegrated Chaos, but in order to get May back we need to grab her and close the portal again before Chaos can-"

"Before I can escape?" Chaos sat behind them looking far too comfortable on the uncomfortable plastic chair.

THIRTY-FOUR
ANTICI-

Chaos had made Sonan's robotic eyes unmentionable. Her artificial hair and skin, too, was unmentionable. The only thing that was not unmentionable about her was her voice and that was becoming so. It sounded like someone hanging by their fingernails off the edge of a chalkboard cliff. I probably shouldn't have mentioned that, actually.

"Listay, I am astounded at your lack of gratitude," Chaos said. "When I possessed Yvonne, I treated you so well."

"You murdered me." Listay charged the anti-matter cannon, hefting it onto her shoulder where, it must be said, it looked a great deal more at home than on Sonan's thin frame.

"I expended nearly all of my remaining energy to bring you back to life because I am a merciful goddess, and rather than worship me, you disintegrated my new body the moment you got the opportunity."

"I did. Why didn't you remain disintegrated?"

"Oh larvling, I'm not going to explain the mysteries of the universe to you," said Chaos sneeringly. She said this because she had no idea, and not knowing things tends to give ancient and powerful entities the willies.

"Right so," Xan fiddled with the photon gun in a way he hoped was intimidating, "what's the current timeline doing? Because I really get the sense that I shouldn't be here, and yet here I am. And is Tuhnt back to existing now?"

This, Chaos had an answer for, and she couldn't wait to tell them.

"I wanted you dead to shut off the command loop in this hard drive which was screeching at me to imprison you. You living or dying had nothing to do with Tuhnt. Back then I was stuck with Yvonne's body and she wouldn't let me destroy the planet until you were off it, so I slipped into the nearest admiral I could find and got you to leave, which had the added bonus of making you think you'd doomed Tuhnt but the clear disadvantage of you continuing to exist. Now. You answer my question: Do you have the fish yet?"

"Do I have..." Xan blinked. "I'm sorry, what?"

"Obviously not. Now if you'll excuse me, I think I'll pop back to the beginning of life on Tuhnt and step on anything that has the spiracles to crawl out of the ocean."

By now, Listay had attempted to discharge the anti-matter cannon once, Aimz had pulled the trigger on the plasma zapper twenty times, and Xan had almost figured out how to turn on the photon gun.

"This is a safety bubble, larvlings. Guns don't work here," Chaos laughed.

Then she stopped.

Aimz had shoved the metal bit into the space between Sonan's artificial neck and shoulders. The android's system, unsure of how to deal with the metal bit pinching some rather important wires, shut itself down.

"Sharp bits of metal still work! Always will. Love a good sharp bit of metal." Aimz smiled, scooping up Sonan's limp body.

Listay set the sphere's coordinates to a few bloops earlier and a touch to the left before taking Sonan from Aimz. "You two retrieve May. I'll keep Chaos off your marks."

"Anything you like, Listy." Aimz tapped open the gate and dragged Xan into the past, pulling him into a bushel of wires which spewed from the back of a computer bank in the silo.

There was no sign of a conflict in the silo. It was pristinely dark, aside from the orange glow of reflected light from the *Audacity* which towered above, pointing toward the heavens and, Xan noted, a closed silo roof.

"Hey, can I just open the roof while we're here? Avoid a few dozen dents and scratches from the start?" Xan whispered. He didn't know why he was whispering.

Aimz grabbed his collar and drew him further back into the shadows behind the computer bank. "No, we're not changing the timeline anymore. You're going to rescue May, and I'm going to smash the time ball, because it's a piece of trok."

"You're giving up on Tuhnt?" Xan asked.

"Of course not! It's not giving up. But you heard Chaos. She was going to destroy Tuhnt anyway. I'm moving on. I mean, I've *been* moved on, it's just I thought maybe there was a possibility of un-moving-on, but there isn't, so I'm just back to where I was alright? Not giving up. Besides, my personal timeline is a disaster because you abducted me onto the *Audacity,* so I would really rather not continue to fiddle with it. Time's not my area of expertise."

"Why don't you take yourself back before I show up and bring you onboard the *Audacity*? Wouldn't that fix your timeline?"

"Because..." Aimz knew there was a perfectly valid reason, but it eluded her. "Oh! Because if I don't distract Chaos or, rather, if I *didn't* distract Chaos she will...or would...or would have? Oh goddess preserve us. If you had taken me back before Chaos appeared, she will have killed you. Got it?"

"I might be going to have got it," Xan chuckled. "Having some trouble with tense?"

Aimz glared at him. "You can't tell me those pedantic linguistic classes prepared you for this exact eventuality."

"Not this exact one, no. But the Handbook of 1001

Tense Formations says-"

"Please spare me from knowing," Aimz said. Then, "Ah! Hush, I heard something."

"I wasn't the one talking," Xan whispered.

"I know, just, shhhhh." Aimz slapped her hand over his mouth and peered around the control panel. The silo door opened.

Her past self, May, and Listay would arrive any minute just to the right of their portal and then, slightly to the right of that, Chaos would appear.

"Okay, here's the plan." She kept her hand clamped over Xan's mouth. "The moment you see May come out, you grab her and bring her through the portal that we just came from. Not the one she came—er, is going to come out of."

Xan pulled her hand away. "Why not that one?"

Aimz thought painfully for half a blip. "I don't know! Just do what I said. Take her back through the one we came out of. I'll help myself hold off Chaos and then come back through the portal we just came out of. Zuut, I hope you take the right version of me onto the *Audacity*."

"You know, I don't remember doing that. I should remember doing that, right?"

"I remember you doing it, so you must have."

"Alright, but couldn't you stay back here and plasma zap Chaos until you and I get away? Then I'll definitely take past Aimz, not current Aimz."

To spite him, she tried to think of a reason why that wouldn't work, but couldn't.

"Okay, agreed."

Another portal opened and Listay entered the silo with May and Aimz's past selves. Aimz gave a satisfied little hum. There had been no mirrors in the whole of Yenuket Municipal; it was nice to see herself again.

"May!" Xan vaulted over the computer bank when he saw her. In the distance, a younger version of himself was exiting the MegaCruiser.

"Right, still alive! Come on." He tried dragging her to the portal he was supposed to go through.

"Xan? Why-" May was interrupted. Admiral Ranken sent

a photon blast sizzling into her thigh.

Xan made the noise he thought May should have made but hadn't. He half carried, half dragged her back to the spaceport, motioning to Aimz who was living out some kind of sniper fantasy behind the computer bank.

After sending off a final, poorly aimed shot in Ranken's direction, Aimz helped heft May into the spaceport and closed the gate.

Listay had maneuvered Sonan's body into a plastic chair and, having nothing to tie her down with, was perched on her lap. "You got May," she noted.

"Yeah, he got me." Xan set her down on the low pile spaceport carpet. "He got me distracted enough that someone put a hole in my leg."

"At least you aren't dead this time," Aimz said.

"At least," May agreed, curiously peeling melted fabric from her thigh.

It looked gross, a hand-sized dark gouge in her thigh that had been cauterized the moment the photons tore into her skin. Not a terribly effective weapon, she thought briefly, one that immediately cauterizes a wound. Still it should have been incredibly painful. Only, it wasn't.

"That looks bad," Xan said, kneeling behind her and prodding the wound helpfully.

"Doesn't it?" May said as if it were a soufflé that hadn't quite turned out.

"I know I'm at risk of sounding a mite obvious here but," he looked from the hole to her curiously calm face and back again, "doesn't that hurt?"

She shrugged, stood, and found that the horrific pain that ought to have shot down her leg did no such thing.

"Not at all." She put all of her weight on the leg now to prove it to herself.

He stared.

"Hey, stop looking at it," she said. "It's fine. You're off the hook on this one."

"If you insist." He stopped staring at it...no he was back on it again. He forced his attention away. "I'm still on several other hooks and also possibly dead."

"I'm not sure about that," said May, grabbing the

manual from the desk and leafing through it again. "How did you get back here?"

"That's really a fantastic question because last I remember, we were going back to the subbar on Trilly to stop me from stealing the *Audacity,* and then I was here and you weren't. Then Aimz showed up."

"Right. That doesn't make sense." May ran her finger down the page, trying to focus on one word at a time to get the translation chip to work.

"Does anything ever?"

"Occasionally."

The sphere shivered, the safety bubble of the spaceport strobing festively before it stabilized again.

"What was that?" asked Aimz.

"Probably the power source failing," said May.

"And the power source is?"

"Oh, just the core of the planet." May showed her a page in the manual with an illustration of New Tuhnt bisected to reveal the cleverly economical and completely safe power grid which had been threaded through the planet's core. "Let's find the MoonHopper Chaos used and get out of here."

"Can't we fix the Gremlin?" Listay asked, twisting over her shoulder, still sitting on Sonan's lap like a living paperweight.

"It didn't..." Xan looked at May like perhaps she'd prefer to give the bad news. She did not. "Didn't fair well."

Listay liked the Gremlins, they were simple and efficient and dependable, so it really was a shame that the last one in existence had perished. Noticing that this news had deflated her, Aimz leapt into the plastic seat beside her.

"I'd wager I could make it work again," she said with a crooked smile.

"You're an engineer?"

"Er, well, I mean I'm an adventure biologist. I could adventure into engineering, though. Have done, too! Didn't go well the first time, but I most definitely learned something from that experience."

"We'll take the MoonHopper." Listay patted Aimz's knee. "But I'm sure you could fix the Gremlin if we had the time."

"Right, let's be off, then. Going to need this." Aimz yanked the metal bit from Sonan's neck and immediately regretted it.

Chaos sizzled through Sonan's wires again, reinvigorated after the short break. The jolt forced Listay up, and, though her nerves were still vibrating from the electricity, she prepared to fight Chaos hand-to-hand.

Chaos shook the android's limbs out to gain control of them again, snatched the plasma zapper from Aimz, and set it to its most gruesome setting.

"I grow tired of playing with you lot," she growled. "So I'm going to exterminate you." Chaos flung Listay aside with a jolt of electricity and opened the gate.

In the silo, an alternate Xan abducted an alternate Aimz whilst an alternate Listay and May went at an alternate Chaos and a further alternate Xan ran after May as another Aimz shot at the whole conglomeration from behind a computer bank.

Admiral Ranken Warders looked on in horrible confusion, occasionally firing into the mess, thinking perhaps that would help.

Chaos reached into the past with the plasma zapper and killed them.

All of them.

The silo went silent.

Chaos smiled, and May smiled too, because this only further confirmed her suspicions. She launched herself into the sphere and pushed it off the desk. It shattered, plunging them into darkness.

THIRTY-FIVE

-PATION

No one saw May's smug expression in the darkness, but she kept it up anyway. It was rare she got to feel smug about something.

Xan was the first to speak. "We're alive?" he asked, wondering idly where the photon gun he had just been holding had gone off to.

"Yes. Also," she felt for the hole in her thigh but did not find it, "leg's healed up."

As her vision adjusted, she found that they weren't exactly in complete darkness. Cracks of light from outside dappled the black floor, the pedestal which had formerly been the desk, a plaque which assured everyone that they were seeing the genuine Sphere of Time, and a row of ride vehicles on an ancient track.

Chaos stood, staring at the remains of the sphere. She was having a hard time accepting what had just happened. She was having a hard time understanding what had just happened.

They should be dead.

She killed them.

Her lack of omniscience was really starting to get to

her.

"It's an attraction, Chaos," May said.

"Pardon?"

"An attraction. These Pontoosa people never actually used it. They just found it and assumed it was a time machine. But it only simulates the past. It's not real."

"How did you know?" asked Listay.

"I was shot in the leg!"

"And?"

"And I was fine. That isn't normal."

"Why won't you pests die?" Chaos raged, shooting the plasma zapper in a wide arc around herself.

In some rare occasions, earthquakes can be a stroke of good luck. For example, if you're so desperate for money that you've just lit a match with which you're about to burn down your house in order to commit insurance fraud and an earthquake suddenly destroys the entire structure.

Or, as was the case here, you're about to be shot point-blank by a plasma zapper and that earthquake causes part of a building to collapse in such a way that the android who is attempting to shoot you is blocked from doing so.

Aimz found the exit first and whistled as a way to point this out to everyone, not waiting to see who was coming before sprinting down the stairs and into the utility corridor.

"Alert: Generator core overheating, explosion imminent," said the planet. This got Aimz to pause for a moment. Xan, not expecting her to stop, tripped into her and she caught him as May came to a grateful halt.

"Did you hear that?" Aimz asked.

"What, the incredibly loud alert which just reverberated from the heart of the very planet? No, did you?"

"Keep going!" May wheezed. The air in that part of the corridor, near the surface but steadily approaching the suspiciously oxygen-rich underground, was still thin and forced May's lungs, which were already over-taxed by all the running, to squeeze every morsel of oxygen like toothpaste from a near-empty tube.

Still, she ran, Aimz and Xan not far behind (and rapidly overtaking her). The background noise of the planet elevated from an agreeable buzz which could almost be mistaken for silence, to an agitated hum, to a tormented growl as they ran. Soon, they were far enough away from Chaos to stop worrying about what they were running from, and begin wondering what they were running to. The MoonHopper, presumably, was somewhere in their general vicinity, but where?

It didn't matter. The geography was about to choose for them.

A three ton slab of rock, slick with something at least a meter thick and chartreuse dislodged itself from the ceiling directly in front of them.

Aimz, undeterred, gave an excited squeak at the obstruction and shoved May and Xan face first into it before sinking into the skrum herself.

May held her breath as it enveloped her, her eyes shut tight. It was a surprisingly amiable way to die, she thought. Warm and comfortingly weighted. Slipping into the chartreuse mucous was like taking a dip in a thick bath. Better to suffocate here than be crushed painfully under shards of cave, she supposed.

She felt a tap on her shoulder.

Hey, unpin it. We're not going to suffocate. It was Aimz's voice but, instead of being in Aimz's head where it belonged, it was in May and Xan's. *It's cave skrum. Highly conductive of thought waves, extremely friendly*, an echoed slurping noise could be heard, *and also delicious.*

Beside May, Aimz lounged in the goo, licking lips which didn't move as she spoke.

I've never seen a colony of skrum this prolific before. Found some in the holding cell and the trash compactor. It's rich in oxygen too, for those fragile Earthling lungs. Taste it!

May licked her lips. The flavor was reminiscent of an expensive, well aged bourbon. May had never had the occasion to taste an expensive, well aged bourbon, and as such she was unable to appreciate the delicacy that was cave skrum.

Right, thought Xan, *your biological asides are unendingly interesting, Aimz, but we're still trapped underground during an earthquake on a planet that's kindly alerted us to its intention to explode. So can you stop thinking about skrum and start looking for a way out of here?*

The corridor trembled, making them shiver like cherries suspended in a Jello salad, then collapsed.

THIRTY-SIX

DELETED

Whose elbow, thought May, *is in my cheek?*

Sorry, that's mine, Xan thought. The elbow extracted itself from her cheek.

When she opened her eyes, she saw nothing but a sharp jut of rock which looked as if it had tried to give her a black eye, but a barrier of skrum a centimeter thick protected her. She couldn't move.

This rock's loose. Aimz thrashed, setting the skrum violently aquiver. Had May had lunch, she might have lost it to the skrum's undulations. The debris shifted, though, and Aimz, using her whole body like a battering ram, pushed rubble out of the way.

After much shimmying, a bit of wiggling, and an unwholesome amount of grunting, the trio flopped wetly onto the detritus of the planet's surface which was now a great deal lower than it had been.

May swiped a handful of thick chartreuse skrum from her eyes so she could stare despondently up at the walls of the steep crater which had formed around them. In the distance, the MoonHopper Chaos had stolen spread itself messily across the new landscape, smoking casually as if it had just had the time of its life and needed to calm down.

"Where's Chaos?" Xan asked after spitting out a mouthful of skrum. He preferred to get the oxygen he needed to survive the normal way—via osmosis.

Aimz swallowed loudly. "Don't worry about Chaos anymore," she said, skrum dripping in thick, wet plops to the dusty earth as she squeezed it from her hair.

"You'll excuse me if I continue to worry about the immortal Chaos goddess who just tried to kill all of us, I hope," he muttered, sloughing layers of skrum from his suit.

"I'd wager anything that Listay got her offline again. She's really the hero type, you know? Strong, smart, sexy, undead. Imagine what she must've been like when she was alive." Aimz began to dig through debris, looking for her favorite zombie.

Exhaustion had been creeping over May since the holding cell, but the moment she noticed it, it slammed into her like a rogue wave. She hadn't eaten for over a rotation and even then, she had eaten ice cream. The skrum, fortunately, provided substantial calories with a satisfying kick of Vitamin B12. She sat on a relatively smooth boulder and licked the gelatinous skrum from her fingers.

It was a strange feeling, not needing to breathe, but it was worlds better than hallucinating, and the taste was growing on her. Like cheap bourbon, but somehow better. Once her fingers were dry, she rested her head in her hands and tried to take a micro-nap.

Xan, not keen on helping Aimz find Listay because she was likely with Chaos, sat behind May.

"Are you alright?" he asked.

"Yeah. Tired." She leaned back on him, dipping in and out of consciousness. "You?"

He gave a noncommittal warble.

"I'm sorry," she said, her words slurring with exhaustion. "Shouldn't have forced you to go to Rhea. Shouldn't have forced you to race, either. Ahhh," May groaned. "I'm the fucking worst."

"Not the fucking worst," he said. "Only, perhaps, trust me next time I tell you we oughtn't do something because generally I'm on to do anything with you unless it's a really horribly awful idea that might possibly end in death or worse for one or both of us."

May patted his knee sleepily. "Trust," she acknowledged.

"And, in a reality where we live through this, I'll tell you absolutely everything there is to know about me."

"That'll take forever."

"Right. Just the relevant information, then?"

"Okay," May said, driftingly.

Behind them, watered perhaps by Aimz's affection, Listay sprouted.

"Hey, Listy! Welcome back to the land of the living," Aimz said. "Or, seeing as we're trapped in a crater with no means of escape, the land of the dying." She laughed, but stopped as if someone had kicked her. "That was insensitive," she said.

Listay brushed off her comment along with a layer of dirt. "Don't worry about it."

"Oh, I wasn't." She watched Listay dust herself as if she were watching a gourmet meal being prepared.

"What happened to Chaos?" Xan shouted over a sleeping May which, of course, meant she was no longer sleeping.

Listay shook her head. "I lost her in the cave-in. Didn't think anyone would mind."

"Not really," May said, awake now. The micro-nap and nutrients were beginning to revive her for a second wind which was really more like her ninth thus far.

"Alright." Listay mounted a protruding rock to survey the area and collect her thoughts. She had collected one thought, and it was this: They were severely zuxed. "We don't have a vehicle, so our only option is to head out on foot. Aimz and I will try to untether the *Audacity*. You two." She nodded toward the pile of collapsed Jenga blocks which were May and Xan. "Look for Precious Butler. He might be willing to help us."

"Alert: Generator core overheating. Explosion

imminent," the planet reminded them.

"'Imminent,'" Listay shouted at the grey sky, "does not give me a time frame!" She loved time frames, and she loved cleverly working within them. Without a time frame, she could only guess that they were disastrously behind schedule. "We need to move. Chaos could still be after us and the core of the planet might explode at any blip."

May tried to gather up all her exhaustion and released it as a prolonged groan. "Okay. I'm ready."

"I could carry you," Xan offered.

"You don't have the stamina, Blueberry. Last time we tried that you got about twenty feet."

Xan tilted his head at her. "I've only ever had two feet."

"I mean we didn't get very far," she said. "Thanks for the offer, though."

Under their feet, beneath a few dozen sizable boulders, in the dense darkness of the planet, Chaos was engaged in a battle for survival. Sonan had detected her. Sonan was doing her best to delete her. Commands descended upon Chaos's consciousness like the upper middle class descending upon Walmart on Black Friday.

Chaos was no longer a demigoddess. She was a virus, and she had to be deleted. Sonan's circuits were realigning; she was restoring order to her mechanical brain. With one final shove, Chaos was out. Nothing more than a filament carried on the wind.

"No Virus Detected," drifted from a crack in the rubble, followed by a shifting of detritus and the pale pink metal fingers of Sonan for she was, once again, Sonan.

Her mechanical voice made Xan shiver and not just with fear. He suddenly felt as though something was with him, lounging across his shoulders like an evil boa. "Aaaand ignoring that—let's shift before she digs herself out, eh? We've got a mission: Find Precious Butler and get out of here."

"He found us," May said, pointing out a MoonHopper which was working its way down the edge of the crater, relieved that she wouldn't have to walk the distance back to the *Audacity.*

MoonHoppers are not great land travelers. They aren't terrific at space travel, either, but once they exit the atmosphere, their complete disregard for aerodynamics and shoddy stabilizers matter slightly less. As such, it took an uncomfortably long time for the MoonHopper to reach the four of them. A time which was made further uncomfortable by Sonan slowly emerging from the ground.

When it finally reached them, Sonan's entire left forearm was wiggling worm-like from the ground. The MoonHopper door slid open, giving the impression of an unmarked, windowless white van without the round, friendly tires.

Precious Butler leaned his head out of the MoonHopper, gave an awkward wave. "Did you folks hear the alert? I lost three shelves of seedlings to that last quake. Where's Sonan?"

No one answered. He'd seen her. Her arm, at least. With a disappointed tsk (which either meant he was disappointed in Sonan for getting herself buried, or that he was disappointed in them for *letting* her get buried), he jumped out of the MoonHopper and lumbered over to her, moving rocks aside until he could get a decent grip on the badly dented android and extract her. He helped her sit on a boulder, ankles crossed politely.

"Oh that's much better, thank you," Sonan said. "I'm not sure what came over me, I do apologize." She surveyed the organic beings who surrounded her now. "Fuck, it is a pleasure to see you again." She nodded to May who nodded stiffly back. "And Xan. Feeling better I see? That's no trouble at all; the *Innocuous* is well stocked with barley tea."

"Terrific," he said, though it was not.

"Sonan," Precious Butler stepped in front of her now, "the planet's unstable, we need to get out of here. I'm taking you to the colony on Not Tuhnt where you can stay with me and the wife as long you need." He moved to scoop her up, but she recoiled.

"That's very kind of you, but I must arrest and imprison

Xan under Carmnia of Trilly on Tuhnt, and on the colony, I don't have that authority."

"Sure, but you could get him arrested."

"Arrested and tried for a vehicle theft which took place a millennium and a half ago on a planet which no longer exists? My larvling, I'm afraid that would be quite impossible. He will stay here with me in the hold of *Innocuous* where he belongs."

The planet, having heard enough, rattled violently beneath them. Its ancient voice issuing a firm reminder. "Alert: Generator core overheating, explosion imminent."

Precious Butler hefted Sonan into his arms and motioned with his head for everyone to follow him to the MoonHopper. Once inside the cockpit of the ship, he set Sonan down in the co-pilot's seat and waited for the others to pile in.

They did not.

He poked his head out once more. "Come on, then. I'll speak with Sonan once we're all safe."

"This is our best option," Listay confirmed with the kind of confidence that could convince a mollusk to take up ballet.

They packed into the MoonHopper and shut the door.

THIRTY-SEVEN

GOODBYE STARSHINE

The MoonHopper lifted from the planet like a rock falling from a great height but backwards.

"The Tuhntian colony is on Rhea I, which isn't far, but we'll need to make a stop off at Yenuket Municipal for fuel," Precious Butler said as he brought the ship into the thin, sickly atmosphere on New Tuhnt. He sat heavily in the pilot's chair, rubbing his forehead. "A thousand orbits wasted on this trok."

Sonan, who had been sitting quietly in the corner and running tests on herself to be sure Chaos was really and truly gone, snapped up.

"Precious Butler, how could you be so offensive? I'm surpr-r-r-r-r-r-"

He knew this day would come. Knew he'd eventually slip up and offend her. But he didn't expect her to take it so hard that she would violently glitch. He set the ship on autopilot and knelt to deal with her.

"R-r-r-r-rest and imprison Xan under Carmnia of Trilly on Tuhnt," Sonan finished, her eyes flicking toward Xan who leaned against the MoonHopper's breaker box, idly combing the skrum out of May's hair.

Xan liked to think that in a situation like this, he would have something meaningful and persuasive to say. "Uhh-um," is what he settled on.

Sonan found the horrific command Chaos had conjured in Sonan's perambulatory files. Horrific though it was, the language of ancient evil and binary were shockingly similar. She sent a command to her lips which made them appear to smile, then stood of her own will for the first time in 1,500 orbits.

"I'm frightfully sorry, but I cannot allow Xan to leave the planet. He is under arrest. I must have him imprisoned aboard the *Innocuous*. Then perhaps a cup of tea to celebrate. Won't that be nice?" Then, calmly in the way an arrow might calmly plow into an eye socket, she thrust her hand through a seam in the MoonHopper's control panel.

The ship shuttered under her command, all unnecessary functions and several necessary ones spluttered offline, and it began to plummet back to the planet.

"Sonan, be reasonable," Precious Butler said in a way that gave no hint that they were hurtling through the sky toward an exploding planet. He tried to coax her hand away from the dashboard, but she yanked it back along with a fistful of live wires which she touched to his sweaty neck.

Precious Butler sizzled, jerked, and dropped to the floor of the MoonHopper. Not dead, but not alive enough to be of much help.

Fortunately, Listay was exactly alive enough. She slid protectively between Sonan and everyone else, then leaned into Aimz. "Do you have the metal piece still?"

Aimz, heartbroken, shook her head. "I lost it; I'm sorry."

"It's alright, mun." Punching was still an option. A rather good option, too, on account of her robotic arm. "Sonan, can you understand me?"

"Yes."

"Then please listen. If we go back to the planet, we will all definitely die. Including you."

"I must arrest and imprison Xan under Carmnia of

Trilly on Tuhnt in accordance with my prime directive."

"Oh, is that all you wanted to do?" Xan said from between Listay's legs. He was between Listay's legs because her body was blocking him from Sonan. "Because if that's the whole plan here, you don't need any of them, right? Just me and you down on the planet?"

May dropped beside him to whisper, "Do you have a plan?" He never, in her experience, had been much on planning.

"Do you?"

"Not exactly."

"Alright, then I'm going to turn myself in, and maybe she'll let the rest of you go."

"That's not a plan, that's giving up."

"I'd prefer to think of it as moving on," he said as the MoonHopper fumbled onto the planet's crumbling crust. "Hey Sonan, you can arrest and imprison me if you leave them with the MoonHopper, alright?"

Sonan tilted her head as the idea processed. The MoonHopper belonged to EnviroDev and was commanded by Precious Butler. Taking it would be vehicular theft which Sonan felt quite strongly about.

"Yes. That is an acceptable arrangement," she said, wires still sizzling in her fist. "Step onto the teledisc and we will return to the *Innocuous* where you belong."

Xan began to crawl out through Listay's legs, but May grabbed his lapel.

"There are four of us! We can take her down *and* get out of here before the planet blows."

"Precious Butler is as big as all four of us combined and she had him out in half a blip," he whispered back. "If I let her do her thing, everyone will be fine, right?"

"*You* won't be."

"Right, but the way I figure it, I'm doomed regardless. I should've been on Tuhnt when it blew up, so I might as well be on New Tuhnt when it does. It's poetic."

"I hate poetry."

"You just haven't read any you liked yet! I wager I can find something you'd like."

"Wager accepted, because you can't make poetry

recommendations if you're dead!" May's jaw hurt and she realized she had been talking through clenched teeth.

Aimz pushed between the two of them, spreading Listay's legs even farther. It was at this point that Listay felt she'd had enough of acting as a living cone of silence and stepped aside.

"I'll be honest," whispered Aimz, "we could probably take her. Have you seen Listay? Positively rippling." She winked at Listay who'd been rather more focused on Sonan but glanced back approvingly anyway.

"See?" said May. "You don't have to die."

"I know! I know we could take her. But, hey, who's to say she won't take one of us while we're at it? I want to go. Better to be blown to beautiful bits now than wither away in a prison on the colony. This face won't wither well," he whispered, the affected alliteration assuaging his anxieties.

"You can't do that!" May shouted, shoving Aimz aside.

"I've spent my entire life doing what other people wanted me to do, and now I'm going to do something nice for myself. *Please* stop being so zuxing stubborn."

May had been sipping a cocktail of fear, sadness, and exhaustion, but now she had a new mixer: spite. The concoction this created evolved into rage on the rocks.

"Fine. I'll be less stubborn *after* I do this." She sprinted at Sonan, ready to rip out her circuits with her nails if she had to.

Something held her back.

Something twisted her into a boa constrictor hug.

Something shoved her into Listay whose arms cinched around her.

"Goodbye, Starshine."

Xan joined Sonan on the teledisc, and they were gone.

A rock dropped from a great height in May's chest, but backwards. The arms encircling her were strong and comforting, but she was not ready to be comforted.

Rage at the pointlessness of everything screamed out of May. She tried to leverage herself against Listay, but the more she pulled away, the tighter she was held, like an oversensitive locking seatbelt.

"Hey, it's alright, shh," and other less helpful platitudes tumbled out of Listay. Aimz hopped over Precious Butler's inert form and into the cockpit of the MoonHopper to bring it back under control, then left the ship on autopilot and sat cross-legged in front of them, searching for the right thing to say.

"At least he'll die quick," was the wrong thing to say, but she said it anyway.

In a feat May herself would never be able to explain or duplicate, she wrenched herself out of Listay's grasp and tackled Aimz, battering her fists against her like an ounce of saltwater battering the hull of an ocean liner.

Aimz caught Listay's gaze and silently asked for assistance.

"You brought that on yourself," Listay mouthed at her.

With a resigned shrug, Aimz laid back and let May beat the shit out of her for awhile. Getting punched in the face repeatedly felt a bit better than ditching Xan on a doomed planet with an insane android, at least.

THIRTY-EIGHT
BEFRIENDING SONAN

It couldn't be said that teleporting was ever a pleasant experience, but teleporting off the MoonHopper with Sonan was singularly wretched. Xan wasn't sure if it was from fear or mingling briefly with Sonan's electric atoms, but when they arrived on the *Innocuous,* his very atoms seemed to vibrate for a few blips before settling back into his body and he shivered on the teledisc for a moment. Sonan waited, visibly unshaken, for the theatrics to end.

Once his atoms collected themselves, Xan gave her an uncomfortable smile. "Back to the holding cell? Or do you want to poison me again?"

"I have someone I'd quite like to see privately first." She began leading him toward the cell. She didn't pull a weapon on him. Didn't drag him along. She knew that he knew that he wasn't going anywhere.

"Who's that?" Making conversation, he figured, would help pass the time until he died.

"Admiral Warders. He'll be pleased to hear the mission is complete."

"He's here?" Xan choked, no longer able to walk casually beside his captor. "But he knows Chaos forced me to steal the ship because she used him to do it! Why does he want me imprisoned?"

"The Admiral is dead." Sonan tapped her head where her hard drive resided. "But he remains in here." She blinked and a recording of Admiral Warders appeared to walk beside them.

"Oh that's..." Xan jogged a little to catch up with the android and the hologram. "That's disarming. Alright." He swallowed, unsure if he was glad that the Admiral wasn't actually there or concerned that the digital ghost of the Admiral was leading him to his grave. He decided he could be both.

If he could be both pleased that May and Aimz were safe and terrified that he'd never see either of them again, he could live in the dualism of being glad that the Admiral no longer existed and concerned about his ghost.

He rolled with it.

There was a chance, however slight, that he could make friends with Sonan.

"I'm sorry to hear about the Admiral. Were you close?" he tried. It would at least be harder for her to let him die if she liked him.

"We still are. He is, as I said, stored in my harddrive."

Clearly Sonan didn't grasp the finality of death in the same way Xan did. That was not the angle to take.

"Right, naturally! So could I...could I meet him? We sort of got off wrong on our first meeting. I mean, I suppose he was possessed at the time, so he might not even remember me-"

"He remembers you. He hates you."

"Well, maybe he wouldn't hate me if he-"

"He hates you," she repeated.

"Right," he said, then chewed his lip as he thought. "Hey! We could take the ship into orbit, couldn't we? Then you could torture me for a lifetime instead of just...well just in between now and the imminent explosion."

"The ship is immobile. We were shot down almost immediately by the *Peacemaker* because there was no distraction rocket to assuage the attack. Which is your fault and the reason that the admiral hates you."

“Hated. I mean, if he’s dead. Past tense,” Xan mumbled. It was more difficult than he had expected to befriend Sonan. He wasn’t sure why he’d assumed he could do it at all. He was still operating under the falsehood that he was a likable person.

Sonan stopped, turned, and led him into the holding cell. He once again walked through the sickly yellow light barrier.

THIRTY-NINE
WILL TO LIVE

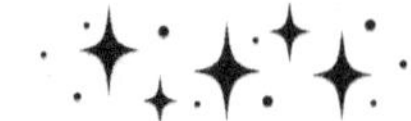

The holding cell aboard the *Innocuous* was built for reflecting. Literally, on account of the aluminum walls, and figuratively because the only entertainment available to anyone locked in the cell was to watch their own memories until they were distorted as a rotting VHS tape.

Xan had found another way to amuse himself. The deadly laser barrier which imprisoned him happened to be on the same electrical circuit as the climate control, and so whenever the ship's climate control unit kicked on, the deadly laser barrier dimmed almost imperceptibly.

Rather than think about what had happened, he started counting these instances.

The light had fluctuated three times.

Four, now.

Xan's eyes were beginning to dry out. If he blinked, he might miss a fluctuation, and if he couldn't even be trusted to count the number of times the power decreased in a laser barrier, he truly was an utter waste of perfectly good organic material.

Five times now, but this time was different. This time, the power had fluctuated due to a tremble in the planet's core.

"Alert: Generator core overheating, explosion imminent," said the planet, densely muffled by the insulated walls of the ship.

"Alright, thank you, I got it. You can stop reminding me." He winked one eye, then the other.

Imminent, it had said.

What did it mean by imminent, anyway? Did he have beoops left to live? A rotation? The only thing that was certain was that Death loomed much closer than he was typically comfortable with.

How, he wondered, would he actually go? Perhaps the ship would first plummet unknown distances to the fiery core of the overheating planet and he would roast.

It was equally likely that the entire thing would shatter into a kazillion bits and he would be skewered on the shrapnel like an unwitting shish kabob.

Or the laser barrier might get him. If the ship were to fall into a crater and land side-ways, gravity would pull him through the barrier like paper through a shredder.

Maybe, if he were really lucky, the collapse of the planet would take a lifetime and he would die of old age before anything more horrific happened.

Six fluctuations.

No, he thought. That would be the unluckiest eventuality of them all. A lifetime of counting minor power variances in the laser barrier to keep from thinking about how impressively he had botched the whole living thing.

At least, he thought, he could craft a nice death for himself. He'd only need to cuddle up to the laser barrier and let it do the work it was made for. If sizzling an entire organic being into non-existence wasn't job satisfaction to a laser barrier, Xan couldn't begin to imagine what would be.

"Alert: Gener--"

"Yep. Yes, I heard you," he told the floor irritably.

"Right, so. May's as safe as she can be. Doesn't have the *Audacity,* sure, but she might have enough gem for a decent racing rocket. Aimz is alive and doing whatever it is that makes her happy which, I assume, involves licking every rock she encounters and probably Listay as well. I don't need to worry about either of them. May can probably teach Aimz to do David Attenborough impressions and Aimz can reach things on high shelves for her. They better stay together; May's too short. Oh Blitheon! I should've told Aimz that May can't reach the high shelves on her own and they need to stay together. Wait, no. That's ridiculous. May can just use the lower shelves. Or climb on something. She's resourceful. Goddess. Who will keep her hair up? Who will fix May's hair?!" he shouted at the laser barrier.

It fluctuated a seventh time in response.

"Someone else. Someone I've never met who's good with hair." He moved close enough to the laser barrier that he could feel the electricity buzzing gently across his skin.

"Alright. I'm doing this for myself. I'm just going to walk right on through this extremely deadly laser barrier and find out what exactly happens when you die because I mean, zuut, who knows really? I'll think of it as an experiment. Aimz would be proud; I'm being very scientific in my last moments. I should probably lick it first, just for her sake. That's what she would do, the zuxing zoup-nog. She'd lick it first and mutter something about its composition." He stuck his tongue out and heard the tongue ring click against his teeth as he did.

"Zuut! I should've returned the tongue ring. That was thoughtless of me. I'm an utter and absolute taagshlorph. Pointless existence. Aimzless, Mayless." He put his tongue away and wondered when exactly he had forgotten how to walk through extremely deadly laser barriers.

He needed to return the tongue ring. There had to be a way out of here and back to Aimz and May, because if there wasn't, Aimz would never get the tongue ring back. He sat, raking his fingers through his hair as he attempted to think his way out.

"Augh, May needs the zuxing *Audacity*, too. Sure, she could get a new rocket but why should she have to? Because I'm a Poslouian-slug-grass-eating-coward. Alright, I'm going to bring it to her. And the tongue ring. Not to her, to Aimz. I'm going to bring the *Audacity* to May so she can keep living her life, and I'm going to return Aimz's tongue ring because I sure as trok refuse to die a thief. But how?" His only plan had involved befriending Sonan and that was clearly out.

The ship pitched to the side as the planet's surface began sinking into itself, flinging Xan toward the laser barrier. Some instinctual push for self preservation convinced him to grasp the rim of the shelf he had been sitting on as gravity coaxed him toward the barrier. It wouldn't be impossible, he thought, to pull himself back onto the shelf. Keep trying just a touch longer. Just in case.

Sweat, or what he would have us believe was sweat, dripped off his face and sizzled on the barrier. May wasn't coming and he wasn't smart enough to escape without her help. And he didn't want her to come, anyway. He wanted her to be safe and he wanted to get what he deserved.

So he let go.

"Alert: Generator core overheating, explosion imminent," the planet said as the chunk of it which was supporting the *Innocuous* crumbled into the depths of the planet.

FORTY

MORE VEHICULAR THEFT

It's rather difficult, May quickly found, to punch someone who's hugging you. There's just not enough room to get a good swing in. Aimz knew this well, having been herself thwarted by a number of hugs.

So Aimz held May on the floor of the MoonHopper until May realized attacking her would do exactly nothing to help the situation.

"I'm beginning to think," said Aimz, "you didn't like what I said."

May sighed but twisted it into a humorless laugh. "Well spotted. I'm sorry. I was mad at Xan, not you. Well, I was a little mad at you."

May rolled off Aimz and sat up, smoothing her hair away from her face. "What the hell am I going to do now? I can't afford a racing rocket, I don't want to go back to Earth, and I'll never get into poetry," she said with a laugh which sounded like a cleverly disguised sob.

"Sonan?" asked Precious Butler, his voice muffled by the metal floor. He curled up, looked around blearily for a moment, realized two of the six who should have been on the ship were not on the ship, realized *who* those two were, and groaned. "What did she do?" He knew.

May took a breath and opened her mouth, but when everyone politely looked at her, she found she could move her lips quite well but getting sound passed them was more challenging than she remembered. Her lips trembled before she pressed them into a tight line.

Listay helped. "Xan sacrificed himself so we could escape. He and Sonan are on the *Innocuous,* and we're almost to Yenuket Municipal."

Precious Butler rubbed the back of his neck and sat down at the control panel. "That's interesting," he said, getting a sense of how close they were to Yenuket Municipal, finding they had nearly passed it, and reversing the thrusters to bring them down. "He didn't strike me as the heroic type."

The MoonHopper docked in one of the nicer docking bays on Yenuket Municipal. You could tell the nice ones from the shady ones by the lines of holographic police tape which crisscrossed the shady ones.

The moment the ship settled, May hopped up as if she'd been spring loaded.

"What's the plan?"

"The plan?" Precious Butler said. "The plan is to fuel up and get to the Tuhntian colony on Rhea." He pulled the fuel cap release lever.

"I mean for saving Xan. Someone's thought of one right?" May looked first to Listay who felt uncharacteristically unprepared, then to Aimz who was studying a rust flake near her shin on the floor of the MoonHopper until she noticed May staring at her.

"Me?" She sat up. "I'm partial to the plan that doesn't involve being on an exploding planet, myself."

"He's your brother!"

"He left me on doomed planet first, so we're settled up now. Besides I have other brothers." She watched a speck of dust float in front of her for a moment. "Hey, Precious Butler, how many Carmnians are left on the colony?"

His massive head bobbed uncertainly. "A few?"

"See! A few is plenty." She gave a crooked smile, then the glimmer of her shoulder spikes caught her eye. "Won't need these anymore." She shrugged off her jacket and began to studiously unscrew the sharp studs.

"I suppose since there are plenty more, I'll just find myself another Carmnian hairstylist who owns a racing rocket, loves old Earth television, and does an outstanding impression of David Attenborough. There must be plenty of those left, right?" May growled at Aimz who had the decency to look hurt for a nanoblip.

"I know a Carmnian who's good with hair, yeah."

"That's great news. Do you have their phone number handy? Because I could use a touch-up!" May ground her teeth.

"I..." Aimz glanced at Listay for help. "What's a phone number?"

"Ten digits including area code. Dash in the mid...No. Okay. Everyone out."

"Out?"

"Out!" May shouted. "If none of you want to help, I'm going back alone. Give me the anchor." She held her hand out to Precious Butler and he haltingly dropped the anchor button for the MoonHopper in her palm. She squeezed into the cockpit and Precious Butler backed away. "Goddamn aliens have no sense of loyalty," she muttered, studying the control panel to get a bearing on how this particular ship worked. Behind her, a statue garden. She spun around. "Would someone please fuel up the ship?"

"You'll, uh..." Precious Butler began. "You'll pick us up when you're done, right?"

"Yeah, I don't want to get stranded here again," said Aimz. "Even the good neighborhoods around these parts are in a bad area."

"I'm going to go with you," Listay said, putting a hand on May's shoulder which May only then realized had been trembling like a Soprano's vocal chords. The hand helped.

"Listaaaay," Aimz whined. "Don't let her intimidate you. Xan is as good as dead. I'm over it. I was over it a thousand orbits ago. You don't have to do this for me."

"I'm not doing it for you; I'm doing it for May. I'm

partially responsible for her being stranded in space. I oversaw the orders to abduct the Earthlings. If she's made something good out of what I did, it's my duty to support her. Besides, Xan was tricked by Chaos just as I was. If he deserves to die, I do, too."

"Alright but you *did* already! He hasn't yet."

"Enough. I'm going to help May."

From the door of the MoonHopper, a lazy knocking. Precious Butler pulled it open to reveal a grey-green Udonian who looked like a turtle that had been removed from his shell standing outside with a digital clipboard.

"Yenuket Municipal, please prepay," he said it like a plea for death.

Listay stepped forward and offered her face for payment, but Precious Butler held her back. "I insist," he said.

She pushed him aside."No, it's alright, I've got it."

"Please, it's the least I can do." Precious Butler angled his face toward the attendant.

"Really, it's fine," Listay out maneuvered him, a flash of blue, and the attendant nodded approvingly and let them out.

While they fiddled with the fuel pump outside, May looked again for a clear and obvious button which would make the MoonHopper go, such as the *Audacity* had. She was beginning to suspect that flying the *Audacity* had been altogether too easy.

There was a checklist, apparently. A list of tasks scrolled across the viewscreen waiting for May to complete them before launch. She ran through the list ferociously, flicking this on, pressing that off, locking the other in, skipping that because what the hell was an intramanual gauge bypass relay? The fuel indicator light turned green as Listay filled the tank, and May opened the fuel booster and held down the engine starter until it sputtered on.

"That's plenty, let's go," May shouted at the open door.

No one came. Not even Listay who had said she would.

May squeezed herself from cockpit and leaned out of the door. There was, she now realized, a very good reason Listay had not joined her.

Listay was being arrested.

"Let me pay; they're in a terrible rush," Precious Butler tried to explain to a chrome Cosmic Constable who was only slightly larger than him but a great deal rounder.

"According to our records General Listay under Rapite of Rhea is dead. Suspect."

"Right, she *was* dead. Now she's not!" Aimz protested.

"May," Listay called to her, "I'm sorry this might take a blip." She jerked her head toward the docking bay exit and mouthed, "Go" at her repeatedly. The Cosmic Constable wasn't built to catch a hint, but May was.

She slammed the door, sealed it, ran to the cockpit and committed vehicular theft.

FORTY-ONE
KA-BOOM

Having a spine was a prerequisite, Xan thought, for acute spinal pain. Continued existence, he also thought, was a prerequisite for thinking at all.

There was not much on the wall opposite the holding cell. Smooth aluminum siding made up the majority of it, but in one place, a breaker-box with a sharply angled handle was affixed to the wall.

This, naturally, had made it an excellent target for Xan's spine.

A spine which, curiously, still existed.

A spine which, even more curiously, was still encased in the rest of him.

Someone was staring at him. He knew this, though his eyes were closed, because even in the darkness of his own mind's eye he could see them. Her, actually.

"Uhm. Hello," he said.

She pursed wispy blue lips at him, shook Her head, and sighed like a breeze exiting a catacomb.

"Not you again," said Death. "What's *with* you?"

"With me?"

"There's something stuck on you. I can't take you like

this!"

"Sorry."

"You're an utter and absolute taagshlorph for calling me out here twice in one rotation, you know that?" She disappeared.

"I am," he agreed with nothingness then paused before adding, "talking to myself now. I am talking to myself. Okay, alright, well." He glanced up at the cell he had just fallen out of and saw that the laser barrier was still on, but looking perhaps a touch disappointed that he had survived it. "That was unsettlingly lucky," he noted, then got to his feet, standing on the ship's wall. "Science experiment: Can I keep that up?" He sprinted into the dark hallway of the ship until he found the nearest teledisc.

He stared at it for a moment. It was on the wall. Well, it was on the floor, but the floor had become the wall.

Teledisc operations may appear somewhat magical, but there are rules. There are always rules. One of these rules is that you must keep all arms and legs inside the telefield created by the disk in order to ensure that you will arrive with the correct number of limbs.

Telediscs were not meant to be used by someone standing on the wall. If he laid down, he could at least get his feet on the disc. That would have to be enough. He had cheated Death a few times now, he was fairly confident he could outsmart Maiming.

"Alright, *Audy*. Going to steal you back for May. Really hope you're not boiling in the core of the planet right now." Then Xan sent the teleport command from his BEAPER.

He remerged on the *Audacity*'s teledisc and sprung to the control loft, flicking on the back-up generator with a button underneath the panel that he had found accidentally enough times to find on purpose now. The first step in untethering the *Audacity* from New Tuhnt, Xan figured, was understanding exactly what had tethered her in the first place.

The warm orange glow of the ship's ambient light flickered on and, for a moment, he could imagine that everything was as it ought to have been.

Xan so wanted to enjoy the sight of the living room of the *Audacity.* To settle onto the worn, rust colored couch and forget everything that had transpired thus far. It had been a rather difficult character arc for him, and he was tired and ready to watch a few episodes of "I Love Lucy" with a carafe of coffee and a sleeping May curled on the other arm of the couch.

But May wasn't there, and at this distance any scraps of radio waves that held episodes of "I Love Lucy" would be shoddy at best. Also, they were low on coffee. Not out, but low. He eyed the coffee maker, considering one last carafe.

The planet felt that it was a good moment to alert him once again that he was in imminent danger of being blown up, and the coffee was forgotten.

He leapt up the stairs of the control loft and reached for the viewscreen switch, ready to see chunks of oatmeal colored land jutting out of the boiling magma which he assumed was now swirling around them.

Instead, he stopped short of turning on the screen when saw an Osculum languidly rolling down the control panel, floating back up to the top, and letting itself roll back down again.

"Osy?"

The sponge creature purred, wafted up to him.

"This whole time you were hiding out on the *Audacity,* never once wondered where we were?"

It stared facelessly at him.

He shook his head and stuffed the sponge into his pocket. "Alright, I'll bring you back to May, too."

Once he switched the screen on, it took him a moment to register what he was seeing outside the ship. It wasn't magma-lit, that was certain. It was dark as death. No, he retracted the analogy; Death had been rather pale, actually. It was dark as a crater. It *was* a crater. Emergency lights on the hull of the *Innocuous* picked out the broken shards of planet they had landed among. Too deep for sunlight to penetrate, not deep enough to be swimming in a red-hot soup of liquified rock and metal.

Good enough.

Xan exited the rocket via the teledisc, stumbling through a pile of loosely packed debris until he got his footing on a largish slab of ground. He walked around the perimeter of the *Audacity* until he found it: the embarrassingly thin line of the tether which had foiled their escape from New Tuhnt looped into one of the ship's round fin vents. He could reach it if he climbed, but then what? Scowl at it? Call it nasty names? Bite it off?

He ran his tongue, or rather, Aimz's tongue (he still felt odd about that but was trying to accept it), over his teeth as he considered what a tether strong enough to hold back the *Audacity* would do to his smile.

He liked his smile. He'd already lost a molar to Yvonne and wasn't keen on losing anything else.

"No, nope, not my teeth. Alright, where do you lead, you horrible string?" he asked it, picking up the thin silver line and freeing it from debris, following it across the shifting and quivering rocks to its source.

With growing dread, he followed the string across the distance between the *Audacity* and the *Innocuous*. At last, he found the source, a featureless box attached to the underbelly of the *Innocuous* with a seam down the middle and a hole like a spider's spinneret from which the tether protruded.

That looked to Xan like a weak point. He almost apologized as he dug two fingers into the hole and began to pry open the tether's casing. It gave perhaps an eighth of a centimeter before he lost feeling in the tips of his fingers. Clearly, that was not an option.

The Osculum wriggled in his pocket and he fished it out, placed it on the seam and watched it gayly roll along the casing. Useless.

Something, perhaps a sharp bit of metal, to leverage it would have been massively useful. So too would have been Ranken Warder's photon gun which he had briefly had. But, on account of the whole Sphere of Time being a sham thing, the photon gun hadn't actually existed.

He tapped the side of the box as he thought, searching the surrounding, poorly lit debris desperately for anything that might help. Rocks, mostly. Rocks were his assets. He pocketed Osy once more, picked up the largest rock he could feasibly throw, and pelted it at the tether box.

Dented! Dented was good. He studied the dent, ran his thumb over it. Not a dent. Just a smudge of dirt.

Another tremor convinced him that if he survived this, he could always get dental implants, so he cinched his teeth around the tether and gave it an enthusiastic gnaw.

Then a less enthusiastic chew.

Eventually, he sat down to nibble, his jaw aching from the effort.

"Hungry?" May sai-

"MAY!" Xan interrupted her dialogue tag and launched into her for a hug. Anticipating this, May had planted herself solidly outside the MoonHopper, her stance wide, her arms open. "I'm not hungry, no, that was terrible." He continued to hug her. "I was just on my way to bring you the *Audacity*. Why do you always insist on saving me?"

"You keep needing to be saved!" she said over his shoulder, the rim of the emergency helmet she'd found on the MoonHopper cutting into her neck.

"I was doing alright." He released her with the sense that he should be offended by that.

"You were chewing on an unbreakable tether."

"I was assessing the situation." He plucked the tether where he'd been chewing on it; aside from being a touch wet, it looked no different. "The situation, I'm fairly certain, is a bad one. Why did you come back? Where's Aimz?"

"I have to show you the haunted Big Mouth Billy Bass! And Aimz didn't want to come."

"Ha! Fish promise. Aimz was right not to come, though. It's dangerous, I'm not worth it."

"You are. I don't make friends easily, so if you're going to die, it better kill me too." She grabbed his hand. "Now come on." She tugged on him and got about as far as a gnat trying to move a marble statue with a rubber band.

"Not planning on dying! I was just going to figure out how to free *Audy* for you so you can keep racing." His eyes pingponged from the *Audacity* to the *Innocuous* and back again. Another good idea would come to him, he figured, if he was patient enough.

New Tuhnt reminded them once more that it was considering ripping itself to pieces in the near future. It had started to feel like an empty threat to Xan, until the planet added a bit of pertinent information. "Explosion," it said, "in five..."

"Five what?!" May squeaked at the planet as she tried to drag Xan to the MoonHopper. "I don't want the *Audacity*; I came back for you. Get in!" She tugged again, and he yielded, but only because the planet rattled violently, tossing them both to the ground.

The quakes, up until now, had been brief, reminiscent of an involuntary muscle twitch. This one kept at it, making it difficult for them to regain their footing on the shifting rock. "Four," said the planet.

"You love the *Audacity!*" he shouted over the tumult of crumbling earth, oblivious to the countdown.

"I love you more, now come *on*!"

Xan stared once more at the beautiful orange ship, her fins half buried in the planet's rubble, until his eyes began to water, which took roughly a nanoblip. "Three," the voice from below them echoed, nearly drowned out by the tumbling of a nearby landslide. Three of anything was not many, and this sufficiently convinced Xan to get a move on.

"Alright, okay, let's skedaddle." They clambered toward the MoonHopper which hovered just over the trembling ground, swaying and bobbing gently as if it had seriously considered leaving without them.

"Two." A shard of granite knifed up in front of them, cutting them off from the MoonHopper and hurling a couple dozen head-sized boulders at their shins. They toppled like bowling pins.

"I've got the anchor!" May shouted, implying that if Xan could get to her and send the teleport signal to the MoonHopper with his BEAPER, they still might survive this.

"Mmphh!" Xan said, implying that he was trying to get to her, but his leg was jammed rather firmly beneath a boulder.

"Shit," May whispered, implying nothing, as she crawled toward him over the shuddering rubble.

"One."

May launched herself at Xan as he sent the teleport command and both of them remerged inside the MoonHopper just as a wall of flame erupted outside from a massive fissure. Xan flung the door shut then was himself flung against the ceiling of the MoonHopper as the blast launched them into orbit, spinning them like wet laundry. Stumbling into the cockpit, May reached for the artificial gravity control and successfully stuck them both to floor.

The viewscreen lit up white, every pixel straining to contain the brightness of what was happening outside the ship.

And then space vacuumed it all up. The entire fiery blaze which had destroyed the planet was gone in an instant, replaced by nothingness peppered with crumbs.

FORTY-TWO

SONAN WINS

"*Explosion in five...*"

Light filtered through the holowindow, picking out the curling forms in the doily on Sonan's tea table. A folder called "Contentment" slowly opened, coaxed out by the warm tea in her hands, and, finding no unsatisfied directives loitering about, flooded the heretofore unused code into her system.

She blinked open an old but well preserved hologram video file which she projected atop the chair in front of her.

Admiral Warders flickered there now, in what had been his usual seat, glittering with sharply pixelated edges and stroking his impeccable facial hair.

"In the event," said the recorded image of the admiral, "in the *likely* event," he amended, his mustache twitching, "that I don't return to you, I have one final request." The memory of Ranken Warders leaned in now across the table, reached for the memory of the handle of a tea cup, brought the cup to his mustache, sipped.

"*Four.*"

"Oh but you must return, Ranken," said Sonan to the

memory, for it was what she had said a millennium ago.

He shook his head. "My larvling, without the *Audacity* we haven't a chance against the *Peacemaker.* I would like you to find the Carmnian that did this to us. Can you do that for me?"

"My dear Admiral, I wouldn't know where to begin." Sonan said, but this time when she said it, it was with a hint of irony and a small smile.

"*Three.*"

"I have complete faith in you, Sonan. Your new priority one directive is to arrest and imprison Xan under Carmnia of Trilly on Tuhnt."

Sonan's mouth cracked into a stiff smile. "Yes, Admiral. It's done, for you." She had been waiting so long to say that; her circuitry could barely contain the pleasure it gave her.

It was difficult to say for sure, but Sonan liked to believe he had winked at her.

"That's my larvling." The recording cut out. That was the last she'd seen of the admiral before the crash.

Sonan drank her tea, the wires at the back of her throat jittering their displeasure.

"*Two.*"

The tea set rattled violently on the table, but this didn't bother Sonan, as it was nothing her gyroscope couldn't account for.

She opened another video file now. This was a live feed from a camera which nestled into the upper corner of Xan's holding cell.

Confusion paused her contentment program. Xan was not where she had left him. Some after-thought of code told her she ought to scrunch her eyebrows downward with concern now, but her hardware wasn't up to it.

"*One.*"

FORTY-THREE

SILENCE

The silence of space is absolute. It's not just a hole waiting to be filled with sound. It's so full of silence that there's no room for sound to wheedle in.

Aboard the *Audacity,* this had never been a problem for May and Xan. They always filled the silence easily with idle chatter or whatever TV signal was wafting around at the time.

Now, staring out of the MoonHopper's viewscreen at the empty space where New Tuhnt and the *Audacity* had been, they were having trouble filling the void.

FORTY-FOUR

THE MOONSHINE CAFE

The Cosmic Constables were unpopular across the galaxy for several reasons. Firstly, they were privately owned, and if they felt they could stand to make a crystal turning someone in or ticketing them, their programming obligated them to do so.

Secondly, they were notoriously touchy. Anxiously chewing on your lip was strike one. A furtive glance, and they would pull a zapper on you. Use a double negative, and you were as good as dead.

Thirdly, they were far too shiny. Their bulging chrome shells were designed to appear strong but trustworthy. Instead, they looked as if they were allergic to bees and had been stung multiple times all over their metallic bodies.

Fourthly, they either didn't understand anything you told them or were simply incapable of listening to reason.

Which is why Listay, Aimz, and Precious Butler were still sitting across from a Cosmic Constable in a broom closet of an office trying to explain that Listay was not dead when the lights went out.

The room, and in fact the entire spaceport, shuddered

with the force of the explosion.

When the lights flickered back on, the Cosmic Constable was alone.

Aimz led the group, sprinting through the spaceport she had had the misfortune of calling home for a millennium and a half.

"Where are we going?" Precious Butler asked from the back of the line, checking behind him for the constable as he ran.

"You'll know when we get there because I'll tell you," Aimz threw back at him, turning down familiar streets, her feet kicking red dust into Listay's face. She skidded to a halt in front of the Moonshine Cafe and smiled. "Right, we're there!"

"A bar?"

"Yes!"

"Are we safe here?"

"The constables hate the robot that works here. Drives them absolutely suicidal, whatever he says. Just don't pay him any attention and we'll be fine." Aimz yanked on the heavy metal door which was mostly rusted shut. It didn't move.

The sound of sirens grew behind them. Listay clutched the door handle beneath Aimz's hands and they were at last able to crack it enough to squeeze inside.

The robot at the counter paused, lifted its head with a depressing creak, then, deciding they weren't worth the attention, pointedly returned to staring at the spot on the bar it insisted on continuing to clean.

"See? Miserable." The trio watched the constable peer in through the window at them with its expressionless vision visor, then seem to sigh and putter away.

"Well done, Aimz," Listay said with a smile as she pulled out a rickety wooden chair and sat at the nearest table to go over their next action plan. Precious Butler and Aimz joined her and once they were all settled around the table, the screen in the center of it lit up with the bar's menu, glowing feebly at them.

They ignored it.

Well, Listay and Precious Butler ignored it. Aimz eagerly

tapped several drinks which materialized blips later on the tiny telediscs set into the table. She gathered all six drinks she had ordered and tasted them each in turn.

Listay watched her curiously, but didn't intervene. "New Tuhnt," Listay began, distracted by Aimz's tongue licking something red from the rim of one of the glasses. She shook her head and addressed Precious Butler instead. "Clearly New Tuhnt has detonated so-"

"Why clearly?" Aimz interrupted, licking her lips now in a way that was further distracting.

"Because," Listay pointedly told Precious Butler, "what else would cause turbulence and outages on a spaceport?"

"Oh plenty of things. Meteorites passing by, nearby planets exploding, meteorites passing by...so that's...you know, that's two things." Aimz finished the second drink and set the empty glass upside down on the teledisc to be whisked away into a cloud of atoms.

"Fine. If we assume that New Tuhnt has exploded, we need to consider the option that May did not make it back in time and we are without a vehicle."

Aimz had leaned back in her chair to finish her third drink. She held up a finger, tossed the glass behind her, and snapped when it landed on a miniature teledisc on the table behind them and fizzled away.

"Aimz please. We've just lost May and Xan-"

"And Sonan," Precious Butler added.

"Yes, and Sonan. We need to find some way back to Rhea I from here without the MoonHopper."

Aimz leaned forward, typed something into her BEAPER and sent it. "There. I told Xan where to find us. I'm sure he'll be along in a blip, and we can get out of here. Between now and then, though..." Aimz slid an opaque white drink over the digital menu to Listay. "Un-pin it, General."

"I cannot un-pin it." She slid the drink back. "Your brother and an innocent human-"

"And an innocent android," said Precious Butler.

"Might be dead, and I need to find some Rhean official who can confirm that I'm not dead so I can use my account again."

Aimz sighed, took the white drink back, and stuck her tongue out at Listay. Not her tongue. Xan's. She missed her tongue ring.

Then, Aimz had a realization: Xan was alive! After orbits of wondering and trying to forget, her favorite brother still existed and that was excellent.

She then, immediately after this, realized something else. If the sexy zombie sitting across from her was to be believed, and Listay hadn't given Aimz a reason not to trust her, he was also not alive and no longer existed. That was not as excellent. She chewed on his tongue.

"Oh Blitheon," she groaned. "Blitheon's zuxing stars." She covered her mouth with her hand, then split her fingers just enough to down the white alcohol, staring wide-eyed at the flaking ceiling of the cafe.

FORTY-FIVE
FISH PROMISE

The MoonHopper nestled into the docking bay on Yenuket Municipal and the pervasive silence at last relaxed its grip on them.

"You love me more than-" Xan stopped, choking on the name of the ship which was something of a sore spot now.

"Of course." May shut off the MoonHopper's engine and twisted around in the seat. "You're the best friend I've ever had."

"Really? You didn't have any friends on Earth?"

"I knew people. Co-workers, I guess. Old friends from high school I'd talk to on occasion because I felt obligated to. It's hard to make friends as an adult."

"Right. I suppose I sort of forced friendship upon you."

She laughed. "I wouldn't say forced. You made it easy, though."

"May, I love-"

"Ah! No, I can say it when I'm trying to get you to give a shit about living, but you can't just go saying it whenever."

"Why not?"

"It's weird."

"In what way is saying 'I love you' weird? I say I love things all the time. I love a good limerick, I love watching movies with you, I love coffee, I love Lucy. Why is that any different?"

May thought about it for a long moment, only coming up with half-formed excuses that really, in this context, made little sense. "Huh," she said. "Alright, go on then."

"I love you more than I love Lucy," he said, wrapping her in a hug.

"More than Lucy? Didn't think that was possible," she laughed.

"Thank you for being so stubborn," he said.

"Anytime. Now let's find everyone else and get off Yenuket."

They locked the MoonHopper and found that the docking bay, like most of Yenuket Municipal, was empty.

May groaned. "Listay got arrested for being dead. They could be anywhere."

"They're at the Moonshine Cafe."

"What makes you say that?"

Xan tapped his BEAPER and the words "We're at the Moonshine Cafe" scrolled across the floating holographic screen.

"I really need to get a BEAPER," May said as they began walking toward the cafe. "My only concern is that it might make life too easy."

"They're distressingly convenient, sure, but I've got one and I can guarantee you it will do no such thing."

"Oh! This." May ran up to a colorfully dripping mailbox and pointed to the poster which appeared to be a stick man and an upright dromedary. "What is this?"

He recoiled at the sight of it. "This must be a really nasty part of the star system if they have to tell people not to do that."

"Do what?"

"Right, well, I promised I'd be honest with you." Then he told her, truthfully, exactly what the poster was describing.

"Okay," May said as they hurried away from the

mailbox which had gurgled delightedly as Xan described to her the meaning. "I appreciate the honesty, but there are some things I'd rather not know."

Bezalbum's Baubles wasn't far now, and May dragged Xan into the damasked front room. Now that May was aware of it, she could hear Big Mouth Billy Bass singing, muffled through the door.

She dinged the bell, pleased with herself for keeping her promise to the wrinkled old Udonian.

"Why are we here? This isn't a cafe," Xan whispered, eyeing the damask as if it might hear him and be offended.

"The haunted Big Mouth Billy Bass. I want you to see it."

"Right, of course! Singing fish promise."

"Exactly. Maybe she's out," May said, leading Xan around the counter and through the back door. Something was different about the back room now. The air was lighter, somehow. The bass, which had been stuck on "Take Me to the River," was now singing through "Don't Worry, Be Happy," and it lifted the mood of the back area enormously.

"Here he is," May pointed to the plastic fish, flopping in time to the music.

Then, as expected, Xan laughed at the wriggling fish and went to take it down. Unexpected, though interesting: the moment he touched the fish's wooden base, it sparked an unmentionable color, stilled, then silenced.

Xan yipped, shaking the electric spark out of his fingers. "Zuut! What was that?"

"Static discharge?"

"I killed him!" Xan gasped, picking up the silent fish now and turning it over to find the battery compartment empty.

May snorted. "He needs batteries. I think you just de-haunted him. Maybe he'll work properly now."

"Can we get him?"

"Yeah," May looked around the stacks. "If I can find Bezal-Ah!"

She was standing behind them.

"Oh now, my dear! You've returned to break the merchandise. Two hundred crystals for the used-to-be-haunted fish person. Two hundred, please dear."

"Alright," May said, the blue flash filling her vision before she had finished enunciating the "t".

"That's right dearie! Now come, come. Such a hurry you were in last time, I didn't show you my collection of stuck together playing cards. If you can unstick them, you can have them! For three crystals each."

Xan tapped May's shoulder and showed her his BEAPER again.

"Hello, this is Listay. If you're getting this, please reply. Aimz is upset and I'm not sure what to do," scrolled over his wrist.

"She's upset! She's worried about me," Xan couldn't keep the smile out of his voice as he tucked the fish under his arm and tapped out a reply. "We ought to go."

"Yes, thank you for the fish," May told Bezalbum whose eyes once again became big and watery.

"Oh my. My dear, it's just been so long since anyone's-"

"I'm sorry we really have to go." Xan was tugging on her arm now.

"Wait! Can't I entice you with a real, legitimate Good Luck Charm? They don't make 'em like this no more, they don't."

May nearly cringed out-loud. "Definitely not, sorry." Xan hadn't heard; he had given up trying to drag her along and instead ran out the door alone.

"Cheap! The both of you. Coming in here, taking advantage of an old widow. How I'll never know do you live with-"

"Sorry!" May shouted back at her as she shut the door and sprinted after Xan.

He didn't know where the cafe was, and she didn't want to lose him in this place.

She caught up to him and they jogged until they found the flickering sign which read "The Moonshine Cafe" and slipped inside.

"I'm here!" Xan announced happily to the table.

"Oh, good. Can I have my tongue ring back?" Aimz was

sitting on the table casually, snacking on something which a hovering black orb deposited one at a time into her hand.

Her magenta eyes were almost difficult to look at, they glowed so fiercely, rimmed with green.

"Aw, Aimz, you were crying!" Xan rushed to her.

"Not at all." She snorted. "What an assumption to make." She tried to continue eating the crisps that the black orb offered her, but Xan had twisted himself around her neck.

May sat across from Precious Butler, beside Listay.

"Is she alright?" May whispered to them.

They looked at each other and shrugged. Neither of them were willing to elaborate.

"Augh, shouldn't have gotten rid of the spikes," Aimz choked, pushing Xan off her and into the chair which had been hers. "You're certainly excited to be here. Found your desire to live again?"

"Yes and this." He showed her the bass.

"Is that a Big Mouth Billy Bass?" Listay asked, horrified, over Aimz's legs.

"Exactly! Isn't he great?"

Listay shook her head. "Don't keep that fish."

"Why not?"

"I..." Listay paused. She couldn't give a logical reason why she hated the fish, but it irked her. It irked her greatly. "I'm not sure. Sorry. You have the MoonHopper?"

"Yeah, it's in the parking bay," May pulled out the anchor and Listay used her BEAPER to teleport the five of them back to the cramped hopper.

Precious Butler slipped into the cockpit and they set off for the Tuhntian colony on Rhea I, which was called Not Tuhnt because that's exactly what it was.

May collapsed against the softest looking wall in the MoonHopper and slid to the cold floor, glad that she didn't have to pilot for once. She closed her eyes, but all she could see was the cyan afterimage of the *Audacity*, so she opened them again, just enough to see Listay's feet planted behind Precious Butler at the cockpit and Aimz's feet flitting around Listay's, and Xan's heading straight for her.

Absently, she snapped the *Audacity's* anchor button off her suit and turned it in her fingers.

"Huh," Xan said, sitting beside her. "It's still connected."

He was right; the green indicator light was still on, pulsing hopefully.

"Hmm."

She agreed, though she was too tired to understand what she was agreeing to. If the anchor button was online, so too was the teledisc which it was linked to.

Snapping the button back on her suit, she closed her eyes again, trying to ignore the ghostly afterimage of the rocket. She rested her head on Xan's shoulder as he hummed something strangely familiar.

THERE'S MORE WHERE THAT CAME FROM!

Go to www.LauraLoup.com
and sign up for my newsletter
to be the first to read

and while you're there, check out *Tarot in Space*, a 78-card Tarot deck inspired by *The Audacity*!

ABOUT THE AUTHOR

Laura Loup is a professional humorologist, illustrator of *Tarot in Space*, and author of *The Audacity* space opera series. She writes technicolor fun in space for adults with a dedication to optimism and good humor that shines through even ridiculously horrible situations.

Connect with me on Twitter or Instagram to see character art, keep up with the process, and get extra content. I'm @LauraLoupArt on both!

Want to chat with Xan? He has a Twitter now, and he's a real chatter-box. Follow @XanOfTuhnt and say hi!